Thomas stares at the test. He's arrived at the last section of a three-hour exam and is mentally exhausted but only has thirty minutes to go. He scans the classroom. Students stretch and moan; they look as drained as he feels. The final section is in creative writing. There is one question left.

#175: You come across a large trunk. What happens next?

Finally, he thinks. Now he can show any college admission's officer what makes him different from the other students. Why else would they put a subjective question on an academic test? There's no measurement, no standard; they want to see where you'll take them. So, what to write? What will get their attention? In his experience, there is a fine line between dazzling people and intimidating them. *Be clever. Be careful.* He taps his pencil on his desk and glances at his classmates, knowing how they'll answer. They're going to write about things. They'll find silly, simple things inside their trunks. He clears his throat and begins.

The trunk is old and weathered with a leather strap running lengthwise around it. A buckle sits at its center; its copper tarnished green. Rust and sediment make it hard to open, but with some pushing and pulling, the lid reluctantly gives way to reveal a dark, empty space.

"Twenty-minute warning class," Mr. Pruitt calls out, snapping Thomas back to reality. A nervous ball of energy forms in his stomach. He's just created the trunk, has hardly gotten it open, and time is running out. Around the room, pencils scratch, and erasers shrink, the clock gobbling up the seconds. He shakes the cramp from his hand and continues to write.

I push the trunk into the sun to help me see, but there's no use. I can't see anything at all. It's too deep, too dark; I'll have to go inside. With backpack in hand, I climb in but slip, falling to a floor that seems much too far away. It smells like the corner of the garage where Dad keeps the mower he doesn't use and the poison we're not supposed to touch. If it's anything like our garage, it's teeming with spiders. I steel myself for the impending cobwebs that I know I'll be covered in, head-to-toe, but I come out clean.

My eyes adjust to see the walls surrounding me, and I get the feeling that while nothing is here, everything is here. My fingers get to work on the cold steel, eager to find something more, but only connect with disappointment. This trunk is empty. There is nothing here other than me, a Thomas-in-the-box. That is what happens next in this essay. I wrote a boy into a box who happens to be me. And now it is time for me to go.

Climbing from my steel coffin, I get partially over its side when my shoelace gets caught-up, and I fall once more. The contents spill from my pockets. Everything scatters except for a single quarter that rolls across the trunk, spinning until it reaches the other side. I keep my ear to the ground, waiting for the plunk, the sound of completion, but it never comes. The breath catches in my throat. No sound means no bottom. And that means that beneath this trunk is a hole. My heart thumps so loudly that I can hear it vibrate off the walls. Thump-thump, thump-thump. But even with the drumming in my head, all I can think about is getting free and getting outside. I've got to see what's underneath me.

I work frantically to free my shoelace from its captor that turns out to be a strange little lever. It fights to lock back into place, and I know that if I let it go, I'll never be able to pull it up again. My dirty backpack is within reach, so I scrummage through it and come up with a black marker that I slip under the latch, propping it up. Sweat drips into my eyes and down my nose as I work against the lever, praying that I don't lose my hold. My fingers ache against the force of my shoelace, and right when I expect it to break, the trunk comes to life. It groans as if waking from a deep sleep, and the walls around me rumble. The floor below me shifts, revealing a tiny sliver of light.

My shoelace slips free, and I climb to my feet as the walls give a final protest and the ground drops away. I stare in awe at the tunnel I'm standing over. Without hesitation, I climb in.

After crawling for several minutes, I emerge in a forest so thick with trees that it's hard to see the sky. Water runs in the distance and bugs click-clack all around me. The smell of pipe smoke floats by, reminding me of my grandfather, who smoked something similar when I was a child.
Following the leathery scent, I find its proprietor, an unusual man by all appearances. He looks wise, somehow, with his

neat black hair and seemingly mindful eyes, yet he wears a rumpled suit that looks out of place.

Like my teachers often do at the end of the day, he leans back in a chair with his feet kicked up on a desk, in that 'nothing to worry about here, folks, way'.

He sees that I've noticed him, and waves me over, laughing at my hesitation. I approach, thinking that the light must be playing tricks on my eyes because he appears to flitter in and out of my vision as if he were transparent one second, and solid the next. The worry that's been working its way up my spine increases when we make eye contact. I am reminded again of someone or something, only this time, I can't place it. The hairs on the back of my neck soldier up, and I know what's bothering me about him. It's his posture, his patience. He knew I was coming, and worse yet, I think he's been waiting for me.

"Good afternoon Thomas," he says. "You're early. Your mother said you wouldn't be here for…well, for years."

"Time's up," Mr. Pruitt calls. "Pencils down and turn in your tests."

Thomas looks up through bleary eyes, his heart tight in his chest. Students make their way to the front of the room to turn in their exams, so he steps into line, dropping his packet on top of the others. Two girls vie for his attention. Thomas doesn't notice. He is interested in one person at this school. If there were a remote possibility that she liked him, he still wouldn't pursue her. His life consists of two things; earning a scholarship and taking care of his little sister because his father has been useless since the disappearance of their mother almost four years ago. It hasn't been easy, but Thomas can finally see the light at the end of the tunnel. He's had his head in the game long enough to know what's essential, and there's no way he's letting a girl—even a beautiful one, derail that. Not a chance.

Mr. Pruitt stands at the back of the room, scanning the class for anything amiss. He makes eye contact with Thomas and nods, saying with what sounds like an afterthought that he's sure Thomas did well on the test. Thomas does well on every test.

The hallway is chaos. Locker doors ricochet over yelling teenagers. Shoes squeak and doors slam in a familiar cacophony.

Thomas blows out a breath. He has no idea what possessed him to write such a bizarre test response. Thank God for creative writing. It's one of the few times you get credit for writing whatever pops into your head, regardless of how weird it might be.

Nicole Casey walks toward him. Blonde tendrils float around her face as if there was a breeze blowing through the hallway. Thomas freezes. Nerves that start somewhere around his kidneys tighten, sending butterflies shooting through his stomach.

"Hi Thomas," she says, blinking gray eyes that remind him of rain. He rubs his shoulders to stop the sudden onset of shivers attacking him and prays she didn't notice.

"That test was brutal. How'd you do?"

"Uh, good, I think," he clears his throat. "It's hard to tell what they're looking for."

"Well, it is on a Scantron. I think you're supposed to pick the right answer."

"No, I know. I meant the writing section. I don't get how that's weighed. If more than one person scores the tests, we could write practically the same thing and get different grades."

"Oh," she frowns, "I hadn't thought about it that way." He stops at her expression, trying not to laugh.

"Don't worry. I'm sure you did fine. That part probably wasn't too important. Plus, you're new here. You might be able to retest."

"God, I hope not. I don't want to sit through that thing again."

"I don't blame you."

"Speaking of tests," she says, cheeks turning crimson. This time Thomas can't help but laugh. She would be horrible at poker. Her face is an open book.

"Hey," she says, snapping her fingers.

"Sorry," Thomas blinks, laughs. "Did you just snap?"

"No," she says. "Or maybe? I didn't mean to. But you were laughing at me."

"I wasn't; I'm not. But you are funny."

"What? How am I funny?"

"Your face," he tries, stopping at her new expression. "I mean, not your face."

"Oh, my God, never mind," she steps backward.

"Wait, wait," Thomas holds his hands up. Dear God, what could I do worse, "I'm sorry? That came out wrong. I'm braindead from that test. What were you going to ask me?"

"Well," she starts, her face flushing.

Here we go, again, he thinks but keeps his mouth shut.

"I've been having a hard time in math, and everyone said that you could help me. That you were really smart."

"Really?" Thomas grins.

"Don't make that face. This is embarrassing for me. I'm a good student. I get good grades, but I can't catch up in math since we moved here so late in the quarter. Between my other classes and unpacking and figuring out where everything is…"

"You don't have to explain," he stops her, "and don't be embarrassed. Changing schools is rough."

"You've done it before?"

"No. But I can imagine."

"Then you'll help me?"

"How could I not? Being so smart and all."

Nicole laughs, shaking her head. "Smart and modest."

"That too," he says, "give me a call so we can figure out a time. I'll write down my number."

"I've already got it. I'll call you this weekend." Turning to walk away, she looks back at his face, smiling. "

That grin," she says, "You might be trouble."

Thomas watches her disappear into the mass of students racing to leave for the day. Blood pulses through every cell of his body. He keeps a steady pace out of school. When he's several streets away, he slumps against the first bench he sees. His body turns to Jello. Sweat drips down his sides; his heart thumps in his chest and head. He hears a strange sound and realizes after a minute that it's his breath he's hearing. He's practically hyperventilating. That was the single most exhilarating moment he has ever had at Westchester High. And that's when it hits him. Nicole cannot happen. She is a terrible idea. Potentially, academic poison.

He feels the air deplete from his body and sags. "What was I thinking?" he mumbles. They spoke for what? Two minutes, three max? And he's wrecked. If his exchange with Nicole had happened before the test, he would have failed. There's no way he could have focused. Unacceptable. His only path out of this town is on the full-ride scholarship bus. Without it, he won't get much farther. Taking care of his sister and struggling every second for everything they have isn't something he wants to do forever. He's already given up most of his childhood to take on the responsibility of being an adult, something that happened to him without his consent. He loves his sister and doesn't resent her for their situation, but he refuses to be powerless again. He's sworn to himself to choose his path. That means no Nicole. It cannot happen. He will not be a slave to any girl. His cracked watch beeps twice, and he laughs to himself—time to pick up his little sister, Madi, from school.

Merrimac Elementary is roughly a half-mile from the high school and is halfway to Thomas and Madi's home. It takes Thomas about twenty minutes to reach her at an easy pace, just as she's released from class. Today, he's halfway there when he realizes that he doesn't remember the walk. It's a frustrating sensation to lose time. It hasn't happened in a while. His mom used to call him a prolific daydreamer. "Earth to Thomas, Earth to Thomas. Come in, Thomas," she'd say in a robot voice. He grieves at the memory of his mother, tugging his mind back to the test he'd just finished.

Where had that essay come from? It felt like the words were already there, that they'd been waiting to be put into existence by the mere sweep of his pencil. And what about the creep who mentioned his mom? Even weirder. Maybe it's time to stop reading so much fantasy. When he was younger, his mother told him he should be learning about history and geography, about why the world is what it is and how it got that way, rather than reading the Sci-fantasy books that obsessed him. Brain-rotter's, she'd called them.

Guess she was right, he thinks. He'd walked halfway to Madi's school completely blank right after writing that crazy essay about a made-up place with a made-up man who talked about his mother. It makes no sense. Still, something about the forest keeps eating at him. There was a quality to it that seemed so real, so...touchable. It's as if one moment he was assaulted by the leftover stink of hot lunch in class, and in the next, he was in the forest.

He swears he could feel the cold dampness from the earth on his skin, could smell the soil mixed with pine—the unmistakable scent of a forest. He knows it isn't possible, yet he's certain he was there.

A car honking nearby pulls him from his daze, and his annoyance dissolves when he hears Amanda Richardson call out his name. Her voice is as shrill as it was the first time they met, in Mrs. Solman's first grade class. They've never been close friends, but Amanda has always been kind to Thomas, and he appreciates her for that.

A scandal can destroy a person, and anything as criminal as a mother leaving her family is one of the uglier things that could happen to a kid. Thomas knows this because it happened to him. His mother was there, and then she wasn't. Everyone knew.

It left a mark on Thomas, an invisible stain that couldn't be cleaned. How bad must he have been that his mother would leave him? Nearly every kid at school pulled away from Thomas, steering clear of his mother's treason. As if it were contagious. Forced isolation by proxy. Luckily, Madi was too young to catch most of the heat. She got to grieve the loss of their mom without the constant whispers and trailing eyes that Thomas felt daily. But there were also people like Amanda who didn't change how they acted toward Thomas. Those that recognized that he was still the same person, albeit wounded. Whether that was unconscious or purposeful, Thomas didn't care. Kindness was kindness, and Amanda gave that to him.

Amanda pulls next to Thomas in a giant gold sedan adorned with equally giant curb feelers.

"Yo," she says.

Thomas examines her car with raised eyebrows. "Wow, Amanda. That's a jazzy car you've got there."

Amanda laughs, "This thing? God, no, it's my grandma's Buick. My car's in the shop."

"Ah, ha. I like the curb finders. Super cool."

"Right? Thinking about getting some for my car," she laughs. Anyway, I hate to ask, but are you still in the paper-writing business?"

Shit. For the past few years, Thomas has been writing papers and doing other students' homework to make money. It's a small, controlled, by referral-only business that he's been able to keep running because very few students know about it. There are a lot of gossips at Westchester High. If word got out what he was up to, the teachers would undoubtedly find out. He could be suspended, or worse. Two weeks ago, a Geography paper he'd written for a student had gotten stuck to the back of an English paper he'd written for himself. Without realizing it, Thomas had turned in both documents. When his teacher came across the Geography paper attached to Thomas's essay, he'd asked Thomas about it in front of the whole classroom.

Thomas quickly made up a story; he'd found the paper on the floor and planned to give it back to the student when he saw him between classes. He must have turned it in by accident. The teacher seemed to buy his story, but it was still a close call. Since then, Thomas hasn't done anyone's work, and it's starting to sting financially. He makes a good deal of money with his business, and his meager funds are running dangerously low. While he doesn't want to jeopardize his college career with a plagiarism scandal, he should hear what Amanda's proposing. They are friendly, after all. The problem is that she isn't a client, and he didn't give anyone permission to tell her about his business. He has a strict referral rule with his clients, and someone broke it.

"Who told you that?" Thomas asks.

"Toby."

Ah yes, her boyfriend, Toby. Thomas can't stand him.

"He said that you'd done a couple of assignments for him before."

"Well, he shouldn't have."

"Why? I'm not going to tell anyone. He only told me because I was complaining about how much work I have. We've been out to dinner every night since my grandparents arrived, so I've fallen behind. Don't be mad at him."

Thomas waves his hands to stop her. "It's fine. Just keep it quiet. And by quiet, I mean that you cannot refer anyone to me without asking me first. Toby is aware of my rule, and because it's you, I'm giving him a pass. But be sure he understands that this will be the only exception."

"Okay. I've got it. I'm sorry. He told me because I was desperate."

"It's fine, Amanda. It's not your fault. I have some time this week. What do you need?"

"I've got a six-page history report and an English paper that's supposed to be between eight and ten pages. If you can knock those out, I will owe you big time."

"No, you'll owe me a hundred bucks," he smiles.

"Pricy," she says, "but worth it. I've been freaking out. Anyway, I have both assignments with me; they're in the back. Where are you headed? I can give you a ride."

"Great. I'm picking up my sister from Merrimac," he says and climbs in, pulling the heavy door shut. A wave of dizziness washes over him, and he's glad he's sitting down. Amanda prattles on, unaware of his discomfort until they make eye contact. She stops mid-sentence.

"Are you okay?" she says. "You turned white."

"I don't know," he glances around the car and shifts in his seat. "It seems weird in here. Don't you feel it?"

"Feel what?"

"The air—it seems like it changed. It's thick somehow. I can feel it in my lungs. Take a breath, move your fingers around. It's, I don't know, prickly."

"It's what?" she looks around the car. "Are you messing with me?"

"I'm not. You seriously don't feel that? The air feels charged. Like when you're on a hill and lightning is coming, you can feel the electricity building."

"That's never happened to me before."

"Really?" he shakes his head, "I used to scare the crap out of my little sister," he laughs, "I'd tell her to hurry and get the barrettes out of her hair, or she'd get zapped. Now she's terrified of storms. She thinks that lightning is after her."

"That's mean."

"Well, ya, in retrospect."

"She sounds like…wait, I think I hear it or feel it, maybe. My ears kind of tickle. It's like a buzzing sound. What do you think it is? Maybe it's coming from the car. Oh God, this thing is so old the battery is probably ready to explode!" She scans the car, whipping her head around so quickly her pony-tail smacks Thomas across the face.

"Shh," Thomas says, squinting at the air above him, "listen a second. The battery isn't going to explode, and if it did, we'd be safe behind the window." A piece of dust lands on his eyelash. He brushes it away, but several more take its place, tickling his nose and mouth. "What's with all this dust?" he asks. "Why am I just seeing this? Hey, Amanda," he says, nudging her side when she doesn't respond. "Did you see this before?"

"I don't—uh, what am I looking for?"

"The crap in the air. You can't see that?" He wipes his eyes, hoping to clear his vision, but it doesn't help. The dust intensifies, and it looks like it's started forming into shapes.

Ants, he thinks; it looks like millions of tiny ants have filled the cab's airspace. He raises his hand to touch them, tapping the air with his finger. It shimmers.

"Oh, my God," Amanda whispers, "what is that?"

"I don't know, but it's spreading. Look."

He points, reaching to the same place as Amanda and their fingers connect in the middle. Everything goes black.

Chapter 2

A red convertible tears down the road, leaving dust in its wake. Thomas blinks open his eyes, studying his surroundings. He is riding in the backseat. He doesn't recognize the car or understand how he got inside. Overwhelmed with confusion, he wracks his brain for an explanation. Wasn't he just in Amanda's Grandma's old tank? But when was that? Maybe the battery exploded after all. They might have been killed or maimed. He could be in a coma, or he's potentially just losing his mind. But his head is throbbing, and his tongue is starting to sweat, sure signs that he's about to be sick. That wouldn't happen if he were dead or in a coma, would it? If he was in a coma, why would his brain bother, and if he were dead there'd be no brain activity at all.

The nausea is so overwhelming he's sure he'll vomit, but his mom's voice pops into his head. You've got to look out at the horizon. She used to tell him that every time he got car sick. Not that his family traveled together often, but when they did, it was always by car, and Thomas was sick every time. Taking a long, drink of air, he gazes toward the horizon and finally notices that he has company.

Driving the shiny convertible, like she had the Buick, is Amanda Richardson. Only now, instead of being seated beside her, Thomas is sitting behind her. Her new front-seat passenger is a guy named Brad Jacobs, who Thomas recognizes from his History class. Brad looks relaxed. One arm dangles out the open window, the other rests comfortably on Amanda's thigh. That's odd, Thomas thinks, because Amanda is together with Toby, a lunatic football player who would smash Brad into little pieces if he saw what Thomas saw right now. Thomas is about to comment on this when it occurs that he has no business commenting on anything. He's lost—in some kind of nightmare inside a dream, or he's been drugged and is experiencing extraordinary hallucinations. If that is the case, he would like to get to a hospital immediately, because this will undoubtedly melt his brain into mush. Infuriated by that idea, he reaches forward to tap Amanda's shoulder when he sees Brad's hand working its way up Amanda's leg. What is going on now? Why did they bring him? He has no interest in these two idiots and what they're up to.

"Excuse me," he yells, the wind dissolving his words into dust. "Hey, assholes," he tries again, slapping his hands together, "what the hell?"

The car burns down the road, with Thomas waiting for an explanation that never comes. In front, Amanda trails her pinky down Brad's face. Her hair floats behind her like silk. Brad runs his fingers through it, smiling at her profile.

"Are you happy?" he asks Amanda.

"Very. My parents think I'm with Lisa, and Toby thinks I'm at my grandma's house."

Brad rolls his eyes, drops his hands into his lap. "Please don't talk about Toby. He's still my best friend. I'm not proud of what we're doing. I thought you were going to end it."

"You said it would mess up training for the team - I didn't tell him because of that." Amanda's eyes water, "You know I would have. I'm not proud of it either, but it's not my fault. He's not the easiest person to talk to; he can be scary."

Brad rubs her shoulder. "I know, babe. I'm sorry. Maybe it'll be better if I handle it."

The sun beats down on Thomas's head like fire. His anger grows steadily with the rising temperature. Why are they doing this to him and how long are they going to keep it up because he's about to snap. Then Brad leans over to kiss Amanda and his gaze falls on Thomas and Thomas understands that something is seriously wrong. This isn't some prank Amanda and Brad are pulling on Thomas. Brad wasn't privy to Thomas's presence. He had no idea that Thomas was even there. Thomas can tell, because the face Brad is makes is not one of humor or malice, it is one of shock.

Brad's jaw goes slack; his eyes work to focus on Thomas. Thomas can see the muscles in Brad's face tick while he works out what he's seeing. Music blasts on the radio, some boy band

Thomas doesn't recognize but knows he will never forget, because at that moment the disc-jockey interrupts the end of the song, drowning out the last few notes before they've played.

That was the Copycat Killers with their smash hit Summertime Girls are Trouble; you can see them live at Trimble's Open-Air Concerts in the park. You're not going to want to miss it, folks. It's the final event of the summer. Now two lucky winners…

Somewhere in the background, Thomas can hear the D.J. over-projecting his voice, but he's stopped listening because he knows that the concert the D.J. is referring to happed months ago. This is not a hallucination. It's a real experience. But it is not one that he is supposed to be sharing with Brand and Amanda. It is like earlier, from today maybe, when he thought he was in the forest even though he knew it wasn't possible. Yet, he's confident he was there, which makes him even more certain of where he is now. He is inside a moment that belongs to Brad or Amanda. Somehow, he has worked himself into one of their consciousnesses, into what seems to be a memory.

Sweat pools under his arms, the stench a slap in the face. There's nothing worse than fear-induced body odor, and he is getting worse by the second. Thomas wants out of the car and away from this scene, the strangeness is too much to process. But he isn't sure what to do. His eyes flick between Brad and Amanda, and Amanda must sense it because she turns toward the backseat, her eyes locking on Thomas. Something between a gasp and a hiccup escapes her lips, the noise so visceral, Thomas knows instantly that the memory belongs to her.

He tries to speak, but nothing comes out, which is just as well, he thinks. What could he possibly say? Pullover and let me out? That's ridiculous. This isn't real; how could it be? And yet, he's still here, and he still wants out.

Amanda doesn't seem ready to help in any shape or form. She looks like a mannequin version of herself. Her face is trained on Thomas while the car continues down the road. Brad must notice the glaze behind her eyes because he grabs the wheel. Amanda doesn't seem to notice or care. She sits frozen in place, dead eyes locked on Thomas.

"Well then," Thomas mumbles, struggling to his feet, "I'm not supposed to be here."

Brad glances at Thomas but quickly returns his focus to the road.

"I'd like to get out now. Please stop the car," he yells as his body is ripped into the air and sent tumbling to the ground.

That was unexpected, Thomas thinks, although he'd had no idea what might happen when he stood up. Still, he was surprised by how strong the wind could be in nothing more than a memory from a moving car. He hadn't anticipated that it could pick him up and toss him into the bushes at roughly forty miles per hour. As he lay on the side of the road covered in dirt and rocks, he welcomes the pain and the taste of his blood. It's the first thing he's sure is real since he found himself in the red convertible.

He is so grateful that he doesn't care that Amanda never slowed the car, even after he was swept from its interior. It takes five minutes to pick most of the gravel from his road rash, and several bits are left behind. They get to come out later when peroxide and tweezers are available. Clutching a branch for support, he struggles to his feet and waits for his body to scream, which it does.

"Well this is great," he spits a mouthful of blood into the dirt and examines his surroundings.

Outside of the bushes that he flattened with his fall; there's no sign that anyone has ever set foot here. It's hard to decide which way to go as he doesn't know where his journey began. But, following Amanda and Brad means that he'd likely have to see them again, something he has no desire to do. With that in mind, he heads in the direction the car came from. It had to come from somewhere, after all.

Twisted bushes line the road with scatterings of dried foliage and dead trees. It looks like a fire has come through recently, and anything left living is fighting to stay that way. Hang on, he thinks, all you need is a little rain and this whole place will turn around—green for days. The sun seems to crank up a notch, and Thomas can't help but think of the sunscreen he'd smelled earlier in the car with Amanda and Brad. He laughs despite himself. How ridiculous.

The twilight zone of doom he's living in trumps a sunburn, yet his brain is hanging on to the things he'd usually be thinking about. He really should be figuring out how he got into that car and ended up here. This is how people go crazy. Or maybe it's what happens to them after they've gotten through the 'going' part. Perhaps he's already gone. If so, then what's the harm with continuing? With letting his guard down and exploring the strangest situation he's ever experienced? He is a natural-born problem solver—at least that's what he tells himself.

"So, what now?" he says out loud, tears clouding his eyes. 'Identify your problem, engineer a solution,' he hears his mother whisper. He is eleven in his memory. A thumb-tack prank was pulled on the teacher and the class is being punished. Until the guilty student comes forward, every student will suffer on his or her behalf with thirty-minutes of after-school detention, beginning the following day. But Thomas cannot have detention after school, he has karate practice. His parents have splurged on this one thing he's always wanted to do, and if he misses a single practice, his father will take it away. Thomas explains what happened in school to his mother, hoping that she will explain the problem to his father. Instead, she tells him no, and gives him advice that will become his life-long mantra. Identify your problem and engineer a solution.

Thomas thinks hard on his mantra that night. In the morning he is ready. He compels every student in the classroom to plead guilty to the charge. When they do along with Thomas, the teacher, while still angered, is softened by the comradery and drops the issue. Thomas is certain she knew who the guilty party was. He thinks most of the students did. But no one wanted to snitch. Either way, he'd solved their problem. *Thank you, mom.*

Someone attempts to whistle. It is a sharp, painful, sound, yet Thomas recognizes the tune. He feels his body tense with unease. Who could be here, and why are they so happy that they're attempting to whistle a rap song? Is this a joke, or something more sinister? It's the type of sound he'd use in a scary movie right before a murder. Shit. Where is it coming from? He stands still listening, ears working to gauge the noise's location when he sees movement. Ahead in the distance, puffs of dust rise into the sky then dissolve silently. Whoever it is, the whistle can't be coming from them; they're much too far away. But seconds later, a figure comes into view, each step sending dirt clouds into the air. It's blurry at first and takes a minute for Thomas to make out any features. When it gets closer, Thomas can see that the figure is a kid. He's walking in Thomas's direction with his head down and earphones in, whistling and singing off-key without constraint or reservation. Thomas watches in fascination at the mirage turned to life.

Bad Whistler, whom Thomas has already dubbed the boy, continues along his absentminded walk and is a few feet away from Thomas before he notices that he's not alone.

"Oh, hey," Bad Whistler says, taking out his earphones.

"Hello," Thomas says, trying not to frown.

"I'm Adam," the whistler holds out his hand. "Everything okay?"

"I'm not sure how to answer that," Thomas says, slowly extending his hand. "I'm Thomas."

Adam chuckles, "Okay, Thomas. Good to meet you. You're looking a bit frazzled. But not to worry. I get it. It's easy to get lost here. You're just south of the Way Station. It's a hundred yards behind you."

"Come again?"

"The Way Station. It's right behind you. Don't worry; you didn't lose it."

"Are you saying weigh station? Like for truckers? I'm not looking for one if that's what you're asking. I don't know why one would be here anyway. These roads look too small for a big truck."

Adam rubs his head. "Wait, what are we talking about?"

"I'm not sure. You keep saying weigh station. I'm trying to get to Westchester. I'm hoping that's it up ahead," he nods toward the road.

Adam looks where Thomas motioned then back at Thomas. "Uh, no. We're nowhere near Westchester. We're up the road from East Way Station."

Thomas sighs. "That again. Sorry, man. I'm not looking for a weigh station; I'm on foot. You know what, never mind. Can I use your phone?" He nods at the earbuds running from Adam's neck to the pocket of his jeans.

Adam follows Thomas's gaze, touches his phone, "Um, yeah. The phone doesn't work here. It's only for music."

"Of course," Thomas says. "Makes perfect sense. Anyhow, I think I'm going to take my chances in town. If that's not Westchester," he points past Adam's shoulder, "then what city is it?"

Adam scrunches his face, takes in Thomas from head to toe. "Dude," he says, "that's not a city. That is where my Broker lives. The Way Station is behind you. That's W-A-Y."

"Friend, I'm not asking about any of that. I just need to know where I am. What city is that?" Thomas says, searching behind Adam.

"It's not a city. Wait, you do realize that you're on the other side, don't you?

"The other side of what?" Thomas says, freezing to watch a pig-sized dragonfly fly toward him. It's beady eyes ooze puss that smells of licorice, and from its' mouth dangles a half-eaten squirrel. The dragonfly struggles against the weight of its kill; his victim bobbing so violently that blood sprays into the air. Thomas jumps backward, hoping to miss the spatter. All but one small droplet hits him, landing below his left eye.

"Jesus," Adam says, "those things get nastier every time I seethem. Hey," he looks at Thomas. "Are you alright? You don't look so good."

The thing about fainting is that some part of you, the primal part knows and accepts that it's coming. The conscious, rational part of you refuses to believe it, but can't do much to stop it. Black spots fill his eyes. Thomas fights to hang on but knows it's no use. His legs buckle, and the world turns dark.

Somewhere in the distance, someone is calling his name. Now they are shaking his arm. It's all Thomas can do not to scream KNOCK IT OFF.

"Thomas? Hey, wake up."

There it goes again, Thomas thinks, his eyes fluttering open. Adam is squatting next to him, uncomfortably close.

"Are you all right?" Adam asks.

Thomas locks eyes on Adam as if seeing him for the first time. "I'm still here?" he reaches to his face, wiping away the blood. Adam nods. "Then no, man. I'm not okay."

Adam cracks his neck to each side and stands up, offering Thomas a hand that he takes, grunting as he rises. "Look, I'm not sure what's going on," Adam says, "but I don't think it's a good idea to leave you here. I was heading home, but I should take you to see my Broker, and he can send you back with me. Or you guys can figure out something else. Maybe he can track down your Broker and you two can work out what happened."

"What are you talking about? What Broker? Like a stockbroker? I don't have any money. Why would I have a broker? And even if I did, what good would he be to me here? I don't need sound financial advice, currently. What I need, is to understand where the hell I am. And what was that thing that flew by with the dead squirrel?"

Adam takes a breath; seems to think through what he plans to say before saying anything.

"This," he gestures around with his hands, "is complicated to explain. I'm not sure what happened to you, but I'm getting the impression that you have no idea where you are. I don't know if you knocked your head on your way here or if your Broker screwed you over, but what I'm about to tell you might not sit well. Or maybe it will. Either way, it's going to be hard to process. I don't expect you to believe most of what I say, so I'm going to keep it brief. That said, whether you believe me or not, this is nowhere to get lost. You will not get out of here without help. So regardless of what you think of me after I explain where we are, you can't leave my side. Understood?"

"Jesus, dude. Spill it."

Adam shakes his head, "I don't know how you got here or who pulled you over, but it's pretty messed up because this isn't something I'd do to my worst enemy. I'm not going to rat out whoever did this to you should I ever find out, the last thing I want to do is make anyone mad, but, because I'm not a total dick, I'm not going to leave you here on your own to wait for the responsible party. Instead, I'll take you to Amos, my Broker, and while you probably won't enjoy that very much, it'll still be better than leaving you alone."

"Wait, if this is so bad, why do we have to go see this guy? You were already leaving. Can't I come with you?"

"You can't. I've never taken anyone through before, and I don't want to kill you."

"Through what? What would kill me? Where the hell are you going?"

"Christ, man, I can't explain everything, but the short version is that I'm going home via the Way Station. And by home, I mean our home," he thumps his hand to his chest, "on Novo. Do you have any idea what I'm talking about?"

Thomas shakes his head no.

"You're on Tendo, Thomas," Adam says. I have no idea how you got here on your own, but you've crossed sides to Tendo. You're in the second world."

Chapter 3

It takes Thomas several minutes to get his breathing under control before he's sure he won't faint again. Adam waits patiently, kicking rocks into the distance. "This can't be happening," Thomas says, his voice shaky.

"Well, it is. And while I know you're probably not ready to get moving, I don't have unlimited time. I have to get back, so we've got to go."

Adam walks away at a crawl but picks up speed when he sees that Thomas has caught up. "Listen," he says, "I understand there's a lot going through your head, but until I say otherwise, your focus needs to be on staying close to me. This section is confusing, and it's easy to get lost."

Thomas matches Adam's speed, not sure whether he should laugh or cry. What kind of day is this? Every few seconds, he risks a glance at Adam, waiting for Adam to blow his cover and reveal who is behind the remarkable prank that Thomas is the subject of. Who would put so much time and effort into such a thing?

"Stop," Adam abruptly halts, holding up his arm. Thomas freezes, just missing contact with another dragonfly, this one larger than the last. By the size of its belly, it has recently finished a meal. Adam waits for the bug to pass and makes a gagging sound.

"Sucklefly. Christ, they stink. Disgusting as all hell, but they do eat the vermin."

"What eats the sucklefly?" Thomas mumbles.

"Sorry," Adam slows, walking next to Thomas. "I guess this is a bit much for you. I was scared the first couple of times I came here, and I'd been prepped, if that's what you call it. Although, how do you prepare for something like this?" He gazes off, lost in thought. Then he's back, life returning to his eyes. "Anyway, try not to get too freaked out. It'll be over before you know it."

"Yeah, then I get to look forward to a lifetime at the insane asylum. Great."

"I wouldn't worry about that," Adam says. "Once Amos figures out how you got here, he'll send you to your Broker, or he'll wipe away your memory. One way or the other, you'll be alright."

"Alright?" Thomas stops. "Those are my only options? On what planet would I be alright?"

"Well, not planet, per se," Adams shakes his head, "sorry, too much info. All I mean is that you'll be fine either way, in either universe."

Thomas shakes his head at the ground. This is ridiculous. Who is this kid? Why is he even listening to him? He should have seen it before. Adam is nuts. Adam watches Thomas try to work it out, pats his back when Thomas doesn't comment.

"I know you think I'm crazy or that you're crazy, but that's beside the point. Whether it's true or not, you are still here, and you need to get home. We are going to figure out how to make that happen. There's no point in fighting it. So, go with it. At the end of this day, you'll either be back with your Broker who can explain what happened or you won't remember a thing."

"Then I guess we'll have to wait and see," Thomas sighs. Adam's right. There's no point in arguing about it. He is out of options and has no idea how to navigate a place where bugs eat squirrels. God only knows what else is running around. Adam is his best option. "So, tell me about this place, Adam. What is it, and what are you doing here?"

"Good question," Adam picks up his pace. Thomas keeps by his side. "As I said, I'm from the same place as you. It's called Novo on this side."

"And you come here a lot?"

"I guess. I use this Way Station to travel back and forth."

"For what?"

"For my Broker."

"Which is?"

"He's the being that runs this territory. My job is to listen to people's thoughts when I'm on our side, then I come here, and Amos takes them from me."

"To listen to thoughts. Seriously?"

"Yep."

"Okay. Let's say that's possible. What happens next? You said he takes them. How does that work?"

"He just drains me of them. I show up with a bunch of thoughts I've gathered, and he takes them away. Then I go back home, and everything is normal until he needs me again."

"So, then you're what? Telepathic?" Thomas raises an eyebrow.

"Sort of, I guess. I know how it sounds. I can't believe I said it out loud. But it's true. And I don't really listen to the thoughts; I only pull pieces of what people are thinking. Then I bring them here, and he takes them away."

"Why? What does he do with them?"

"He and the other Brokers use them, somehow. I'm not sure for what, exactly, but I do know that it's crucial for both sides that the thoughts make it here."

"But if it's that important, shouldn't you know why? I mean, what do you get out of it? At least if you knew why you were doing it, you'd have an incentive."

Adams' eyes twinkle. "Oh, there's an incentive."

"Which is?"

"I get to make my life better. When my dad divorced my step-mother, they split me and step-brother up, and then my dad moved us to another town. He works non-stop, so I never got to see him or my old family. Everything turned to shit, and my consolation prize was blowing my chances at medical school because I let my grades slip to deal with my family. It was pretty much over for me until I came here. And now, because of this place, I get to shape my life into exactly what I want it to be. And pretty soon, my family will understand how important I am; and that I do matter and that I always have."

"I'm sure you mattered before," Thomas says.

"No, not like this. Not like I do now."

"What do you mean?"

"That their crap almost cost me everything I'd dreamt about as a kid. I'd always been a good student; I'd always planned to be a doctor and thought I was working toward it. Then everything got in the way, and they forgot about me. There's too much to cover. But when today is over, I hope you get a chance to come back. This place gives you the possibility to be the best version of yourself and see the world in a new way. And as much as you think that you're here by chance, I don't buy it. They've got an endless pick of people to choose from. If you're here, you're supposed to be; maybe not now, but eventually. So, keep that in mind."

"But I didn't ask to be here. You keep making it sound so amazing, but so far, I've seen some scary-ass animals and a bunch of bushes. If that's what this 'universe' is, I guess I'll stick with mine. For all I know, I'm hallucinating." Freaking Amanda, he thinks. She probably drugged me.

"Thomas, you're in another world. I mean, what more is there to say? Don't you get the magnitude of it?"

"I don't because I can't. Seriously, Adam, I don't know what we're talking about. I don't understand what this is."

Adam stares into the sky. "No, sorry, you're right. It's impossible to explain. Let's talk to Amos and figure out how to get you home. Then if you're meant to return, it'll happen."

"If you say so. Anyway, thank you for helping me. You don't even know me."

"No worries, I was heading home anyway. I'm just glad I found you when I did."

"See, that worries me. You keep making it sound dangerous to be here."

"Na, not if you know what you're doing. Let's get moving. One thing, though," he looks at Thomas, "when we get to Amos's place, be quiet. Don't ask questions, don't say anything."

"Why? Is he that bad?"

"No, it's not that. He's not patient. And he doesn't like surprises."

"Then why do you keep coming?"

"You'll see, but we've got to go. This is taking too long."

"Holy shit, that's right," Thomas stops, "I have no idea how long I've been here. I was on my way to pick up my little sister. She's probably freaking out."

Adam holds up his hands. "Don't worry about it. Time is different here; it's probably only been seconds on the other side, if that. I doubt anyone's noticed."

Thomas lets out his breath. "Thank God. Christ, what a nightmare." He's moving before Adam starts walking.

"Hey," Adam catches his stride, "I'm serious. Stay close."

The patch of land ahead reminds Thomas of a National Geographic video he watched in science a few months back. A few steps in and they're entrenched in a jungle so dense it makes him claustrophobic. He tells himself not to panic just as Adam glances back at him and shrugs as if to agree that it's unsettling. He can smell that there are animals nearby, but based on the sounds, nothing seems out of the ordinary. Light forces its way in where it can, illuminating greenery and berry bushes with an alien glow so unsettling Thomas reminds himself to breathe.

"So, we're going to your Broker's house?" Thomas asks. If he doesn't distract himself soon, he'll start hyperventilating.

"Something like that. If Amos isn't there, his assistant might be able to help."

"Great," Thomas mumbles under his breath. "I'm sure his secretary will be thrilled to help out."

Adam smiles over his shoulder. "It'll be fine, okay? I can tell you're stressing, but I won't let anything happen to you out here. I've been coming here long enough to know how to handle whatever comes up. There's one thing, though, that you should probably know."

"What?" he stops, waiting to hear the bad news.

"It's nothing to worry about, but something you should be aware of. It's uh, well, as we get a little deeper into the bush, you need to try to be calm, peaceful, if you can."

"Peaceful?"

"Ya, I know how it sounds. But I think that this place reacts to me, to how I'm acting, or feeling. The calmer I am, the easier things seem to go for me."

"Really?"

"I think so. It could be a coincidence, but that's how it's gone for a while now. It took me a long time to figure it out."

"But isn't that how life works or is supposed to anyway? The better you behave, or the more you disrupt, effects how the world treats you in turn?"

"True. It could be that, too. But it just seems more intense here, like you can see the change in dynamics right away."

"Then I'm on board. No reason to cause any friction. I'll be cool as cucumbers."

Adam snorts, "my dad says that." He smiles at Thomas and picks up his pace.

"So did my grandpa," Thomas smiles back, keeping up with Adam. The forest tightens along the path. Vines tear at their pants and shirts, Thomas pulls one free from his arm, gaping at the swath of white ants left crawling down his forearm. When he goes to wipe them free, Adam smacks his hand away.

"Don't. They don't bite unless you're aggressive."

"I wasn't aggressive. They started it."

"Blow them off," Adam says, waiting until Thomas has blown the last ant from his body.

"That wasn't one hundred percent calm."

After walking what seems an eternity, the trees thin out, and the path widens, giving Thomas a view of the sky that is the oddest shade of blue imaginable. He feels the earth shift below his feet and looks down, watching as the ground grows softer with every step he takes. He stops to push his foot around in the fine white powder covering his shoes.

"This looks like sugar."

"It's not," Adam says and disappears under a canopy of palm trees that Thomas could swear didn't exist before.

"Adam?" he tilts his head to the sky to take in the size of the trees. Those are higher than the ones we were just in, he thinks. Should palm trees be that tall? They've got to be seven hundred feet. "Hey Adam, do these trees have coconuts?" Adam laughs from somewhere past the tree line. "Adam?" Thomas yells, and something hisses next to his feet. Thomas rushes into the canopy, colliding so hard with Adam that they bump heads.

"Ouch," Adam rubs the back of his head.

"Sorry," Thomas pants. "Something's out there; it hissed at me. And Christ, it's dark in here. What are we doing?"

"Give it a second," Adam says.

"Give what a second?"

"Shh. Stop talking and wait."

A light flashes near Thomas. Adam whispers to wait. Another light blinks by their feet. It's quickly joined by ten others that form a circle around Thomas. Dread tightens around Thomas's throat. He's ready to flee when there is a single, brilliant flash, and billions of tiny lights spring to life illuminating a tree canopy so long and dense it appears as if they are in an underground tunnel. Thomas gapes at the swaying masterpiece.

"The lights," he says, "are they moving?" The glowing lights shimmer and undulate, dropping to the ground and bouncing off the trees.

"Uh-huh."

Thomas leans forward to examine a light on the wall. "But how? They look like; I don't know…"

"Tiny hummingbirds?" Adam says, his toothy smile glowing white under the lights. "They are. Aren't they amazing? They're not even half the size of bee hummingbirds."

"But how did they get in here so fast? Where did they come from?"

"They were already here. They needed to, well, turn on. Your noisy entrance helped."

"What?" Thomas turns to Adam's illuminated face.

"We'll be at my beach in a minute, and I'll show you why they light up. It's called bioluminescence. I saw a show in science about how during certain times of the year, the waves on the West Coast glow when the phytoplankton gets disturbed. The same thing must happen to the ocean here except that it's all the time because after the hummingbirds drink it, they turn into little flashlights. Every time I come through the trees, this whole place lights up."

"This is the coolest thing I've ever seen," Thomas spins around, careful not to step on any birds. Every movement he makes sends them fluttering around, changing patterns and directions that mimic his own.

"I know. It's killer. This is one of my favorite parts."

"One of them? You mean there's more?" Thomas asks.

"You asked what I got out of all of this, and this doesn't even scratch the surface. Be prepared to have your mind blown."

"Too late for that," Thomas says.

"You have no idea," Adam's eyes flash.

Adam leads the way, Thomas following behind, playing with the birds who have covered his entire body. Adam turns and laughs. He's done the same thing on more than one occasion.

"Start shaking them off," he tells Thomas then steps from the cave into the sun. Thomas spins once, gently freeing the birds from his clothes, then he's standing in the daylight next to Adam. He's confused; he was sure the walk through the tunnel would take much longer. He's about to ask about it when they step onto a beach stretch so beautiful the question dies on his tongue. Powdery sand runs from the trees to the waterline and beyond, forming bridges and islands as far as the eye can see.

"Right?" Adam gazes at the sea.

"It's indescribable," Thomas says.

"I know," Adam says. "Only try."

"Huh?"

"Try to describe it. What does the water remind you of?" Adam asks.

Thomas blows air through his lips. "I don't know, lava? It looks like we're watching a volcano erupt on television"

Adam laughs, nodding his approval. "That's it; he says," his eyes dancing. "I mean, it is water, but it looks like lava. It turned out exactly as I planned."

Thomas snorts, "Yeah, right. You made that," he points to toward the glowing sea. "Great job."

"Thank you. I agree. And I did make it, smart-ass. A few years back, my step-brother got me a lava-lamp for my birthday. When Amos told me to think of something beautiful, I imagined the lamp. And voila!"

"Seriously?"

"Yes, seriously. I'm not joking. I made this part," he gestures around. "The beach, the ocean. It's mine. Amos lets me build here."

"How? And why? I mean, I still don't get it. What is this place?"

Adam searches the sky, turning back to Thomas, his eyes intense. "Watch," he says, grabbing a handful of sand and squeezing his eyes shut. Thomas waits, mesmerized by tufts of smoke that drift from Adam's fingers. Adam opens his eyes and smiles. "Look," he slowly opens his hand. Resting on his palm is tiny scorpion figurine, its skin the color of onyx. Thomas reaches for it with wide eyes. The scorpion flexes its tail, prepared to strike.

"Holy shit," Thomas pulls his hand back, "it's alive?"

Adam grins, blowing gently on the creature, turning it back into sand.

"Na, not alive per se, I'm not God. I can't bring things to life. But I can make some cool stuff. That particular creature could have stung you by the way. Do you always reach for scorpions? That's not very smart. Just saying."

Once more, Thomas sways on his feet. Adam catches his arm. "It was just sand. Relax. In the grand scheme of things, it's not a big deal, but I think you're starting to get the point. Anything and everything are possible here. This is where unrealized potential lives. If you can dream it, you can have it. That is what this place is. And beyond the coolness of that, this place is important. Crucial even. Without Tendo, there is no Novo and vice versa. One does not work without the other. I don't know how much of a role the thoughts play, but I know it's a big one. So, not only is this the most amazing place that I have, or you will ever see, but our existence depends on it. I am a part of that. Sometimes it's too much to process—like it'll eat me up if I let it. But I won't let that scare me. I could never go back to my old life after this."

"Well, that's the thing; if this place needs us, or you so bad, then why is it a secret? How come more people aren't involved? Why aren't we working together?"

"I don't know. I guess if the Brokers let too many people come here, it could get chaotic, so they have to be selective."

"Meaning you were chosen. How?"

"Amos came to me in a dream, told me how to get to the Way Station. It took five times before I believed it might be real, and that I hadn't just dreamt it. I went to the coordinates he gave me feeling like an idiot and not expecting anything but ended up here. Amos was waiting for me."

"Then I'm definitely not supposed to be here. Nothing like that happened to me. I got into a car with a girl, and then I blacked out and pretty much ran into you. This whole thing is a mistake, so after I get home, I guess I'll forget it all."

Adam's mouth drops. "You'd be okay with that? To go back to your old boring life?"

"I don't think I have a choice. And anyway, I don't think I could get used to hearing people's thoughts. I bet you hear some sick shit."

"Yeah, well, everything has a price, doesn't it? And it's not like that. You listen for a second to some fleeting thought, and then Amos takes it away for the most part."

"For the most part?"

"He leaves a tiny portion behind, almost like the resin left behind when you pull a sticker off something. You can tell by its shape what kind of sticker it was even though you can't see it. So, it's not so bad. He's never left anything horrible behind and told me he never would."

"Well, that makes it all better then. It's not like you're exploiting people if you can't remember every detail."

"Look," Adam's face darkens, "I don't love that part of it, but there are two things you need to consider. First, someone's gotta do it, so why not me? And second, this doesn't last forever. My time will come to an end here as it does for everyone, and when that happens, it'll be worth it. I assure you."

"I don't mean any offense. I don't even know what I'm saying. I'm sure you know what you're doing. I'm here by mistake, remember, and then it's done for me. It'll be like I had a crazy dream and forgot it before I woke up."

"Wow," Adam says. "I can't believe that knowing all of this might be taken away from you isn't making you crazy. It would kill me."

"There's nothing I can do about it."

"I guess," Adam shrugs. "Who knows? But in the end, we both have the same plan, and that's to get home. So, let's go."

Chapter 4

Walking along the beach, Thomas is struck by how normal its general components look compared to all of the unworldly elements. The sand slopes toward the water, where it disappears after a gradual decline. Palms line the sand in the distance, dancing with an invisible breeze. But then there is the unearthly color of the water and sand, so strangely spectacular that it brings tears to his eyes. The swaying palms on the beach, standard anywhere but here, look like dragons roaring green fire into the sky. If Adam created this, Thomas could see where he started. The brilliance of its infrastructure, the ordered chaos of its planning, a creation by an imagination developed through years of books and movies, cartoons and make-believe, dreams, and nightmares.

Adam taps Thomas's shoulder, urging him forward. Thomas desperately wants to stay and gawk, but across the water, he spots a structure he knows will be far more interesting than the beach. It's too far to make out any details, but it's clear that it's massive even at this distance. "Are we heading to that building or whatever that is way out in the ocean?"

"Yes."

"Are we taking a boat?"

"No."

"Then how…" he begins, stopping in confusion when his feet meet with hard rock. They have arrived at the base of a mountain made of stone. Thomas stares up the wall, his eyes blurring into focus. He gasps, whispers, "that's not a mountain."

"Of course not," Adam says. "It's a skyscraper."

For Thomas, everything leading up to this seems less significant, somehow. The sheer size of the building is overwhelming, and in every second that follows, he spots something stranger and more exciting than the last. While there appear to be no windows, the shale texture of pink and green reflects the sky so perfectly that the structure itself seems translucent. Invisibility cloak, Thomas finds himself thinking and wishing that Madi were here to see this. One of their favorite games is how best to hide objects without hiding them at all.

"So, how do we get in?" Thomas asks, "I don't see an entrance."

Without a word, Adam points at the front of the building, and as if the building heard his silent request, two black columns solidify on its surface, revealing an entrance, that like the columns themselves, stretches into the sky.

"Christ," Thomas takes a jittery step back, "I can't believe you've done this before. First, there's no building, then this giant thing appears and now we're supposed to walk through an entrance that comes and goes? This is nuts."

Still focused on the tower, Adam says, "Space or place or whatever you want to call it is tricky, here. Don't try to make sense of it. There is no point. And the building was there the whole time. We just moved very far, very quickly. It's not like this everywhere, but it is in this section because Amos wants it that way. The closer we get to his palace, the faster we travel. It saves time. As for the columns and the opening, you're right. They're sketchy. But keep calm, remember?"

"Right," Thomas mumbles. "Because everything is listening. So, what part of this place did you build?"

"None of it. My construction stops at the water. But the cool thing is that every time I come here, something's been altered, so I never know what to expect. Well, outside of the main structure, anyway. That stays intact. But I can always find something new. For instance, those columns," he nods "when I left earlier, were made of fire. This time they look like lead or something. I'm not sure what that material is."

Thomas coughs. "Of fire? Really?"

Adam rolls his eyes. "Mm, hmm. Anyway, this is the final walkway before Amos's chamber, so remember what I said. I'll do the talking."

"Fine by me," he says, following Adam into a hallway where vertigo forces him to stop. Sea life surrounds him in every direction. "My God," he spins around. "This is incredible. I feel like I walked into a fish tank. Is that what the walls are made of?"

"Yes. Keep moving."

"Wait, we've got to stop for a second. This is insane. It looks like we're in one of those walk-through aquarium tubes you see in movies; only they're not tubes, right? I can't see an ending or beginning. They're like vertical infinity pools. Does this part change too?"

"No. What's inside does, but not the walls."

Mesmerized, Thomas stares into the tanks. "You've got to be kidding me. This is amazing. The glass is perfect. It's so clear I feel like I'm underwater. I've never seen so many colors in my life."

A school of fish passes by, one peeling off and approaching the window, its eyes fixed on Thomas. Now just inches away from Thomas, Thomas can make out its details, the intricate circles of black surrounding orange on a white backdrop, glowing golden eyes lined in black, fangs exposed in what could be a smile or snarl. The only difference between a jaguar and the fish staring back at him is its appendages, fins instead of paws. Mouth quivering and ears pounding, Thomas takes a step forward, his eyes no more than an inch from the fish. In response, the tiny jaguar moves closer to Thomas, its whiskers pressing against the glass; its face smashed into a blur. Thomas is about to laugh

when the glass bulges out, only to snap back into place, sending
the fish scurrying away.

"Did the glass just, uh…" Thomas reaches out. Somewhere
behind him, he hears Adam.

"Thomas, don't."

But it's too late. Thomas's finger touches the glass and
presses through it. What he thought was a wall isn't glass at
all. It's water, liquid, and solid at the same time. The water
pulses, sending ripples around his finger.

"Oh God," he pulls his finger out and expects the entire
wall to collapse to the ground, but it pulls back into its
original shape. "Whoa," he says, reaching forward to do it
again, but Adam catches his arm, pulling him away from the wall
and down the hallway.

"Are you crazy?" Adam whispers. "I said to be cool. Amos is
crazy about his water-wall. It's the fastest way to piss him
off, which we don't want, remember?"

"Sorry. I did not mean to do that."

"I know. Just don't touch anything else."

He walks away without waiting for a response.

The hallway opens into a massive circular cave, so perfect
in shape that it reminds Thomas of the crop circles that pop up
around the world. It isn't cold, but he shivers. Something feels
very wrong here. To the left is a pool, also circular, and even
from the other side of the cave, Thomas can see the sea life it
contains as if it were lit up from below. Behind Thomas, Adam
calls out for Amos, who doesn't respond, so Adam walks to the
wall and pushes a buzzer that immediately buzzes two beeps back.

"Nice," Adam says, visibly relaxing. "Amos left, but his
assistant is here. I'll go see if she knows what to do."

Thomas arches his eyebrows. "Is that a good idea?"

"It's fine. I'd rather deal with her than Amos about this.
He was testy today."

"How's that?"

"I don't know; he's hard to read. He's serious and expects efficiency. But he can also be cool; and then he can flip into awful without warning. Usually, he's just serious Amos, and that's who I want to work with. You know what to expect and he expects the same from you. Whatever I do, I don't waste his time, because that's the surest way to make him mad. Anyway, he seemed like he might be having a shitty day earlier so seeing the assistant will be better. Plus, she's super cool. The Way Stations are complicated. She knows that. She'll probably think you just got lost."

"You're not going to tell her how I got here?"

"I don't know how you got here. Do you?"

"Good point. So, what now?"

"Wait here. I'll be gone for a few minutes."

"Will do," Thomas looks at his feet and around the cave.

"Seriously. Stay right there."

"I'm not going anywhere. Go talk to her."

Adam raises his eyebrows at Thomas, then turns and walks directly into the pool without slowing and disappears. Thomas mentally paces, wishing Adam would hurry up. He has no interest in meeting Amos and prays that he doesn't return. Gurgling sounds come from the hallway, and Thomas knows he shouldn't leave but walks the short distance to check it out. The left side of the water wall pulses sending the visible fish scattering. A second pulse follows, only this time, the middle of the wall presses out, growing like a pregnant bubble. Thomas expects it to explode, but a hand bursts through, into the air. It struggles forward, followed by an arm, and Thomas thinks Adam's shoulder will appear but instead, a fish comes to the surface. Its eyes bulge as it thrashes around, its body working its way free from the water until it falls to the ground with a loud thwack.

Terrified, it flops across the hallway and is absorbed back into the water when it touches the wall on the other side. The fish is so distracting that Thomas misses most of Adam's resurfacing but turns in time to see him climb sideways out of the water-wall from the waist down. Completely dry, Adam adjusts his shirt and walks over.

"I hate doing that," he says. "It's sketchy inside the water. Things change really fast."

"Did you see that fish? It just—"

Adam grimaces, reaching into his pants. He struggles for a minute before ripping his arm free. Clutched in his hand, is a black, foot-long fish with razor-sharp teeth. It flaps around in Adam's grip, growling and snapping its jaw.

"Grab it," Adam yells.

Thomas does, catching the angler by its gills. It whips and thrashes in Thomas's hand, a tooth tearing across his palm. Thomas pauses at the sight of blood, but the fish continues to fight. Adam grabs the fish from Thomas, and like he's throwing a baseball, pitches the fish at the water-wall where it sticks and is slowly reabsorbed. Thomas expects it to race away, but instead, it stays at the edge of the wall, swimming back and forth like it's pacing, its eyes never leaving Adam.

"I hate those things," Adam says. "I should have banked it off the ground before it hit the water. How bad did it get you?"

"It's a scratch. I'm fine," he says. He'd rather not think about it. "What happened? Did you see the assistant? Does she live in there?"

"I saw her. I don't know where she lives, but she spends a lot of time in the water walls. It's pretty weird when you think about it, but she's nice. Her name's L."

"L., like the letter? That is weird. Is she a Broker, too?"

"She's not a Broker; I'm not sure what her story is other than that she's important to Amos. And it's not 'L' the letter; it's just what I call her because I've only met her underwater and it's hard to understand everything she says, especially her name. Anyway, she told me I could bring you through the Way Station like normal, but to hold on to you until we'd passed through, so you didn't slip out somewhere else. So that's what we'll do. She also told me to give you this," he hands Thomas what looks like a pill.

"Me? Why, what is it?"

"I don't know. I didn't ask. She just handed it to me and told me to give it to the traveler."

"What do I do with it?"

"Take it, I guess. I don't ask a lot of questions around here. I just do what I'm told."

"And you'd take a pill from a stranger that lives underwater if you were me?"

Adam rolls his eyes.

"Oh," Thomas says, "I think that fish got you, too."

"Huh?"

"The fish that cut my hand. Your cheek is bleeding." Thomas points towards Adam's face while Adam reaches for his check, their fingers touching. Everything goes black.

Thomas is back at the entrance to the skyscraper; then he's passing the columns and traveling through the water hallway before walking straight into the pool. *Oh no*. This is like what happened with Amanda, only now I'm in Adam's memory from when we got to the palace. For the love of God, is this whole thing starting over?

Fish of every color and shape swim around; each one is as unusual as the next. A school of fish with ram-horns swims by, each one bumping the other from behind. A white stingray matching the sand skims across Adam's foot. He sees it force its eyeballs attached to long eel-like strands out of their sockets to watch him. One eye tries to get a better look and detaches. It floats in front of Adam's face. Adam gags, blowing bits of vomit into the water that the ram-fish circle back for and devour in seconds. The landscape is magical and terrifying at once. There is a person up ahead; the assistant, Thomas guesses. The underwater forest is so thick she's barely visible, and while her voice is muddled, most of her words are understandable when they arrive in bubbles and pop near his ears.

"Hello, Adam. This is unexpected," her words pop. "What brings you in?"

"Hi L. I have a courier with me who got turned around in the Way Stations. He can't reach his Broker and needs to get back. I thought he might be able to come through with me but wanted to make sure that would work."

Adam's words float over to her, and he sees her nod in understanding.

"Interesting," a bubble floats from her mouth, making its way to Adam, "a lost courier. You sure you're not up to something?" pop-pop, pop-pop.

"I—no, not at all. He's just a kid who got lost. I was going to ask Amos what to do."

Pop, pop, pop. "I'm kidding Adam, I trust you. I haven't used a Way Station in years, but remember that they were confusing. Just hang on to him until you're sure you've completely crossed; when the light has retracted. And be thankful Amos wasn't here. He wouldn't have liked this." Pop-pop, pop-pop-pop. She starts to float backward but then returns. "Wait," she says, "what's his name? The boy?"

"Thomas," Adam says, watching her features change when his bubbles arrive. "L.? You okay?" L. pulls a container from her pocket and rushes forward, pushing it into Adam's hand.

"Give him this," she says, floating in the water, her green gown swirling around her. Confused but compliant, Adam takes the pill, looking up when a shadow passes overhead. Thousands of jagged teeth flash white in the water above him. He can't tell what creature they belong to, only that it's massive, stretching hundreds of feet. He freezes in place, his eyes snapping shut for fear of blinking. There is nothing worse than the things that can live in this water. L. speaks at Adam, the current taking her words on a bumpy ride. When they finally arrive and pop by his ears, her gentle voice soothes away most of his fear.

"Earth to Adam, Earth to Adam," they say. "Come in, Adam." Pop-pop, pop-pop.

Thomas feels his knees wobble and struggles to stay upright. He braces his weight against his thighs, breaking the connection with Adam.

"Thomas? You okay?" Adam blinks. "You look like you saw a ghost."

Thomas shakes his head, mutters, "I'm fine, Adam."

Breathe, Thomas, breathe, he tells himself. Get out of here. Don't think about it yet. Not yet. But it's no use. There's no escaping the truth. That was her in the water; in Adam's memory. That was my mom.

Chapter 5

The walk back is less impressive than the walk in, yet for Thomas, more jarring. He can hardly contain his emotions. Adam doesn't seem to notice, or, if he does, he keeps it to himself. They walk like ghosts might, quiet and reflective. "So, we're going to the Station that will take me home?" Thomas steadies his voice. He has a million questions about his mother but isn't sure what to say. "That's what the assistant said?"

"Yep. It sounds easy enough." He scratches his head. "L. said it was a good thing Amos wasn't there; that he would have been angry. We got lucky."

"Why? What's his deal? Is she scared of him? What's she doing in there anyway? Can she leave?"

"I don't know. I guess so. I don't get in the middle of their relationship." Thomas stops, the vein in his neck bulging. "Their relationship? Like they're together?"

"Yuck. No, not like that. Why do you care, anyway?"

"I don't. I don't know. It just seems bizarre, and I'm curious about this whole place." He shoves his hands into his pants, hoping Adam didn't see them shake.

"Well, I wouldn't worry about her. It's not like you'll ever see her again."

Thomas winces, hoping his face didn't show it. "But what if I want to? I mean, maybe I am supposed to be here. You said that if this was just a fluke that I wouldn't be able to remember, and there's no way I'm forgetting this because I didn't even see Amos. Wasn't he the one who was going to make me forget?"

Adam's eyebrows pull up. "He'd just wipe you in your sleep or pull you back in and wipe you then, but I do like the sudden interest. Water walls change your mind?"

"Yep. Water walls. So, what do you think? What are the chances that I get to come back?"

"I have no idea. You're supposed to have a Broker to get here, but that didn't happen with you, or maybe it did, but something got messed up along the way. All I know is the first time I came, I was dreaming, so I wasn't here, per se. But after that, Amos explained how to use the Way Stations, and I've been coming since."

"But if we use the Station today, I'll know how to get here again."

"You won't. They don't work the same for everyone. Your entry spot would be different than mine. That's how they keep them safe. Even if you could find one, there'd be no point coming here without having a Broker. You'd be lost. Seriously, I don't think you understand how confusing it can be here. Anyway, L. said to hurry. I've been here too long today. You run?" he grins, racing away before Thomas can answer.

Thomas groans but keeps up. He hates running and imagines they'll be at it forever but is pleasantly surprised a few minutes later when Adam comes to a stop in front of a run-down building that reminds Thomas of an old gas Station. Of the windows remaining on the creaky shack, all but one is broken. There's a sign dangling from a single hook with EAST printed in the middle. Thomas wrinkles his face, looks at Adam.

"This can't be it."

Adam laughs. "What?" he says.

"I just expected, with what everyone can do here, it'd be…"

"Nicer? Yeah, that makes sense," he bows, gesturing for Thomas to enter. "If you think the outside is bad, wait until you see the inside."

Thomas hesitates, but steps through the doorway. He is assaulted by the smell of something burning, like old papers or leaves. When his eyes adjust to the dim light, he sees ashes floating in the air, confirming paper was indeed burning, only they don't fall to the ground. Instead, they hold their positions, floating in front of his face. He leans in for a closer look, gagging when he accidentally sucks a glob of material into his mouth. Adam's eyes widen to saucers and fill with tears.

"Spit it out, you moron," he yells, eyes fixed on Thomas.

Thomas spits the blob out with such ferocity that it travels through the air, smacking Adam in the chest, who is now roaring with laughter.

"Arrgghh," Thomas screams, wiping his tongue with his shirt. "What was that?"

Adam has doubled over to laugh and stands, wiping the tears from his eyes. "Why'd you suck one into your mouth, you nutjob? What did you think it was?" Adam asks, incredulously. He can't stop laughing.

"Ashes," Thomas says, staring at the tiny floating jellyfish he'd just had in his mouth. It turns red and starts to shake violently. Thomas reaches for it, not sure what else to do, and it splits in half, forming two perfect tiny jellyfish. They wiggle and stretch, before the shaking starts again, and the two creatures split into four. Four quickly become sixteen, and in less than a minute, millions of ghostly creatures surround Thomas.

"Let's go," Adam floats by, a smile swallowing most of his face. Thomas watches in disbelief as Adam summersaults through empty air, an eerie pink light trailing his every move. He waves to Adam, and the jellyfish surround his arm in a gentle cradle before lifting him from the ground. The higher he rises, the tighter he's encompassed by their warm, rubbery bodies. Up ahead, Adam sails around the room, a clumsy ballerina without a dance to practice. A little ball bumps Thomas's nose and glares at him.

"Ouch," Thomas yells, fighting to keep his balance. Adam mock swims over, sees Thomas holding his nose, and looks around.

"Oh shit," he points at the ball making its way toward them, "that blob is coming for you. Don't let it get ya," he backstrokes away, laughing so hard he clutches his stomach in pain.

"Why! What was that?" Thomas tries Adam's technique to back swim away from the little ball, but it has the reverse effect, sending him in the wrong direction toward what must be certain doom. He yells for Adam in a panic. Adam returns and pumps his hands through the air, forcing the blob away on an invisible current. His laughter has taken on a hyena-like quality that Thomas wants to smack from his face.

"What the hell was that thing?" Thomas yells.

"That was the mini-sun," Adam cackles. "You shouldn't let it burn you."

"I didn't let it!"

"I know," Adam gathers himself, "just kidding. That thing's a serious jerk. Didn't you notice the jellies trying to avoid it?"

"No, I didn't. A lot is going on here in case you didn't notice. Christ." A ball spins by Adam, blowing his hair back before moving on.

"Jupiter," Adam says. "Fast and stormy, but she won't bother you."

"Is the entire solar system in here?"

"Shh," Adam stops him. "It's time to go."

"What? How do you know?"

"I can feel it. Amos sensed that I'm here. He's going to push me through. Hold on to me, and don't let go."

There is darkness, then piercing white light, and sounds of ragged breath.

"We made it," Thomas hears Adam say. "This is your stop. I'll see you soon."

"What? How?" Thomas sits in darkness, disoriented.

"You said Westchester earlier."

"Yeah?"

"My step-brother goes to school in Westchester. I'm a town over with my dad. Ugly divorce, but I still visit."

"Small world," Thomas says and hears Adam snort.

"Nothing small about it. See you around."

Thomas opens his eyes. Sitting across from him in the old beat-up Buick is Amanda, their fingers still touching. She blinks several times as the shimmer surrounding them dissipates. They drop their hands and stare at each other. Amanda shakes her head, and her eyes come into focus.

"What just happened?" Tears fill her eyes, "how did you do that?"

"I didn't do that. I have no idea what just happened."

Amanda's breathing grows erratic; her chest hitches as she frantically looks around.

"Hey, slow down," Thomas says. "You're hyperventilating. You've got to get a hold of your breathing."

Amanda nods, squeezing her eyes shut. Thomas counts slowly backward from ten, prompting her to count along. They continue the exercise several minutes until Amanda's breathing returns to normal.

"Better?" Thomas asks.

Amanda shakes her head. "I guess." He tries to smile, pats her leg.

"Listen, whatever just happened was crazy, and I know we need to talk about it, but I've got to go get my sister."

Amanda tears up again, "Of course," she says. "I'll drive you."

"Thanks," Thomas grabs his bag, "but I don't think you should drive for a while. Maybe just sit here for a few minutes. Get your bearings."

"Okay," she mumbles. He climbs from the car, feeling a tickle in his ears and hears, *he was there. It doesn't make any sense, but Thomas was in the car. He saw me with Brad.* He looks in at Amanda with her hands frozen on the wheel, white knuckles unmoving, and it hits him like a train. She hadn't moved a muscle. She didn't say a word—but she'd thought them, and he *heard* her.

"Hey," he leans into the car. "Don't worry about any of this. Your secret is safe with me."

Amanda looks up with wide eyes. "What?"

"Nothing. Never mind. I just don't want you to worry about anything. And get some rest, okay?" He tosses his backpack over his shoulder and walks away. At the end of the street, he glances back once and can see Amanda sitting in the car, her hands still locked on the wheel.

Chapter 6

With its red bricks and bright white trim, Merrimac Elementary looks like an advertisement in a real estate magazine. The remainder of Westchester isn't much to look at, but they got the elementary school right. Pine trees line the left side of the building that is surrounded by a manicured lawn. Behind the school is a new play structure that was recently installed. There seems to be an endless fund for improving this place. Thomas likes coming here as much as he did when it was his school. The day is warm and sticky. Thomas picks a shady spot under a tree, dropping his backpack beside him. Somehow there are several minutes left before Madi gets out of school. Adam's words run through his mind. Time and space are tricky here; it's probably only been seconds on Novo. Everything feels strange and new, like he sees the world through different eyes.

"Thomas?" A tap against his foot startles him, and he blinks open his eyes to Madi standing above him. She tosses her bag aside and plops down next to him, wearing a chocolate-smeared grin. "Are you going to answer?" She licks at the chocolate on her cheeks.

"Huh? Oh, hey, Madi. Sorry, I must have zoned out. That big test I told you about was today, and it was a long one. How was school? What's on your face?"

"Jenna Martin had her birthday. Her mom brought cupcakes for the whole class."

"I see you had vanilla?"

"Nope, chocolate," she says, licking her face again. "They were delicious. I had two."

They walk home slowly, Madi kicking leaves from the sidewalk on what will likely be one of the last warm days this year. Thomas listens while she talks and spins, her sugar high in full effect. The fourth grade has had an eventful day. They're revving up for a play. She'll need a costume. Thomas sighs, knowing there's no money for a costume. He'll figure something out; he always does.

"Think he'll come home tonight?" Madi asks.

"Whoa. Where'd that come from?" Thomas says.

"I don't know. We haven't seen dad for a while. Maybe he misses us."

"He doesn't. If he wanted to see us, he would."

"You don't know that. Maybe he can't get home."

"He could if he wanted to. Madi, Jimmy's not a good guy. I hate to say that, but it's true. The sooner you realize that, the better."

"Don't call him that. You're supposed to call him dad. Kids don't call their parents by their first names. It's weird."

"Those kids have parents. If Jimmy acted like one, I'd give him proper billing, but he doesn't; so, Jimmy it is."

"You still call her mom."

Thomas stops in his tracks. "That's not fair, Madi. It's not even close to the same thing, and you know it. And she didn't leave us. Something happened to her."

"You don't know that," Madi says.

"I do, Madi. So, let it go."

"Geeze, okay. I'm sorry. Don't be mad. I know how you feel about mom. But she hasn't been back once. At least dad comes home sometimes, and you hate him but not her."

"I don't hate him. Just forget it. You're too young to be talking about this. Focus on the things you need to take care of, like memorizing lines for your play. I'll worry about the rest and believe me; things are going to change soon. I'm sorry that I said anything, and I'm not mad at you."

"Promise me if he comes home, you'll be nice."

"I'll be how I always am with him. If he's decent, I'll be decent. But if he's nasty, like usual, I'll ask him to leave. I don't like him around you anymore."

"Why? He would never hurt us. He's our dad. You used to get mad that he was gone, and now you get mad when he comes home. Don't you want him back? Don't you want to be a family again?"

"I used to, but I don't think he can be a good person again. And we are a family, Madi. We may not have a lot, but we're getting by, and we have each other. We don't need him."

Madi's head drops, and he wonders why he said all of that. It would have been so easy to appease her. A simple white lie and the conversation would have been over. But no, not him. He had to be right, as usual. Of course, she misses him. She's a little kid with a skewed perception of who their father is. She remembers the good times with Jim before he started to change into what he's become. It's something for her to hold on to because she still thinks the old Jim, the family man, can come back. What's the harm in that? Jim's rarely around, anyway. Thomas can manage this for her, along with everything else. Thank, God, Madi's personality takes after their mother's and not their father's, because otherwise there's no way he could have survived the frustration of taking care of her all this time.

Their house, or cabin as Madi calls it, sits on a tiny, unkempt piece of land that backs up to a stream that's frozen half the year. It has two bedrooms, a small living room, and kitchen. Being the furthest house on the east side of town, only a handful of neighbors live nearby, and all are senior citizens with zero interest in Thomas or Madi. And while it sometimes seems desolate, Thomas is grateful, because no one has bothered to call child protective services about their lack of supervision. Apparently, seeing Jim from time to time is enough to squash any curiosity that might have arisen in the neighborhood. It's still warm out, but the cabin has been getting cold at night, and mornings have grown frigid. Thomas builds a fire in the pot-belly stove and pours Madi a glass of milk. He searches the kitchen for something to make for dinner.

"Hey kid," Thomas says, "you're in luck. I found some Mac-n-cheese. Why don't you start your homework while it cooks, and I'll help you with math after we eat?"

"You don't have to. It's easy."

"Thank God, I'm wrecked. Can you grab the mail?"

Madi returns with both backpacks and a stack of mail. A pink power bill drops to the ground. Madi looks at Thomas.

"Uh, oh."

"Don't worry about it, Madi. I'm working on it."

"How? Are they going to turn our power off?"

"They're not. It's just a warning, and I've got some work lined up for this week."

"But—"

"No buts. It's fine. Start your homework." She does. A few minutes later, Thomas sets a bowl of hot noodles in front of her. "Eat your noodles."

"They're hot. Can I play a game on your cell phone while they cool? There's a new one, and it's free."

"You can't. I had to stop the service for a while. I'll turn it back on soon."

"But my friends. How will I—"

"You can call them on the landline. It works fine, and it's cheap."

"But I don't know their numbers."

"I have their numbers stored in the cell phone. The address book works, you just can't call from it. Now eat your noodles."

Later that evening, Madi sets off to bed, leaving Thomas to his thoughts. He plops down at the table with his head in his hands. He lied. There isn't any work lined up. They're nearly out of food and money. He counts backward from ten, tells himself to get up and find a solution. When that's done, he can think through what's happened. It's going to take some brainpower. He looks around the cabin, through the cupboard and fridge, then opens the bills and assesses their situation.

Twenty minutes later, he's called a cluster of students he's done homework for in the past. Everyone bites, and they promise to be diligent with how they handle his work. Anything he hand writes has to be rewritten. Only typed work can be turned in directly to the teacher. With his recent close call, he can't chance getting caught in a forgery scandal. Still, thank God for these lazy students. Without them, he'd be broke. He takes a few more notes, jotting down a reminder to check with the neighbors across the street tomorrow about any odd jobs they might have for him. Yesterday, they had a cord of wood delivered and there's no way that Bill is planning to chop and stack it all by himself. He's got to be eighty years old.

Glancing at his list, he relaxes a bit. Way to go, he thinks. Fatigue fights to overtake him. He's bought them a few more weeks of food and electricity, along with the luxury of not freezing or starving to death. Terrific. Resting his head on the table, he lets his eyes close. Thomas hears his name called and yells for Madi to go to sleep. Then hears it again. Groggy and annoyed, he pulls open his eyes to check on his sister. Pink snow covers the hillside he's sitting on.

"Hello Thomas," the man from the forest says.

Thomas scrambles backward, sending snow into the air.

The man raises an eyebrow. "If you disturb the snow, it'll turn blue and cold. I suggest you leave it alone."

Thomas sits still. The cold blue spots that were forming around his body return to pink. The man smiles.

"Am I dreaming?" Thomas says.

"You are not. Your body is sleeping, but you are here."

"And here is?"

"Let's not waste time, Thomas. This is a short visit."

"What do—"

Against his will, Thomas's mouth is forced shut. His eyes gape against the strain. It feels as if there's a hand over his mouth.

"Yes. I can do that," the man says. "Now, I'm trying to decide if you'd be of service to me. You certainly showed some gumption getting to the forest on your own, but then again, you could be troublesome."

Thomas pinches his eyebrows in confusion, thinking, then why bring me here?

"See," the man says. "Just then, you questioned my judgment in your thoughts. That is disrespectful, and I cannot have it."

Thomas feels anger stir in his stomach. This man reminds him of his father. He is a man who wants respect without earning it. He's judging Thomas based on a single thought, yet he knows nothing about him. They've just met.

The man laughs. "I do not need to judge anyone, Thomas. Your life makes no difference to me, but the superiority you feel is unsettling. Because you're smarter than most you feel entitled; to what, I'm not certain. Still, your brain intrigues me. It's a maze of compartments, something I've never seen before. It could prove useful to me."

Thomas's nostrils flare. What is this guy talking about? Can't he just say what he wants?

"What I want is for you to keep your thoughts quiet while I think," the man says, pacing. He stops to study Thomas, a crooked grin forming on his lips. "What I think is that, until I see how you perform, I won't be able to decide. Therefore, I'm giving you twenty-four hours to collect thoughts, at which time I'll bring you back and make my decision."

He releases his hold over Thomas's mouth and steps back. Thomas gulps down air, but the strange smell of the man's invisible grip refuses to dissipate. Thomas is fearful that the scent might never leave him; that he'll be forever connected to this unknown man from the strange forest, yet the only thing worse he can imagine is not being able to return. Because the man has just said the words Thomas was so desperate to hear. That Thomas is to collect thoughts; and the place where those thoughts will go is where his mother happens to be. This creature is his key to the other side. Thomas breathes deeply, relaxing his demeanor and mind.

"I'm not sure what to do," Thomas says. He cannot mess this up.

"You're to listen to thoughts."

"How do I do that?" Thomas says.

"Oh please. You've already done it. Now do it again, and I'll be watching. Try not to have too much fun."

"What does that mean?"

The man winks, his skin flutters light and dark.

"Who are you?" Thomas says, waves of dread replacing nausea.

He blinks and opens his eyes to the familiar dining table he's sitting at. It was just a dream.

"Dammit," he yells, punching the table. His eyes fall on the sheet of paper he pulled out earlier, except the writing on it is nothing like his own and what's been written pushes the air from his lungs. Tick-tock, Thomas. We'll meet again soon. - Simon.

"Holy shit," he scrambles away from the table, remembering too late that Madi is sleeping and knocks over a chair.

"Thomas?" Madi calls.

"Sorry," Thomas peeks through her cracked door. "I didn't mean to wake you."

"It's okay. Can you stay until I fall asleep?"

"Sure thing, kid," he says, rubbing his eyes. Dropping into the worn bean bag on the floor, he's asleep before Madi.

Chapter 7

The cabin is freezing. Thomas cracks open an eye to the early light flooding into Madi's room. He's cocooned by the overstuffed cushion he fell asleep in. His feet are numb in their worn socks, but he's not sore from the awkward position he slept in. Climbing to his feet, he pulls the covers over Madi and pads into the living room where he builds a fire in the pot-belly stove. His father might not have made the best choices, but buying the stove was a good call. It gets hot fast and heats the entire cabin in minutes.

Madi wakes when the house is warm and joins Thomas for peanut butter toast, and milk, their standard breakfast. Neither is a morning person, today being no exception. They eat quietly while wood crackles in the living room.

The note from last night stares up at him from the table, reminding him of everything that happened yesterday. It doesn't seem possible. Did it really happen? And if so, what is he supposed to do? Try to hear people's thoughts? It's preposterous. He thinks it happened with Amanda, but that was different. The whole experience was something he'd never be able to replicate. He wouldn't know where to begin.

"Are you done?" Madi stands with her dish, holding her hand toward Thomas's empty glass.

"Yeah," Thomas hands her his glass, "thanks for the help," he says, and it occurs to him that he does need help. Unfortunately, the only person that can help him is Adam. Adam had said that his step-brother lives in Westchester, but Thomas has no idea who he is. With Simon's tight deadline, Thomas doesn't have time to look for him. He still has to work today. There might be this fantastical thing he's supposed to do that may or may not result in him getting to the other side, but he has a life here and sister that depends on him. She comes first. So, while he's making his rounds with clients today, he'll mention a boy named Adam whose step-brother goes to Westchester. It's unlikely, but maybe he'll get lucky.

"Madi," he calls, dialing the phone. "Pack up some things. I'm going to drop you at the Gleeson's if it's okay. I should have called Mary last night."

"Yes," Madi says, pumping her fists and running to her room.

Once their mother's best friend, is now a surrogate parent to Madi. Mary Gleeson watches her several times a week while Madi plays with Mary's twin daughters. The work-related accident that took her husband's life several years earlier left Mary a hefty settlement along with what Thomas thinks is the empathy about losing a parent that's kept her from reporting Jim to Child Protective Services. After Jim started disappearing for weeks or more at a time, Thomas was sure she would, but instead, she took them in. During the last year, with the condition that they would ask for help if needed, Mary let Thomas and Madi move home. So far, he's proven capable of the task. Mary opens the door with a broad smile after the first knock. The smell of cinnamon wafts out the door and fills the entryway. Thomas's mouth waters.

"That was fast," Mary says. "Head on back and see the girls, Madi. They're awake." She steps to the side to let Madi slip by.

"Hey, Mary. Sorry for the late notice. You sure she's okay here for a few hours?"

Her expression answers his question.

"Okay, then," he says. "Thank you."

"No problem. Have you both eaten?"

"Yep, we just ate."

"At least take a couple of muffins for the road. I made a ton, and if they sit here, I'll eat them."

"Thanks," he says, as a door slams from the back of the house, followed by giggles. "And thanks for watching her."

"No problemo. Join us for dinner?"

"Can I let you know later? I've got a lot to get done, and it might go past dinner. How late can Madi stay?"

"You can leave her overnight. The girls have already been at me about it. Dinner is around six o'clock if you can make it. What are you up to today?"

"Some odd jobs. We've got a couple of bills coming up."

Mary's frown signals to Thomas that a lecture is coming. "Why don't you let me take care of them this month? It's Saturday. Take a day off."

"Mary," Thomas softens his voice, "you know why. My grandpa's trust is barely existent, but the interest it generates usually covers our bills. When it doesn't, I have to make up the difference. It's not the end of the world."

"But—" she starts.

"I know you want to help," he holds up his hand, "but unless we need it, we're not taking any more money from you. Watching her is enough; you help us all the time. I'm not a bum like my father; I can take care of us. So yeah, giving up my weekend's sucks, but in the grand scheme of things, it's minor."

Mary wraps her arms around him in a bear hug. "I know you're not a bum, and you're right, you're nothing like your father. I just hate seeing you miss your childhood. It's not fair. But I understand that you've got to do what you've got to do," she steps back, planting her hands on her hips.

"Now come and get some muffins before I get started again."

Armed with a backpack filled with muffins and snacks, Thomas heads towards his first client of the day, a student he despises and has the bad fortune of sharing four classes with.

Toby Walker lives with his family on the west side of town, in the most upscale community in Westchester. Theirs is one of the nicer houses with a large gated yard and a swimming pool befitting a hotel, flush with fountains and waterfalls cascading over manufactured rock structures. Thomas cringes. It is gaudy in its size and grandeur, so remarkably out of place that it's silly, yet he still feels pangs of envy. How could anyone own such a thing? The house sits atop a winding hill, and the entire walk takes Thomas an hour. When he reaches the gate, Thomas sees

Toby spot him out of the window and nod. A buzzer sounds, and the gate lock clicks open. The front door is ajar, and Nicole steps onto the porch as Thomas arrives. They freeze.

"What are you doing here?" Thomas asks louder than he intended. He wasn't prepared to see her at Toby's.

"Excuse me?" Nicole says, sticking her hand on her hip.

Thomas's face explodes with color. He searches his brain, comes up with "Um."

She laughs, dropping her hand. "Kidding. I was on my way out. I babysit for Toby's little sister, sometimes. My dad works with their dad."

"Right. Sorry. I was just surprised to see you. Thought I'd gone to the wrong house. Why doesn't Toby watch her?"

"Nope. Right house. I think he watches her when he can, but he's usually at football. I guess it's easier to have me. My schedule doesn't change. What are you doing here?"

"I'm helping him with some schoolwork."

"Oh. That's nice. I didn't realize you were friends."

"We're not. Not anymore, anyway. We used to be when I wrestled. I don't have time for that now."

"Why is that?"

"It's a long story and not very interesting. I just don't have time for things outside of school. My life is complicated."

Nicole raises her eyebrows.

"What?" Thomas says.

"Isn't everyone's to some extent?"

"Uh, yeah," he scratches his head, "sorry, I guess you're right."

Toby steps onto the porch, says, "hey," with indifference, looking between the two. "Am I interrupting something?"

Thomas rolls his eyes at Toby, then looks back at Nicole.

"Kinda," he says, grinning.

"Dude," Toby says.

"Yes," Thomas narrows his eyes.

"Ok then," Nicole slips between the guys and gently presses Thomas back a few steps. "Play nice, boys," she says.

Thomas relaxes, dropping his shoulders. Toby does the same. They both look at Nicole. She smiles, shaking her head.

"Right," she says, "and on that note, I've got to get home. Tell Chloe I'll see her next week," she tells Toby, then turns to Thomas. "And I'll see you soon?"

"Absolutely," Thomas says. "How about tomorrow?"

"Yeah, sounds good. Call me in the morning?"

"Will do," she smiles and walks away. Thomas watches her leave, unaware of the grin on his face.

"Wow," Toby says after a minute. "She's gone. Take a breath. I didn't realize that was a thing."

Thomas blinks several times and clears his throat, embarrassed that Toby saw the exchange. He can't stand Toby. If he didn't need the money, he wouldn't be there.

"Not your business."

"Okay, okay, relax," Toby smirks. "Give me a minute; I'll get the paper."

He steps inside, leaving Thomas on the porch. Toby has a mean streak in him. Thomas has never been on the other end of it, but he's seen it. It's like Toby is in a constant rage that he keeps pressed just below the surface. Once in a while, he lets out a little aggression on some poor kid who doesn't deserve it, and everyone looks the other way because it's Toby, after all. He's the football star; he can hurt you if he wants to. It will be easy for him, so it's best not to agitate him. Let him go back to his privileged life until it happens again but to someone else. Everyone knows that it's coming, that it is inevitable. One of these days, Toby will explode, and God help whoever's in his way. Toby returns to the porch and hands Thomas several wrinkled papers.

"What am I doing for you again?" Thomas looks over the papers.

"The trig assignment we talked about, and I put in an outline for a report I need if you can swing it."

"I can. It'll be a hundred."

"Pricy," Toby whistles. "You've got quite the racket going."

"Yeah, well, you get what you pay for. Or not. It's your call," Thomas says.

"I'm in, take it easy." Toby peels a hundred-dollar bill off a stack from his sweats. "I don't need the paper until Tuesday. Get a B this time instead of an A. The last time, Mr. Pruitt gave me attitude. He knows it's not my work but won't do anything about it if I don't push him. The teachers all want me focused on the season. I'd like to keep that going."

"Sure, whatever. See you next week."

Thomas turns and walks away, the front door clapping shut before he reaches the gate. Flashes of the forest interrupt his thoughts and curses himself. He forgot to ask if Toby knew anyone at school with a stepbrother named Adam. What a moron. He considers going back but decides against it. Toby's an asshole. Thomas doubts he pays enough attention to anyone at their school to know anything about them. If it isn't about Toby, then Toby doesn't care. He might feel differently about his girlfriend, Amanda, but even that's questionable. Whatever it is she sees in him, Thomas will never understand. Thinking back on his time with Amanda, he remembers the feeling he had when he heard her thinking. If he could figure out how to do it again, he wouldn't have to worry about finding Adam. But at present, he feels useless, a sensation that infuriates him because it reminds him of his past.

For Thomas's fourteenth birthday, his father took him to Zinger's Indoor Batting Cages, something Thomas had begged to do for months. Having never been a particularly kind man, Thomas was dumbstruck when Jim O'Malley suggested they 'knock some balls' together. He even claimed to take care of all the arrangements, to Thomas's amazement. And on a sunny, Sunday morning, they loaded into Jim's dusty work truck and made the six-mile drive to the batting cases, much like a typical father and son might do. But as they pulled into the empty parking lot and read Zinger's sign apologizing for their 'dust and closure' due to a remodel, Thomas felt his heart drop. He knew he'd never set foot in Zinger's with his father, remodel or not because a sideways glance at his father told Thomas things were going to get ugly.

"Didn't you check to see if they were open?" Jim spit, as if in disbelief.

"I didn't know I was supposed to."

"Shut it," Jim's eyes narrowed on Thomas.

"This is your fault. I tried to do something nice for your birthday, and you ruined it. Now get out."

"I'm sorry," Thomas fought to stop the tears from spilling down his cheeks.

"You're not as sorry as you are useless. Now get out of the car. You've got a long walk home, and it'll be dark soon."

Thomas plays the scene over in his head; how much he'd hated Jim that night, and how he'd never be like him. He also knew that he wouldn't put himself in a position of weakness the moment he climbed out of the truck. Thomas was not useless, and he would never feel that way. Good riddance to anyone who tried to make him think otherwise.

A greyhound passes by, slowing to stop for half a dozen people waiting at the bus stop. Thomas gets an idea and runs to catch it, climbing in as the doors close behind him. He isn't sure where the bus is heading, but he's not a passenger with a destination; he's interested in the people on board. Buses are noisy and cramped, something that should provide him with enough anonymity to study those around him without being noticed.

Thomas stares at person after person for minutes at a time, looking away when they notice. Ten stops, and almost an hour later, every passenger he boarded with has cleared the bus, and he hasn't been able to hear a single thought. He tries again on a group of old women who climb onboard at the town-center stop. All he gains for his efforts are a few dirty looks and a headache. Climbing off at the next stop, he rubs his head. What a bust. He should have given up a while back. He can't hear what people are thinking. It was silly to believe any of this had been real. It might be time to see a doctor. He's lost it.

The car driving toward him taps the horn and pulls over. Mary rolls down her window. From the back seat, Madi does the same.

"Thomas," Madi squeals. "We're going out to eat. Want to come?"

"Hi, guys. Thanks, but I'm beat. I'm calling it a day. I was just coming to get you, Madi. Why don't you come with me and I'll fix you something when we get home?"

"But I thought I got to spend the night. Can't I at least go to the diner?"

"Come on Madi, I'm already on this side of town, and you don't need another sleepover."

"Why don't you join us, Thomas," Mary says, "then I'll drop you both at home."

"Thanks, Mary, but I should go. I need to grab some groceries anyway."

"Oh, good Lord. I'll run you by the store after. Now hop in."

"Okay. Sounds good," he says, loosening the scowl from his face but groaning inwardly at the thought of sitting through a meal.

Debra's Diner makes the best milkshakes in town, so it comes as no surprise that it's where they head. The restaurant is bustling when they enter but they quickly find a booth and slide in. As usual, too much food is ordered by everyone but Thomas, who inhales his burger and fries before finishing two-thirds of Madi's pot pie she barely touched. Mary must have been stuffing muffins down her throat all morning.

"Are you still hungry, Thomas?" Mary says. "Order something else. They have the best soup."

"I'm good Mary, thanks."

As if on cue, their waitress walks over. Thomas can see their check sticking out of her pocket. Clearly, she is ready for them to leave. A flash of butterflies tickles his stomach, the sensation reminding him of driving over the side of a steep hill.
Could these people take any longer?

His head snaps up in surprise. Did our waitress seriously say that to us?

You eat your burger, pay your bill, and leave. It's not rocket science.

The realization hits him. His world slows to a stop. She didn't say it. *She thought it*. It had happened the same way with Amanda. He'd felt a strange sensation, like stomach butterflies happening without a cause. In both cases, there was kind of a *tickle*. Then it happened, the thing he'd been trying for all day. And now he knew that the precursor to the *hearing* was the tickle. *Oh, my, God*. He can't pull the smile from his face.

"Will there be anything else?" the waitress asks the table, oblivious to Thomas's sudden joy.

"Yes, actually," Thomas's voice is triumphant. Everyone looks at him. Madi frowns. One of the twin's snorts, nearly choking on a fry. Thomas tries to relax, then changes his mind. He'd rather annoy the waitress. She was rude.

"I'll take a piece of the pie," he smiles, "warmed, with some ice cream on the side. If that's okay with you, Mary?"

"Of course," Mary nearly shouts. She loves feeding people. "Sounds great. I'd order the same if I wouldn't gain ten pounds. Girls? Room for pie or milkshakes?"

All three girls order at once. The waitress rolls her eyes. *For God's sake*, she thinks, walking away.

Holy shit, Thomas thinks, then an ice cube slides down the back of his shirt. He yells and jumps up, shaking it free. Madi and the twins' roar with laughter. Soon he's laughing too. Thank God, he came here.

By the time he finishes his pie, he's riddled with excitement. His future is looking up. As promised, Mary drives them home, stopping on the way for groceries. She offers to take Madi the following day, which saves him the trouble of asking.

Back at home, Thomas unpacks the supplies, belching when he bends down to put away the milk. He'd eaten way too much but is thankful he did; he'd needed it. Remembering that he didn't see several of his clients, he calls each one and apologizes, then promises to catch up with them tomorrow. Madi ducks into bed with a book but is asleep a few minutes later when Thomas checks on her. She must have had a busy morning with the twins. Taking a seat next to her bed, he watches her sleep and lets the day unfold in his mind.

"You have no idea what's coming, Madi," he whispers. "Things are going to change for us. We might finally get the life we deserve."

Before heading to what used to be his parent's room, Thomas throws a final log into the fire and pulls on a cap to keep warm. No doubt the house will be cold tomorrow. Once inside the bedroom, he frees the pill Adam gave him from his pocket; it's been on his mind all day. He sits down and examines the black capsule, contemplating what to do. It seems like he's changed his mind about whether to take it or not a million times. When Adam gave it to him, he planned to take it without question. But then he couldn't be sure that it really came from his mother. She didn't know it was Thomas, did she? And if she had, then why didn't she come out to see him? Maybe she thought Adam was in danger, and the pill was meant to keep away those that didn't belong in Tendo. Tendo, he thinks. Has it been there all of this time? Is it real? He rolls the pill between his fingers, terrified of what will happen if he takes it, but is more frightened of what will happen if he doesn't. Steeling himself for what's to come, he places the pill on his tongue and swallows it dry.

Chapter 8

A breeze that smells of peppermint tickles his eyelashes, waking Thomas from his sleep. He blinks open his eyes to an icy landscape, blinded by piercing sunlight. Using his hands as a shield, he takes in his surroundings and is struck with an overwhelming sense of déjà vu.

"What is this place?" he whispers. "I know it somehow. But from when?"

"There isn't much time."

The voice nearly stops his heart. Thomas turns toward it; and looks directly at his mother standing less than a foot away. He can't speak. His words have turned to dust and floated away from his grasp. He can only stare.

"Hello Thomas," Lilian says, her eyes glassy.

Thomas reaches for her, his arms connecting with air.

"If you see this, then you swallowed the v-tac. I'm so sorry, but it had to be this way. While I appear real, I am a recording, made today, after I learned of my fate here on Tendo. I will keep the v-tac with me always, hoping that one day, you will cross to this side and I can give it to you. That you are watching this means you've done that. My only hope is that it hasn't been too long for you, something that troubles me beyond words. There is no way to know how long it will take or if you'll ever come, but if I'm right, you are a courier, like me. And if that is the case, you will find me."

Tears sting his eyes. "Why didn't you tell me? If couriers can travel here, why couldn't you send this information to me before now?" he says to the hologram. She could have sent the v-tac with Adam, he wants to cry out, but he knows the answer. She couldn't tell him until she knew whether he was like her or not. If he weren't a courier, he'd have never taken a strange pill from a stranger claiming to know his mother. He wasn't crazy. She knew him better than he knew himself.

"I know that this is hard, Thomas, but remember that I love you and your sister more than anything else. Everything I did, I did for you. Tendo is a magical place. I bear it no bad will for what has happened to me. I was using it to make our lives better and to help others. It is a remarkable world, and I allowed myself to grow so accustomed to it that I forgot how differently it works from our own. My time here had come to an end, Thomas.

I was preparing to return to you and Madi permanently, but while securing the closure of my contract, I misplaced my trust. In doing so, my contract was breached, and now I'm bearing the responsibility for my mistake.

At the time of this recording, I have been granted asylum by a Broker named Amos. Under his protection, no one knows who I am, and better yet, who you or Madi are. But the second I step into a Way Station, I will be detected and destroyed, and you and Madi will be exposed. There is no safe way for me to return without putting us all in danger, and I refuse to do that. As long as I remain here, in this hidden place, I am safe, and more importantly, you and Madi are safe.

"I know that you have questions, Thomas, but you must understand that everything I have done has been to protect you both." Her form flickers in the light, and Thomas thinks she'll disappear.

"You are my whole world, Thomas. You are the very point of my existence. And while the agony I feel being separated from you both is unbearable; it doesn't compare to what I'd feel if anything happened to you. I could not control if, or when, you'd be sensed by a Broker and pulled in, but by agreeing to remain on this side, I could control the one outcome I had to be sure of. The master of the palace I reside in would never seek you, nor would he know you as my son. And unlike other couriers, if you did arrive here, you would bear no obligation to any Broker.

"You are free to return home and never return to this side again, which is what you must do. I do not want this world for you, and I have sacrificed everything to keep you away from it. It changes you. You will not notice it happen, but bit by bit, you will be dismantled. You will become a little less of yourself every time you are here, and at some point, you will stop being you. You will become a version of yourself that you were not meant to be. I can't have that, Thomas, and you shouldn't allow it either. And the only way I can assure this won't happen to you is by separating myself from your world. It is the last thing I want, but the only thing I can do. I love you, Thomas.

"Go now, and never come back. Be with Madi and your father. Create the life you've imagined. You deserve it. I hope that Jim's good to you; that he's helped to ease the pain that I've caused. But know that I did it for you. I love you." She flashes twice and is gone.

Thomas feels his legs buckle but doesn't fight it. He falls to the ground, sobbing. His body convulses as pain and rage squeeze his stomach like a vise. When his mouth starts to water, he opens his eyes to a spinning room and lunges for the garbage. Black bile spews from his throat and nose, nearly filling the can. After his nausea subsides enough for him to move, he makes his way to the bathroom to splash cold water on his face. Staring at his reflection, he drops his head and sobs. What the hell does he do now?

There isn't much time to think about it. The smoke alarm goes off in the hallway, pulling Thomas back to his reality. It's then he notices the smell from the kitchen, the unmistakable scent of burning toast.

"Madi," he yells, running to the kitchen in his boxers, freezing when he enters. Nicole is at the counter, frantically unplugging the toaster while Madi is fanning the front door open and closed. Thomas grabs a towel and runs into the hall to fan the air under the alarm. When it finally shuts off, Nicole and Madi are standing in the hallway. Nicole starts to say something, glances at Thomas in his underwear and backs into the kitchen. Nearly speechless, Thomas mumbles to Madi that he'll be back in a minute as he runs down the hall.

From his room, he can hear Madi laughing and talking in rapid bursts like she does when she gets excited. Nicole seems to keep up with the conversation, the two talking like they've been friends forever. After brushing his teeth and taking the fastest shower of his life, he gathers his nerve and joins the girls in the kitchen. Nicole is making a new round of toast, and Madi is putting plates out.

"Hi," Nicole says. "Sorry about the smoke. I wasn't paying attention. The toast nearly caught fire."

"Don't feel bad," Madi tells Nicole. "Thomas always burns it."

Nicole laughs and turns back to the counter, but not before Thomas sees her hands shake. She's as nervous as he is.

"So, what's happening here?" he says, glancing at Madi.

"You don't remember?" Nicole spins around. "At Toby's, you said the morning was good for you."

"It is. But how'd you find me?"

"Madi gave me the address when I called this morning. Oh, my God, I'm sorry, I should have asked for an actual time that worked. It was getting late, so I figured I'd better get here before lunch."

"Lunch? What time is it?" Thomas asks but checks the time on the stove. "It's nearly noon?" he asks Madi. "Why didn't you wake me?"

"I don't know," Madi takes a bite of toast and drops into her seat.

"I'm sorry," Nicole says. "I can come back later."

"No," Thomas rubs his eyes. "You're fine. I don't usually sleep so late. I'm glad you came. Who knows how long I would have slept if you hadn't turned up?" he glares at Madi.
She laughs.

"Okay then," he spreads peanut butter on toast and takes a swallow of milk, "let's take a look at that math."

"Oh, already?" Nicole leans forward to grab her bag from his chair, thinking to herself how good he smells.

Thomas chokes, coughing milk onto the table. Both girls look at him.

"Are you okay?" Nicole and Madi say in unison. He shakes his head yes and holds up his hand until his coughing subsides.

"Sorry," he says and gets up to grab a wet towel. "Wrong pipe."

After they eat, Madi clears the table to the best of her adolescent ability, while Thomas and Nicole work through her math problems. When they finish, she packs up her things and looks around the kitchen.

"Do your parents work on weekends?"

"Huh?" he says.

"Madi said only you were home when she answered the door."

"That's usually the case. It's just me and Madi. My dad's not around very much."

"Oh. I'm sorry, I didn't mean to pry."

He holds up his hand, "It's fine. Old business. How about you? Big family?"

"Not really. It's only my parents and me. We moved here for my dad's job. The rest of our family is back home. Or, what used to home."

"Right. Do you like it here so far?"

She smiles. "I miss my friends, but it's getting better."

Madi yells from her room that she's getting packed to go to the twins' house.

"Don't forget clothes for tomorrow," Thomas yells back. Nicole makes a face that he instantly understands. He acts more like a parent to Madi than a brother. It must seem weird to people who don't know them. "She's staying at a friend's tonight. I'm taking her in a bit."

"Well, I should go. I just showed up. I didn't even ask if you were busy."

"I wasn't. Don't worry about it."

"Okay, thanks. Did you guys want a ride somewhere? I've got my dad's car."

"That's alright. I have some things to do before we leave, but thanks."

"Then I guess that's it. Thanks, Thomas."

She walks outside and climbs into her car. As she pulls away, she waves. He waves back and closes the door, yelling for Madi that it's time to go. He's already wasted enough time, and with the distraction of this morning, though a good one, he hasn't had time to think about everything his mother said. But even while he was working with Nicole, pieces of Lilian's words found their way to him. By the time Nicole left, Thomas already knew what he'd planned to do.

He would learn to be a courier for Simon, and when he'd learned enough to move around in the other world, he'd bring his mother home.

Chapter 9

The day flies by after he's deposited Madi at the Gleeson's. He sees three students and manages to pull a few small thoughts from the first two by sheer accident. One was yelling at her mother when he'd felt the tickle begin, and the other had a dropped a book on her foot, the corner connecting just so. Thomas had thought she'd cussed so loudly that he expected a parent to storm in, but then realized that she'd *thought* it loudly.

On his way to meet with a fourth student, he decides to take a break, stopping in town. At almost 80 degrees, it's unseasonably warm, and while everyone he passes is in shorts and tank tops, he's dressed for cold weather. He takes a seat on the fountain in the middle of town and pulls off his sweatshirt.

A light breeze cools the sweat beading on his forehead, but the sun is relentless, and he's reminded of the angry globe that burnt his foot. It seems like something that happened in a dream, to another person, a lifetime ago. Silence settles throughout the town, surrounding him. Thomas climbs to his feet, fear prickling the back of his neck. It's as if the town has been swallowed whole. Everything is still, the air's turned dry and stagnant. Birds have stopped chirping, kids aren't laughing; all sounds have vanished as if they were never there. It's Sunday. People should be here; they just were. Something is very, very wrong.

Across the street, the perpetually busy coffee shop looks deserted. Thomas walks over, peering through the window. All of the appliances appear to be on but nobody's inside. Half-eaten plates of food and sweating drinks sit around empty tables, something that he finds horribly disturbing. Taking a deep breath, he makes his way to the next shop and sees the same thing; the lights are on, without a soul in sight. The town is empty.

A gust of wind ruffles his shirt, and he spins, expecting to see a tumbleweed roll by or hear a crow caw in the distance, but neither happens. He laughs despite himself. *Okay, so I'm not in a western horror show.* Still, he shudders. The sudden onslaught of silence is creepy.

The fountain turns on, spitting and gurgling, beckoning him to come back. Thomas fights the urge to run but knows he has to look inside. It's probably nothing. It sounds the same as it did last year when the water level got so low that the pump burned out. A maintenance worker forgot to refill it during an exceptionally hot month, and most of the water evaporated, leaving the engine exposed. Rather than see the man fired for such a costly oversight, Thomas's school had bake sales for a month to help the city pay for it. That must be what's happening now. There's nothing to be afraid of; it's just the pump again.

Reaching the fountain on wobbly legs, Thomas peers in and is overcome with relief to see that it's full of water, but something still nags at him. Something is out of place. It takes him a minute to figure out what it is. Inside the gray basin of the city fountain, the water is spinning in the wrong direction. It gurgles along like it should, but it's moving counterclockwise. *Coriolis effect.* If he was in the southern hemisphere this would make sense. But he isn't.

The strange movement of the water is so hypnotic that he reaches for it without thinking and catches a reflection on the surface; only it's not his reflection he sees. It's Simon's. Thomas dives in.

A sea of blue fills his eyes. The air smells of freshly mowed grass. Thomas sits still, trying to regain his equilibrium. He fights for balance after the stress of switching scenery so quickly.

"Eh hum," Simon clears his throat and rests a newspaper at the base of the lawn chair he's reclining in. Like before, he's dressed inexplicably in a rumpled suit and peers at Thomas with sparkling eyes that seem to demand attention.

"Hello?" Thomas says.

"Is that a question or a greeting?" Simon climbs to his feet so fast that Thomas scoots backward.

"Tsk, tsk," Simon clicks his tongue, "I hate to tease, Thomas, but you spook quite easily."

"Sorry, it wasn't you, it's just hard to change places like that. I didn't have much warning at the fountain that I'd be coming here. Did I fall asleep again?"

"You did not."

"Then I'm—uh."

"You are here, Thomas, the place known to your kind as Tendo."

"And what happens now?"

"Patience, Thomas."

"Sorry, but I have a million questions. Did I really go through the fountain to get here? Was that some kind of door?"

"Thomas, your manner of addressing me is unacceptable. You haven't had the proper time to learn respect for the arrangement between us, which is why I'm giving you a pass this time. It won't happen again. Do you understand?"

Crap, Thomas thinks, fear working through his veins. If he plans to keep coming here, Simon is the key. Whatever Thomas has done to annoy him so quickly isn't clear, but it's best to play along. He takes a deep breath and shuts his mouth.

"That's better," Simon says. "I can feel your anxiety slowing. You have good control of your emotions when you want to. I like that." He rises from his chair and paces. "As you've gathered, my name is Simon, Thomas. I am a Thought Broker, and you are a courier. Everybody has one, only I am yours, and you are mine."

"Then I passed the...I don't know, twenty-four-hour trial?"

"Enough," Simon sighs. "I am the Broker. You are a courier. I am your superior. Normally we wouldn't have to go through this. It doesn't work this way, but with you, everything is backward. You know too much and too little at the same time." He rubs his eyes and clears his throat. "I'm going to allow your questions because this is our first real meeting, but you'll speak when spoken to after that. Understood?" Thomas fights the urge to say something sarcastic and nods instead. Simon paces before him. "Now then, ask your questions."

"How many Brokers are there, and how many couriers come here?" Thomas asks.

"There are many Brokers of varying rank, but there are relatively few couriers. You see, couriers are hard to locate, and even those that make it here may be non-productive."

"Non-productive, how?"

"Meaning that not every person who gains access to a Broker can pull thoughts. Those that cannot are sent back."

"If they can't do it, then how'd you find them to begin with?"

"They are sensed by a Broker who then seeks them in a non-conscious manner, a dream, if you will. If the courier receives the electrical input sent from the Broker, they are tested. If they pass, they come here, and if they mentally survive their exchange here, they are given their agreement."

"Well, that's assuming they choose to participate," Thomas says. Simon raises his eyebrows.

"Excuse me?"

"Nothing. Never mind."

"Young Thomas, are you under the impression that a courier has a choice in the matter?"

"Obviously. Everyone has a choice."

"That's not true. There is no choice to be made, so a choice is not given. The survival of both worlds depends on the participation of both Brokers and couriers. Humans are a selfish bunch. We learned long ago that you would do whatever benefitted you without regard for the welfare of others. Because of that, it was decided that if you were able, you would participate, no questions asked. At the same time, as your participation is mandatory, Brokers thought it fair that you be rewarded or given benefits. Of sorts."

"What kind of benefits?"

"You'll figure it out. Humans always do. It's different for each one of you. That is why we don't discuss it. And now it's time to go back and to get to work."

"But what if I can't do it again? I never know when it will work."

Simon smiles. "You've collected thoughts several times. It just didn't happen every time you tried. It will get easier, but I'm afraid you have to learn your own extraction method."

"But the thoughts. What do you do with them?"

His eyes flash. "Even if you could understand how and why the thoughts were used, it wouldn't change anything. They are a necessity, like us. All you need to know is that we are in a partnership now, and I will do whatever it takes for our partnership to be productive. I can become anyone or anything necessary to ensure that. There's no turning back." He sits and crosses his legs. "I don't require much of you, only that you do what is asked of you. We can be a good team. You'll see."

"But we haven't even worked anything out. I haven't agreed to anything."

"Thomas," Simon folds his hands in his lap. "I'm not asking. It is done."

"But wait, please," his resolve to stay quiet evaporates. "I need more information. How often will I come here, and do I get any say as to when? Will I always come physically here, or will you pull me in during some," he makes air quotes, "unconscious state. You can't expect to send me back and forth between my life and here without any warning. What if I'm somewhere noticeable or dangerous? Do you have any idea what I'm even doing on my side? If I were swimming and you pulled me in, would I drown? And if something like that happened, where would I end up? Would I be alive on this side but dead on my side—my body floating in some pool?"

"Good lord," Simon frowns, "that's a curious question. Why would you ask something like that?"

"Because you pulled me in during class," Thomas snaps. "I was in the middle of a test, and then I was standing in the forest. I'm pretty sure I didn't just vanish from my seat then reappear without anyone noticing. God only knows how long I was sitting there, or if that's even what happened that day. That seems a bit reckless, doesn't it? Pulling me in when I'm in public?"

"That's not how it works, Thomas," Simon says, leaning back in his chair. "I will eventually show you how to come here on your own, but in the meantime, I can bring you here physically or mentally. With both, I can sense what you're doing when I bring you to me. Your attention loses clarity; it gets fuzzy if you will, softer, more malleable. When you're like that, daydreaming or sleeping, I can feel it. You're no good to me dead. I know when it's safe to summon you."

"I get when I'm dreaming, but during class?" Thomas paces, trying to keep calm. "You thought that was an okay time to summon me?"

"No, Thomas, that one is for the record books. I was hibernating your test day; I'd been like that for many years, having lost my drive a while ago. I might have stayed that way indefinitely; but you walked right into my life that day. Remember?" Simon's mouth twitches into a grin. "Oh, Thomas, I didn't pull you in. Quite the opposite. You came to me. You wrote me into your story."

Nearby, a balloon pops. Thomas breaks through the surface of the water, climbing onto the side of the fountain. He coughs up water, steam rising from his soaked clothing. All around him, people bustle with laughter. No one seems to have noticed a thing. Several kids run toward the fountain, peeling off their clothes as if they plan to jump in. What a genius. He'd given them a great idea. Why hadn't they thought of it earlier? Parent's clap and laugh while city workers watch and shake their heads. No one wants to tell squealing children they can't jump in the fountain like the big idiot who just did. Other's ignore the fountain altogether. They shop and eat at outdoor cafes. Women push strollers with babies, children walk dogs and kick balls. For everyone, things are ordinary; straightforward, like they should be except for Thomas, who lies wet and exhausted on the concrete fountain. He's caught a glimpse of his future. And it is wild.

Chapter 10

The scent of Mexican food fills the air, making Thomas's stomach growl. Paco's Tacos, he guesses by the smell. Two girls stroll by carrying Paco's bags, confirming his suspicion. Checking the time, he realizes that it's much later than he expected to be in town, and, while he knows he shouldn't be spending money on fast food, he can't resist. Paco's is delicious. If he doesn't get some soon, he'll think about their burritos all night.

It's not quite lunch or dinner when Thomas arrives. The restaurant is quiet outside of a single table that appears to be occupied by a large family. While they eat and talk, Thomas watches, straining to hear a single thought that doesn't come. His burrito is demolished, but he stays longer to focus on a booth where two new customers have taken a seat. He doesn't realize that he's staring until the younger of the two tells him to take a picture. That not only will it, in fact, last longer, but it'll be way less creepy. Mortified, he jumps to his feet, explaining that he's sorry, that he'd zoned out and was staring off into space, not at them.

Fumbling with his tray, he apologizes once more and walks from the restaurant. Christ, he thinks. He'd better get control of how to do this thing he must do because that was embarrassing.

Later that night, staring at the ceiling fan from the comfort of his worn couch, his thoughts turn from Nicole to his mother, then eventually to Simon and back again. Brain weary, it's impossible to concentrate. Images of Nicole in his kitchen earlier haunt him. He pictures her by the counter, face flushed and lovely. She'd worn jeans and a red shirt and had her hair piled in a loose bun, little wisps of blonde sneaking out around her face. Outside of the burnt toast that permeated the house, he could smell the soap on her skin when she sat next to him. Clean and sweet, like the night jasmine on the bushes outside. And then she'd thought that he smelled good, too.

He sits up in bed, heart thumping. He'd *heard* her. He hadn't wished it or imagined it. But why? What was it that let him *listen* to her? Except for Amanda and the waitress, he'd picked up nothing more than fragments from a few students. But with Nicole, something was different. It was as if she'd whispered into his ear. With the others, the meaningless pieces of thoughts he'd gathered had been jarring, as if the mere act of taking them into his head had caused a minor concussion. And they were exhausting. He hadn't realized how much of his energy they'd sucked away until the third time he fell asleep against his will. But why the difference? The answer is crucial, and he knows it's right in front of him, but he's missing it. And once again, he's too tired to focus and decides on a quick nap. Fresh eyes will be waiting when he wakes up.

In his dream, Thomas rides in the back of the red convertible again, watching Amanda and Brad play out their roles with precision. But this time in the car, something is very, very different. He glances to his left and jerks back. Sitting next to him is Amanda's boyfriend Toby, who is also watching the Amanda and Brad show. Toby's face is twisted in a grimace. His knuckles clenched so tightly that they've turned white. Fury burns from his eyes that stay glued to the couple. Thomas fears those eyes might light everyone on fire. Up ahead, a lake comes into view. A million diamonds appear on the horizon as the sun glints off the water. Thomas admires the beauty for a second, forgetting where he is. He's played this part before. On cue, Brad leans across to kiss Amanda and Thomas steels himself, knowing what is about to happen and that it will be much worse than last time. Amanda turns her head and sees Thomas. She screams.

Thomas closes his eyes and waits for her to see Toby, knowing it's happened when her screams turn guttural. He opens his eyes in time to see the car swerve across the road. Panic sets in. If Toby gets out of the car, things will be bad for everyone. Somehow, Amanda manages to pull the vehicle to a halt. She throws open the door and runs a zigzag pattern into the woods, screaming the entire way. Toby and Brad don't move; they sit frozen in place, their roles over, their scripts played out.

Thomas jumps from the car, catching up to her near the lake. He yells at her to stop and grabs her shoulder, spinning her around, but when she turns, it's not Amanda anymore; there's no face at all. Thomas screams.

Screeching crickets swarm the house, pulling Thomas from a deep sleep. They quiet down for no more than a second before starting up again, tiny violin legs filling the house with metallic music. For Pete's sake, Thomas thinks, rubbing his

eyes. Struggling to his feet he finds the culprit in yesterday's
jeans, his beat-up cell phone that no longer makes calls but is
still an excellent alarm clock. The display says 6:45 a.m. He'd
slept the entire night, and it's time for school.

Great. It'll be so easy to focus. He has nothing going on
in his life right now to be concerned with. Except, he thinks,
being at school might give him a unique opportunity to practice
his new skill. Trying to figure it out in town had been
impossible. People tend to be suspicious when someone is staring
at them. But sitting in the back of the class where no one could
see how weird he was being made perfect sense. Grabbing an apple
from the counter, Thomas tosses it into his backpack and some
water for later. He finishes getting ready and locks the door on
the way out, tripping over Amanda as he turns onto the front
step.

"Geeze," he jumps back. "Where did you come from?"

Amanda stares at him with puffy, red eyes. Uh oh, he
thinks.

"What did you do, Thomas?" She spits one word after another
at him, seemingly oblivious to the joggers who've stopped what
they were doing to watch the unfolding scene.

"Take it easy," he says, and her face contorts with what
looks like both pain and rage. "Sorry," he holds his hands out
in peaceful protest, "I forgot how mad girls get when you say
that. Why is that, anyway?" She turns purple. "Okay, okay,
sorry. I was kidding—bad timing. But seriously, what is going
on? Do you want to come in? We can skip first period."

She seems to think it over, then her face drops, and tears
spill from her eyes. "What did you tell Toby?" she says, her
words bursting through sobs. "He's so angry he won't talk to
me."

"What do you mean? I haven't talked to Toby since I saw
you."

"But he knows, Thomas. He knows!"

"You need to calm down, Amanda, I didn't tell Toby
anything, and I don't plan to. Tell me exactly what happened."

She wipes her eyes, appearing to gather some control. "I woke up this morning to him banging on my window so hard that I thought it was going to break. I only opened it so that my dad wouldn't hear him. He looked crazy. He said he knew what happened. About Brad and me in the car. You're the only other person that knew Thomas. What did you tell him?"

Thomas's stomach clenches. Oh, my God, my dream. Did Toby dream that with me? Did I somehow pull him in? Jesus.

"I didn't tell him, Amanda," he says. "I swear to you. I didn't say a word."

Amanda's shoulders slump in defeat. For lack of a better idea, Thomas suggests they walk to school. She nods, and they walk along at the same pace, both too uncomfortable to break the stride that's already been set. Every twenty seconds or so, he sees her look over at him, but she doesn't say anything. Even so, he can feel the battle between anger and sadness raging behind her eyes.

"I didn't talk to Toby," Thomas says, mustering up the courage to speak. "I mean, I talked to him, but it was about homework. Whatever happened with you two has nothing to do with me. He probably just figured it out. Maybe you misheard him, or you're feeling guilty."

Amanda winces, but Thomas continues. "I don't know what else to say. You need to come clean with him. Do whatever you need to do to make yourself whole, I guess. You can't carry around this guilt, and you were going to end it anyway. I mean, I'm no shrink, but you've got to figure out how to get past this. Stuff like this will fester if you let it, and believe me, I know. It isn't good for you. I wish that there was something more that I could say or do to help you, but there is some crazy going down in my own life right now that I can barely wrap my arms around. I'm no good to you for the time being. But you've got this, you're a smart girl, and I know you'll be fine."

Amanda's gaze falls to the ground, her tears with it. "Great pep talk, Thomas," she mumbles, "but we're screwed."

After what seems an eternity to Thomas, she finally looks up, their eyes locking once again. Only this time, Amanda's have such a dark, glazed look that it hurts Thomas's heart. She is broken, and he is partially responsible. Together they walk blankly along, the destination is forgotten until they reach the perimeter of the school. Thomas keeps walking, not stopping until Amanda peels away to follow her undisclosed path. He calls after her several times, but she keeps walking without looking back.

Christ. What an asshole, he thinks. He didn't even try to help her other than offering some Dr. Phil garbage that couldn't possibly help. And Toby is a serious problem. He is a bomb waiting to be detonated, and there is no way to predict how or when it will happen. Will he come as a carpet bomb, tearing the ground out from under anyone close to the explosion, or will he go nuclear and wipe out everything in his path? That is the problem with muscle-headed narcissists. They don't have the skillset to understand explosives. Bombs are games to simple minds that cannot see the big picture. The gravity of the destruction is relative to the importance of the gesture, and it is the only way to win. How else do you show how important you are? How much something matters to you? That is Toby, and he is terrifying. And Thomas just left Amanda in his hands. For the love of God. Amanda is right; she is screwed. And so is Brad, and most of the people in this town, thanks to Thomas. Yet he let her go like she was nothing more than collateral damage. What an asshole. Maybe he's worse than Toby. Perhaps Thomas is the bomb.

School is a nightmare. There's no possibility of hearing thoughts; he can't even focus on the teachers. He makes it to lunch and leaves for the day, heading to the town where he spends the next few hours in the bookstore, trying to clear his mind. On his way out, he's surprised to bump into Toby's mother who gives him a disapproving look. Of all people, he thinks. It's the wicked witch in the flesh. He doesn't expect her to say anything and is surprised when she addresses him.

"I know you," she says. "You're that boy who wrestled with Toby in elementary school."

"We were on the same team. I didn't wrestle him."

"Don't be a smart mouth."

"Ma'am?" Thomas says, incredulously. She's never been a sweet lady, but she hardly knows him, and her tone was vicious.

"You're supposed to be in school. A boy needs guidance at this point in his life. I see that isn't happening here. Perhaps I'll place a call to your father."

It's all Thomas can do to contain himself. Who the hell does she think she is? Her son's a psychopath. He tries to stop the explosion that's building inside him when he hears it; rather, *he hears her.*

As if placing a call to that father of his would do any good. He has no chance with a family like that. Why do I bother trying to help? I'm just too empathetic for those with so little. I always have been.

Thomas bursts out laughing.

"My God; you think you're empathetic?" he says, wiping his eyes. "Lady, I don't think you know what that word means. And please do call my father. He'd be thrilled to hear from you." He walks away, saying 'empathetic' loud enough for her to hear, which sets him off laughing again.

There's a payphone at the coffee shop across the street that Thomas hopes works; he's never seen anyone use it but decides to take his chances. When he hears a dial tone, he plunks in two quarters and dials Mary. She picks up after two rings.

"Hello?" she says.

"Hi Mary, it's Thomas."

"Thomas? Is everything okay?"

"Yes, everything's fine. I know you've had Madi a lot lately, but I have a huge assignment. I'm calling from the coffee shop by the bookstore. I skipped out early to do some research. Anyway, can you keep Madi one more night? I'll probably be working pretty late."

"Yes, that's fine. Are you sure everything's okay?"

"Yep, great actually. But I need to get this done. I can bring her some clothes later."

"Don't worry about that. She can borrow something from one of the girls. Take care of what you need to, and don't forget to eat dinner."

Thomas hangs up the phone, feeling like a new person, all thanks to Toby's rude mother. She'd made him very angry, very quickly, and it was as if someone had snuck up behind him and plucked invisible plugs from his ears and replaced them with antennas. It had felt similar with the waitress, only that time, he hadn't realized the sheer annoyance he'd been feeling. He'd thought it a fluke. With Nicole, he'd felt joy or desire or admiration; he wasn't sure and didn't care. He'd never use his ability with her again. It had, like the other times, been an accident. But now that he can somewhat grasp how it works, he vows to focus on hearing the thoughts of people who deserve it. The ones he dislikes the most. He knows exactly where to start.

Terri Reed's house is only a few minutes away, but Thomas extends his walk by stopping in a few stores throughout town. He putts around the sports store, testing out basketballs, and spends a minute at the speed bag before hitting the library to scan wanted ads posted in the window. The school would have just gotten out, and he's giving time for Terri to get home. His stomach tightens ever so slightly. He's almost looking forward to seeing her. Terri is awful. This meeting with her will not be pleasant, but if anyone can make him mad, it's her. There's no better candidate. Hopefully, her thoughts come quickly; he has no desire to extend their time together. With that in mind, he tells himself not to overdo it; to get what he needs and leave. There's no reason to engage outside of that. This is a business transaction.

The walk is lovely, but chilly. Thomas finds himself looking forward to the first snow. If all goes well, his mom might be home for it. Lost in a daze, Thomas reaches Terri's house without thinking about his destination. At the front door, he reaches for the knocker and nearly falls when the door is whipped open.

"What are you doing here?" Terri says. Her eyes remind Thomas of a possum's. He giggles.

"I uh…sorry," he clears his throat. "Hi, Terri. I'm here for the assignment we talked about. Remember?"

Terri glares at him, tapping her foot on the ground. He glances at the porch. It's a nice place, something his mother would like. Ceramic pots filled with flowers surround a small seating area. A book he recognizes lies open on a loveseat, and below it sits a pair of slippers. He liked that book a great deal and finds himself wondering who in this house might be reading it. It couldn't be Terri. She'd never read something so illuminating. How could Terri live in a charming place with someone who reads the kind of books Thomas likes and still be Terri?

Terri coughs. Thomas blinks.

"Oh, sorry, do you have a paper for me?" he winks.

Her eyes tighten to slits. He tries not to grin but fails.

"You're late. This was supposed to happen over the weekend, but I guess I'll let you do it. I know you're hard up for money. Wait here," she slams the door.

Thomas rocks on his feet, waiting. After several minutes, he grows annoyed and rings the doorbell. He can hear stomping from inside the house, so he starts whistling. Terri rips open the door.

"Geeze, you're pretty strong. You almost pulled the door off its hinges," he says.

She thrusts the paper at him so hard he's forced to take a step back. "Here."

Thomas looks at the paper and back at Terri.

"Take it," she says. "I don't have all day. Some of us have social lives. We don't have to waste our time on things like this." She smirks, blinking her beady eyes at him.

There it is, he thinks. He's startled by how quickly he reacted to her but is delighted. Welcome anger bubbles through his body, accompanied by several of her hideous thoughts. He stays on the porch, listening to her think hateful things about him, breaking himself free when he can't listen any longer. She seriously dislikes him.

"Sorry," he says. "I'm afraid I can't do that paper for you. But you have a lovely day, Terri."

"What are you doing?" she yells as he walks away. "We had a deal. Get back here. You'll be sorry, loser."

The door slams behind him, but not before Terri squeezes in a final thought. This one is violent, involving blood. His, for that matter, so he files it away. She's a bad apple. It might not be a good idea to screw with her.

"Nice gal," he says, glancing back and shudders.

Chapter 11

Twiggy's Mini-Mart carries at least thirty kinds of frozen burritos. It also happens to be on the way to Rob Greer's house, where Thomas has decided to stop next to pick up another homework assignment he missed over the weekend. Rob's a good guy, so Thomas doesn't mind making the stop after Terri's horrific visit. He has no plans to use Rob in his latest pursuit. Plus, he's hungry, so it's a win-win situation.

Twiggy's payload is in the back of the store, inside its massive freezer. Thomas grabs his favorite snack, a chimichanga, and tosses it into one of three industrial microwaves. While time ticks away cooking his burrito, he whistles along to the song playing overhead and freezes when warm tingles spread through his stomach. *Nicole.*

"Oh no," Nicole says, rounding the corner with a pile of junk food balanced in her arms. Items being falling to the floor. Thomas catches a bag of potato chips and takes a gallon of ice cream from her hands. Two candy bars smack the ground, sliding under the condiment bar.

"Good lord. This is what you eat?" he says, laughing at her expression.

"It's not all for me, I swear," she looks horrified, like a robber, rather than a patron. "I came to get some treats for Amanda, to cheer her up. She wasn't at school today, but I just talked to her. She sounded awful. Anyway, it probably won't do any good but who says no to junk food?"

The microwave dings. Thomas's stomach drops. He turns to grab the burrito without saying anything in fear that Nicole will see the guilt on his face.

"Thomas? Are you okay?"

"Yeah, sorry. I'm cool. Just hungry." He keeps his face down.

"Oh. Okay then. I guess I'll see you around." She walks away.

"Take care, Nicole," Thomas says in her direction, but she doesn't look back. He wraps the burrito in a napkin then leaves the store after giving her a head start.

I suck. *What a coward*, he thinks, taking a bite of burrito although he's lost his appetite. The bushes to his side rustle and Mike Little, best friend of Craig Bateman, the worst human Thomas has ever met, emerges. Mike is an ass to everyone for no reason other than to make Craig like him. Thomas grew up with both guys and remembers a time when Mike was still cool and made his own decisions. That made watching Craig turn Mike into a bully especially hard for Thomas. And while the duo morphed into complete scumbags, Mike is nowhere near Craig's league. Craig is a special kind of bully. A few years back, Craig tripped Thomas in the parking lot so close to the sidewalk that, had his backpack not fallen first, Thomas would have undoubtedly broken his nose. Mike just stood and watched. Thomas remembers looking up at Mike and thinking he'd offer help, but Mike didn't.

The worst part for Thomas was knowing he could take either of them with ease, but he couldn't risk getting into trouble.

Thomas looks at Mike and is surprised at the anger he feels. It makes him smile because it's an opportunity. And the face Mike makes at Thomas's smile is epic. Thomas can't help himself. He laughs until tears drip down his face. The problem is that with his laughter taking over, his anger begins to dissipate. He's got to do something fast.

With a voice nothing like his own, Thomas hears himself say to Mike, "Where ya going, little man?"

Mike's head jerks back as Thomas expected. Mike has always been annoyed by his last name. It's a well-known weakness to everyone at school and one that warrants semi-frequent whispers at Mike's expense when he isn't looking. Not that he hasn't earned it.

"What'd you say to me?" Mike says, his face darkening.

Thomas isn't sure if he's embarrassed or pissed. Probably both. Thomas smiles at the prickling he feels, the anger that's building. He can't stand Mike anymore, mainly because of who he's become. When Mike's brain suddenly blossoms for Thomas to see, Thomas isn't surprised. He races through Mike's thoughts as quickly they pour in. Without intention, he digs deeper; his mind making quick work of Mike's head, pulling apart and squishing through layers of unconsciousness, as if it was a thing he did daily.

A recurring thought makes Thomas pause. Mike thinks about Craig frequently; only the feelings aren't friendly, they're romantic. *Oh.* Of all the people Mike could like, he picks the worst guy at this school, in this town for that matter. Craig wouldn't want Mike thinking those things about him. Mike's thoughts shift to his father and how his father would react to his feelings about Craig. It's bad.

He thinks awful things about his father, and Thomas breaks away, not wanting to see anything else. No one deserves a father like that, even someone as horrible as Mike. Thomas knows all too well what it's like, and he wouldn't wish it on anyone.

"Hey Mike, snap—" Thomas starts, but something hard smacks the back of his head. A feeling of warmth spreads down his neck. He reaches up to touch it and when he pulls his hand away, it's covered in blood. Confused, he looks at Mike, who looks equally confused.

"Mike?"

Mike blinks but doesn't answer. He didn't expect that, either, Thomas thinks. Mike is as surprised as I am.

Laughter starts behind him, and Thomas knows who it belongs to before he turns around. What surprises him is seeing the bloody shovel handle poking out of Craig's hand that he keeps slapping against his palm.

"Terri called," Craig says. "You do know she's my friend, right? So, my guess is that you were hoping to get your ass kicked?"

"I don't—" Thomas tries.

"So you know," Craig says, his eyes sizzling, "the next time you tell her you'll do something, you'll do it."

The world turns black.

The noises that surround me are unlike anything that I've heard before. The air is so thick it has texture. I can see the sounds vibrating in bubbles toward me before they explode to reveal what they are. One by one, they detonate, shrill bird screeches, rabid rats gnawing through their latest prize, razor-sharp snake scales slicing through trees, and only God knows what else. I don't bother to run. There's nowhere to go. Simon is here.

I rub my head that has stopped bleeding but still hurts. I can't believe Craig hit me with that thing; he could have killed me, that moron. An electric current running through the air forces the hairs on my arm to stand up, and I'm pulled away from my reprieve. I'm in a much more dangerous place now than I was with Craig. I can feel it. I should not be here.

"Come out then," I say, sounding braver than I feel.

"Thank you for the invitation Thomas," I hear before he steps from behind a tree. It's not Simon. And although I've never met him, I know it's Amos. It must be. I can sense Adam on him like a dog can smell where his master has been. Then I get a good look at him, and I'm baffled. He's just a kid, no more than eleven or twelve; and he's dazzling, like he stepped off the front cover of a children's magazine. His shiny gold hair and tanned skin make him look like a pre-teen Barbie doll. He doesn't look like someone with power; he looks like an altar boy. Then he smiles at me with sharp black fangs, and I understand what evil looks like. Oh, Adam, I think. What have you gotten yourself into?

"Hello, Thomas. I'm Amos. A pleasure to make your acquaintance. I typically don't travel for meetings. Couriers come to me. But I had to meet the person who walked into my home without being invited." He snaps his fangs tight before offering a broad smile that makes my stomach twist, a sensation that feels like my organs are fighting for pole position to escape.

Oh shit. This is bad. I hope Adam didn't piss him off by helping me. I need to be more careful with my decisions, regardless of how this plays out.

"Shh," he says, "quiet now, little bird."

"What?" I think, "did that kid just call me—"

A hand grips my neck. Moments ago, I was several feet away from where Amos stood, yet now he's pinned me against a tree by my neck at least two feet in the air. My eyes bulge, and I stare into his face, wishing that I could catch a breath. I'm suffocating. This is it. If he doesn't break my neck, he'll strangle me to death. The black spots I'm getting familiar with return, and I feel like my head is going to explode. I wonder where I'll end up after I die. Will I stay here in this awful place, or will I die on the other side? What is happening over there, anyway? Am I lying in the middle of the road? Are Craig and Mike kicking my unconscious body?

I'm dropped to the ground like a sack of potatoes, and my lungs fill with air. I don't know why he let me go and I don't care. Air has never tasted better, even this sick, rotten air. I lie on the ground gulping it down, hungry for more.

"Unbelievable," he laughs. "You can't turn that brain of yours off for anything. Not even death. I could feel your life fizzling out and still, you questioned, questioned, questioned. And for what? For answers that make no difference to you."

"I'm sorry, I didn't mean to. It won't happen again."

"I know it won't," Amos says. He stares into my eyes and I think I might be sick. There's an energy around him that feels off. I felt it when I was in his palace, the sensation growing strongest in the cave. It almost feels like holding a battery to a tooth filling; it's not exactly painful, yet it feels bad enough in a strange way that you don't want to feel it again.

"Amos, there's been a terrible mistake. Both times I've been here were by accident. The first still makes no sense, and this time I was knocked unconscious, but I never meant to go to your home or come here without permission. And Adam helping me is totally on me. I was lost, and he didn't know what to do so he tried to tell you, but you weren't there. It's not his fault. It's mine, and if you let me leave now, you'll never have to see me again."

Amos paces, rubbing his shiny, stubble-free chin. He smiles and frowns, turning his head this way and that, and I think he's contemplating my plea. That's when he makes a sound so awful that bile rises in my throat. And when I realize that the noise coming from him is laughter, I cannot contain my fear any longer and vomit down my shirt. He stops laughing and looks at me with disgust.

"What I'm trying to understand Thomas," he says, "is how a courier that doesn't know how to use a Way Station waltzes into my home, and then gets a free ride out. It doesn't add up. For you to be traveling on this side without assistance, to bump into my courier, use my assistant, and then leave without meeting me, is ridiculous at best. I guess what I'm saying Thomas, is that I don't believe it for a second. I want to know who sent you and why. And until we've sorted it out, I'll be keeping an eye you."

He stops and watches me again, then sighs. "Any idea of how I might do that?"

"I'm not sure," I say. I wish he'd tell me what he wants and let me go.

Amos laughs. "Very well, Thomas. If you'd like for me to get to the point, I will. You'll be collecting thoughts for me until I say otherwise."

"But—"

"Get busy," he says.

"Thomas, can you hear me? Wake up. Thomas, wake up, are you okay?" a voice asks. When the gentle nudging of his shoulder grows more frantic, Thomas opens his eyes. Standing above him is Rob Greer, wearing a look of concern on his face.

"Where am I?" Thomas searches the sky for answers. When it doesn't provide any, he finds Rob again, staring down at him. Rob is slow to reply, and blurry memories start to surface. He was walking, and Mike came out of the bushes. His head throbs, making him wince.

Rob seems to notice. "Take it easy, man. You're bleeding. I was about to call for help," he pulls a phone from his pocket.

Thomas forces himself to sit up. "No, don't do that. I'll be okay. I just need a minute." Rob hesitates but puts the phone away.

"What happened?"

"Mike and Craig. They've got some beef with me about Terri."

"Did you get into a fight? You're bleeding pretty bad."

"I wouldn't call it a fight. Craig hit me with a stick or something when I wasn't looking." Thomas touches the back of his head. The bleeding has slowed but there's still blood.

"That guy's such an asshole. Sucker-punches you with a weapon? You should call the cops."

"And get into it with my dad? No way. He'd be mad I didn't see it coming. I'll be fine." Getting to his feet is excruciating. The ground spins in front of him. He nearly falls, but Rob steadies him.

"I think you should sit down for a while. You look like shit," Rob says.

"No, I can't. It'll pass. I need to walk." He takes a shaky step forward. "See that? I'm off to a running start."

"Yep. You're flying." Rob keeps their painfully slow pace. "I still think you should report it. That guy never gets in trouble and should be sitting in juvey, maybe jail. He's seventeen, and that was assault."

"There's no point. It'll take all day, and his dad will get him out of it like always. I'll deal with Craig when I have the time, but he's at the bottom of my priority list. What are you doing here, anyway? I was on my way to your house to pick up your homework."

"I was walking home from school. I had to stay late."

Thomas stumbles when his head thumps. He catches himself before he falls.

"You all right?" Rob asks.

"I'm good. I could use an aspirin."

"My house is up the street. I'll give you a ride home if my mom's back with the car."

"That'd be great, thanks."

Rob tells him no problem, then spews sports stats that last the remainder of the walk. Thomas nods but doesn't pay attention. His head is throbbing. He'd rather go home and lay down, but there's too much to do. By the time they reach Rob's house, Thomas feels like he might crumble.

"Crap. I don't think she's here," Rob says, as if reading Thomas's mind. He cuts across the lawn to the garage and jumps up to look through the window.

"Sorry, Thomas. I thought she'd be home by now. You can hang out if you want, and I'll take you when she gets back."

"No, that's cool. I've got to get home. Did you still want me to do that assignment?" Thomas asks, swaying.

"Don't worry about that. I'll do it. I was being lazy," Rob says.

"I could use the money," Thomas mumbles, his eye roaming for something to lock on. He's got to get ahold of himself.

Rob blushes, jumps up. "Sure man. I left it in the kitchen. I'll grab it. Do you want anything? A coke?"

"Yes, coke—or whatever, please," Thomas says, stepping inside the house.

The modest living room looks comfortable, and well cared for. A mirror hangs above the fireplace with a mantle littered with pictures, undoubtedly of family. Thomas feels a pang of envy and listens to Rob bang around in the kitchen.

Rob returns with coke and aspirin that he hands to Thomas. "You're sure you don't want to wait? You don't look so good."

"No, I'm good. But I should get out of here before I get blood on anything."

"Don't worry about it." He hands Thomas his paper and some cash. "I don't need the paper for a few days, so if you change your mind, it's cool."

"Ok," Thomas says, feeling weird. He's not used to people being nice to him. At least not so often. He feels remarkably awkward, so he beelines to the door and catches his breath when he gets outside. He turns to leave but can't decide whether to offer his hand as a shake, or to wave, so he shoves it into his pocket.

Rob laughs, stepping forward to open the door. He's felt awkward before, too. "Ok then, he says, "see ya around, Thomas," and closes the door.

Every step is agonizing. It feels like someone is playing the drums on his head. What was he thinking? He should have waited for a ride. The walk home takes nearly an hour, and when he steps onto their property, Thomas can tell that their father is back.

There was a time in Thomas's life when he adored his father. He'd thought the world of him and would have been thrilled to have him home. Jim had been present and eager to be a part of Thomas and Madi's lives and spent as much time with them possible. Then one day, with no warning or apparent reason, Jim began to change. He stopped coming home, and when he did show up, he was distracted. There was some new plan in his life that didn't involve his family, and with it came a dark side to Jim that sickened Thomas. Thomas prayed that the old Jim would return. Instead, the unthinkable happened; Lilian disappeared. Whatever might have been left of the old Jim completely evaporated. Since then, Thomas hasn't seen an ounce of humanity from Jim. He's grown into a monster, and Thomas doesn't expect anything to change.

Breathe, Thomas tells himself and turns the doorknob, knowing it will be unlocked. It spins with ease. His father's presence radiates off their home. He stands clutching the door and waits for a sound; for the floor to creak and the house to whisper where his father is hiding, but there's only silence.

The light grows pale and the world turns quiet. He steps inside to violence.

One minute he's walking, and the next everything is a blur, as he's shoved from behind. Thomas flies across the room, landing against the couch. Behind him, his father speaks through bursts of laughter.

"Boy, you are clumsy as an ox. Je-sus, that was good," he laughs.

"Are you out of your mind?" Thomas says, climbing to his feet and adjusting his shirt. He stares at his father. "I'm already bleeding. What the hell is wrong with you?"

"Oh, settle down, I was goofing around. Don't be a—"

Here it comes, Thomas thinks, "—little girl." Anger floods his body. He knew what his father was going to say, expected it, yet he can't stop the rage he feels.

"Are you going to cry now?" Jim laughs.

Thomas closes his eyes and counts to three. Slowly the anger is replaced by disgust, and he's able to see Jim truly; to take all of him in. Dressed in a tailored suit with pearl cufflinks and black leather shoes, Thomas has never seen his father look better. He leans against the front door with his arms folded across his chest, watching Thomas with a broad Cheshire cat smile. Thomas can't make sense of what he's seeing. Jim doesn't have the money to pay for nice clothes. And he's groomed, clean-shaven with a fresh haircut. He looks amazing. They make eye contact, and Thomas feels his world spin. Jim's gotten to the trust fund and drained it; he's here to celebrate his crime.

"Still the same old Thomas I see," his father says. "A little bit of blood and the world is coming to an end."

Thomas rolls his eyes. He remembers this, the taunting, the goading. His father has done it to him most of his life, with it getting worse after his mother vanished. Jim loves to tease, loves to make others feel small. There are so many people who act that way. Those who feel so inadequate that they try to beat the importance out of those around them; wasting potential rather than seeing it. They are the people that live in their own stories instead of joining the stories around them. How sad.

But, it's fine with Thomas. Jim can stay in his own, ugly story and rot. In fact, Jim can go away and never come back. He means nothing to their family. Thomas can support them. He'll find a way. He always does. The only thing that matters is getting his mother back and taking care of Madi. Thinking of her makes him smile.

"What the hell are you smiling about?" Jim squints his eyes.

"I'm smiling at a waste of a person, Jim. Now get out of my house."

"Your house?" Jim steps toward Thomas, the muscles in his jaw ticking.

"Try it, Jimmy, you'll regret it."

"Is that right?" Jim takes a step. "Went and got yourself a spine did ya?"

"What are you talking about, old man? You are crazier than ever, Jim; something that I didn't think was possible. Regardless, you are not welcome here, and it is time for you to leave. Now."

Jim's expression changes to furry. He starts toward Thomas, but his eyes glaze over and he drops to the ground. Thomas takes a seat and enters Jim's head. Jim's thoughts and dreams are broken and disturbing. It's surprising that he was ever a husband or father. That's he's ever been loved, or that he's loved anyone. It's heartbreaking. Where did he go? When did he grow so violent, or was he always that way? Did having Lilian around neutralize him? Nothing makes sense. Jim's thoughts are so fractured that it's challenging for Thomas to make sense of them. Bits and pieces come together in spurts and show little more than a wasted life. How can someone who started so good turn so bad? Who is this man and what happened to his brain?

Thomas searches for answers until his head feels ready to explode. Giving up, he pulls free from Jim's murky thoughts and is assaulted with a migraine. Nearly incapacitated, he takes in shallow breaths, hoping to ease his pain, but it doesn't help. Finally, he gives in to the agony and collapses into a chair across from his slumped father.

Facing his father's blank face, Thomas is disgusted.

"Even with everything I saw," Thomas whispers, "from the endless half-ideas, to your great plans for the future, you didn't think of us once. There wasn't a single memory of Madi. Of me. I've watched you get worse and worse for years, but I had no idea how rotten you'd become."

Jim moans; his eyelids flutter.

"You're not welcome here, Jim. I don't want you around Madi."

Opening his eyes completely, Jim staggers to his feet.

"What happened? What's going on?"

"You fainted. Now you're awake. Please leave."

"You ungrateful little—"

"I have never been ungrateful, Jim. I have always wanted you back the way you were, but not like this. Look at yourself, wearing fancy clothes paid for with stolen money. That money belonged to Madi and I. We depended on it. And you still don't care. I doubt you ever will. But enough is enough, Jim. I'm asking you to leave."

Jim twitches. "Oh, okay, Thomas. I'll just shimmy up the highway, and let you get back to it, then. Whatever you say. You're the boss, hoss." He smiles, but his body looks like it's rumbling.

"I mean it, Jim. I will call the police."

"You wouldn't. They'd split you two up and you know it, or you'd have already called."

"I will. I'm seventeen, and I'll file to be Madi's guardian or Mary will take us until I'm eighteen. Either way, you'll be in jail. I should have let Mary put you—hell, I should have put you there a long time ago, but I didn't want to be a burden on anyone, something you're unfamiliar with."

Jim starts to speak, and Thomas knows this won't be an easy fight. He can see it on Jim's face and his anger returns. He thinks about losing Madi and all the bad things Jim has done to them since Lilian. At first, he'd disappear for a day or less, but that quickly grew into weeks or months. The longer he was gone, the crueler he was when he returned, as if the absence nurtured his blossoming malevolence. Thomas despises him. Get out of here, Jim, he thinks with fury. I want to make you hurt and you're about to get your nose broken.

Jim's head snaps back as if he's been punched. Blood trickles from his nose. Stunned, he looks to Thomas for an explanation, but Thomas doesn't say a word. He doesn't have to. Resignation settles on Jim's face. His time here is over. He leaves the house for what Thomas hopes will be the last time.

The relief is as gratifying as it is overwhelming. Thomas walks to the bathroom and takes some aspirin, staring at his reflection. He has no idea how he broke Jim's nose without touching him, but it felt good. He wishes he'd learned that trick before.

The strain of the day washes over him, so he lies down to think things through, but he's asleep before he has the chance. Time speeds by and slows down; the sun disappears and rises. Thomas wakes and looks at the clock. He's slept fourteen hours. School started an hour ago.

Outside, birds chirp and crickets squeak, while inside, the refrigerator moans and grumbles. Cars race up and down the street and throughout the neighborhood with distinct melodies; there goes Mrs. Adams in her wagon, boy, is she late; here comes Austin, always cutting school. I hope he didn't find another cat to torture in the forest behind my house. I'll step in next time; my impunity from myself is wearing thin. There's a second that everything seems normal. Then he remembers yesterday and reality settles in. Screw it. It's only Tuesday, he thinks. I'm going back to bed.

His stomach wakes him with more of a churning than a gurgle. Even with everything that's happened, his body manages to stay true to itself, shouting its needs. He's starving. He pulls bread and peanut butter from the cupboard and eats without thinking, then makes several more sandwiches for later. The angle of light on the table tells him it's about time to pick up Madi. He heads out.

Rounding the bend before Madi's school, Thomas feels the sensation that has been becoming commonplace. *Nicole*. Ahead, a car drives toward him, stopping across the road. Nicole leans out the window.

"Hey," she says. "What are you doing out here? Are you okay? I thought you were sick. You weren't in school."

"Hi," he says. "No, I'm good. I needed a day off."

"Oh. Well, can I give you a ride somewhere?"

"That's okay. I'm almost there. Just picking up my sister. Thanks, though."

"Sure. Next time," she smiles and drives away, but not before he hears her thinking about spending time with him.

Screw it; he decides as she drives away. He can see her if he wants to. With all the pressure resting on his shoulders, he deserves to be happy, too. God only knows where his life is heading, and this could be his last chance.

Chapter 12

Classes seem to pass in an instant the following week. Thomas climbs from his desk at the end of every day completely exhausted. Since his confrontation with Toby's mom, he's gotten good at hearing thoughts without much effort. These days, he spends more time in class listening to students thinking than to his teachers. Adam was right. At first, hearing private things was awful, sickening. But after time, he learned how to listen passively by not interacting with whomever he was listening to. Only his own emotions needed to be manipulated, not theirs. It takes nothing more than thinking about his father or Craig Bateman for a few seconds to allow him to hear anyone he wants.

What troubles Thomas now is that people have begun to look simple to him. That's a lousy feeling to have about your peers. He reminds himself that there is more to them than the bits of information he pulls, but it's becoming a challenge to keep that perspective. People are not made up of singular thoughts. They are so much more than that, and it's disheartening to feel this way. He would hate it if someone judged Madi on one moment, instead of her entire life, well-lived.

Today, oblivious students pass by him in the hallway, completely unaware that their thoughts and emotions are being broadcast. The same is true for much of the town. Everyone is clueless about the turmoil surrounding them; that the universe is nothing like what they perceive. Everything could be taken from them instantly, and they would be powerless to stop it from happening. Thomas is still uneasy about invading people's privacy, but it's for the greater good. If they understood what was happening, they'd probably line up.

A group of girls pass by with Terri leading the way. Her eyes find Thomas and she quickly looks away. She says something to the girl next to her and they laugh. *Here we go, always the same Terri.* Terri says something else and all the girls look over their shoulders at him. Now he's annoyed, but more at himself than Terri. He's above this and should not care what she thinks. Yet, somehow, he does. His eyes stay fixed on Terri's and he listens.

Samantha's not even that pretty. She must be a tramp like her sister. That's why Craig likes her. Kate is starting to bug me. Maybe I'll remind everyone that her dad went to jail, for like, some Ponzi scheme. That might make her less smug.

He chokes back a laugh after several minutes and his body relaxes. That should be enough information for one day. At least it came from Terri, the mental cesspool. Walking from school, he feels lighter than he has in weeks, especially now that he's been productive for both Brokers. The last time he saw Amos, Thomas's diligence was praised.

A little more than three weeks pass before Thomas notices how large his pool of subjects has grown along with the weariness that's taken root. There's no indication of how long he'll have to keep this up, and so far, he's noticed no changes on Tendo other than how the Brokers treat him. He's prepared to continue as long as it takes but the constant effort is taking its toll. The one benefit he's experienced, is always knowing which students need his help. They pay whatever he asks because he listens to their decision process while he sells his service. It might not be ethical, but neither is passing off someone's work as your own. Money is still an issue, but not like it was a few months ago.

Walking into the grocery store after school, Thomas sees Nicole pulling out of the parking lot. When she sees him, she slows to a stop and rolls down the window.

"Hi," Nicole says. "How have you been? I've barely seen you at school."

"I know. Sorry I haven't called. I've been buried. It should be easing up soon, though. What's new with you?"

"Not too much. My aunt's in town, so I'm picking up some supplies."

"That's too bad."

"Why?" she says.

"I was going to ask you over for dinner. I make a mean burger."

"Oh, I was getting stuff for breakfast tomorrow; they're going out tonight. But I can come over for dinner, I think. I just need to check. What time were you thinking?"

"Six o'clock?"

"Sounds great. I'll call you after I ask—oh shoot, your phone, it wouldn't work the last time I tried to call it."

"I have another number," he jots it down and hands it to her. "Call me if you can't make it. Otherwise, I'll see you at 6:00." He winks and walks away, feeling his mood improve exponentially. Madi gets out of class later than usual. She runs into Thomas as she's leaving the building. She looks off, somehow. Thomas feels a pang in his gut.

"You're pretty late Madi, is everything okay?" Madi's head hangs.

"I don't want to talk about it."

"If something is going on, I need to know about it. You can tell me anything. You know that."

"It's not a big deal, and I don't want you to feel bad," Madi says.

"Mads, you're not going to make me feel bad. I can take it. What I can't take is you keeping something from me."

She sighs, finally meeting his eyes. "I'm not in trouble or anything, so don't freak out. I had to meet with my teacher. I got into an argument with a girl in my class. I've told you about her before. Cindy Miller."

"What about her? What happened?"

"She keeps making fun of me and my clothes, but I never say anything. Today, when she spilled paint all over herself, I called her a crybaby, and everyone laughed. My teacher wanted to talk to me about it, but it's not fair. Everyone hears what Cindy says to me, and she never gets in trouble, but when I say one little thing, it's like this huge deal."

It feels like the wind is knocked from his chest. All this time, it didn't occur to him that Madi might be having issues at school. She's so mild-mannered, so seemingly indifferent to their situation that he's never bothered to ask. Apparently, that's not the case. This has been going on for some time which is easy to believe since he hasn't paid much attention to her lately. He's been completely self-absorbed. What a jerk. She's getting older, she's almost in fifth grade now. Girls care about their clothes. Bending down to her level, he gently squeezes her shoulder.

"I haven't been around much lately, have I?"

Madi shrugs him off, picking at her nails.

"It's okay. I know I haven't been, and I'm sorry. I got caught up in my stuff and figured that everything was fine with you because you've never said anything. And that's not your fault, it's mine, so I won't do it anymore, okay? We're a team. From now on, I want to know what's going on with you. And not only when things are bad."

Madi nods.

"And this thing with the girl, Cindy. Don't worry about it. Everything will be fine, so don't get pulled into her game. I know she's been harassing you, but hopefully, after this, she leaves you alone. If I'd known this was going on, I would have shut it down before it got to this point. You didn't do anything horrible but calling people names can hurt. I know that it hurt me when dad did it."

Madi flinches like she's been slapped.

"I didn't mean it like that. You'd never intentionally hurt someone. I'm only making a point. If someone is a jerk, it doesn't mean you have to be one back. You're better than that, and you're not a bully. Okay?"

"I guess."

"Seriously, Madi."

"Okay, okay. I get it. But anyway, the twins asked—"

"Sorry, Madi, not tonight."

"What? I didn't even finish."

"I know Mads, and I'm sorry, but not tonight."

"But, Thomas!"

"Let me guess, they invited us to dinner?"

"Uh-huh."

"Madi, the Gleeson's invite us to dinner almost every night. We're overextending our welcome, and we can't do it tonight. Besides, I have someone coming over."

"Then why do I have to come?"

"Because it's Nicole, and I think she'd be more comfortable with you here. You liked her, right?"

Madi's eyes grow wide, and Thomas can tell she's excited. They haven't had many guests since before their mom left. It's all he can do to keep her from bouncing off the walls, so he keeps her busy with setting the table and getting the house ready. By the time dinner rolls around, Madi and Nicole are deep in conversation with Thomas fighting to get a word in. When Nicole pops the last bite of burger into her mouth, Thomas jumps at the break in the conversation.

"I should have bought more meat," he says, regretting it instantly. Nicole flushes and Madi shoots Thomas a dirty look.

"Nice one," Madi says. "Girls love to be teased about how much they eat."

Thomas freezes, looking back and forth between the girls, his impulse to flee growing by the second. Then Nicole and Madi burst out laughing, and it's Thomas's turn to blush. Madi laughs a minute more, gives Thomas a sly grin, and gets up from the table.

"I'm going to watch T.V.," Madi says, then drops her dish into the sink. "Thanks for dinner, Thomas. I'm glad you came, Nicole. Can you come back soon?"

"I hope," Nicole says, blushing harder when she sees Thomas watching her. After they clean up, they join Madi for a movie in the living room and everyone falls asleep on the couch. Far up the road at the edge of town, the church bell chimes ten times. It's faint, but loud enough to wake Thomas and Nicole.

"Oh, my God, I can't believe how late it is. I've got to get home," Nicole says, scrambling for her things. "I'm sorry."

"It's only ten o'clock."

"I know, but my dad's super strict about me driving at night which makes no sense because it gets dark here at like five during winter. I think he says that to keep my curfew early," she says pulling on a shoe. "Anyway, if I'm on time the next few months he'll lighten up." She pulls on her coat and faces Thomas. "Thanks for dinner and everything."

"Anytime. I'm glad you came." His heart thumps as he walks her to the car. She spins and kisses him lightly, then slides into her car before he can react. As the car drives off, she waves, and he waves back, thinking that this was the best day of his life.

Sleep comes quickly, and for the first time in months, Thomas isn't plagued with dreams. He wakes late in the morning shivering and grabs a pile of junk mail to start a fire. The small teepee of kindling he builds lights instantly, and he continues to feed paper into the fire until the shiny, red envelope falls to the ground. Swallowing down the knot in his chest, he opens the bill but already knows what's inside. In the middle of the chaos that's become his life, he forgot to pay the power bill.

"Madi," he yells on his way to get dressed, "get up. We've got to go." It takes him three tries to get her up.

"I don't know why you can't call them. It's Saturday. Are they even open?" Madi says, rubbing her eyes as she walks into the kitchen.

"They're open until noon and I need to get down there to explain that I forgot. I can't pay all the late fees."

"Can you drop me at Mary's then? I'm hungry."

"No. You're coming with me. Put on something warm and I'll make you some toast." Madi shrugs and walks away, returning when her toast is ready.

"Awesome. Toast."

"Not today, okay. I'm doing the best I can." She looks at the ground and tucks her hands into her pockets.

"Sorry. I know you've been busy. I thought you earned all that money for the power. Maybe we shouldn't have had the burgers last night."

"Probably not, but that has nothing to do with it. I forgot to pay the bill. It happens. And I've been working my butt off. I think that's sufficient cause for a burger. Eat your breakfast, okay? I need a minute."

He rummages through the house and his jeans, gathering up all the money he can find. Hopefully, the power company will waive the extra charges. They walk to town, not stopping until they reach Westchester Power and Gas. Madi takes a seat by the entrance.

"Can I help you?" a young teller asks Thomas. Thomas shows her the bill and launches into the story he concocted on the walk.

"Hi. I'm embarrassed about this, but I forgot to pay our bill. My mother usually takes care of it, but she's been in the hospital. If she finds out that I didn't pay it, I'm gonna be in trouble. She's being released tonight. The last thing I want to do is upset her."

The teller clicks away at her computer, not looking up.

"If there's any way you can…"

Thomas stops when he hears her think, *oh my God, what did I do? I think I deleted this kid's entire account. That's my third screw up this week. They're going to fire me.*

Thomas considers her problem. Although it feels a bit smarmy, he makes his decision.

"I'm running a bit late, ma'am," he says. "If you'd like to get the manager for me to talk to, that's fine. I'm sure you could show them the account."

A co-worker passes behind her and asks if everything is all right. The teller's hands shake above the keyboard.

"Everything is fine, we're all set here," the teller says over her shoulder but keeps her eyes on the screen. She looks up at Thomas. "I set up a new account for this young man. Dispatch will get technicians to his house today."

"It says Dispatch tentatively scheduled their power to be cut next week," the co-worker says, peering at the computer.

"That's my fault. I keyed the wrong code but already fixed it."

"Yep, it's been fixed," Thomas says to the co-worker who shrugs and walks away.

Thomas tells the teller thanks for her help, and, with a skip in his step, he pulls Madi from her seat and they walk to town. Over the next few hours and in between conversations with Madi he listens in to a dozen people. It's become so easy he can do it and still hold down a conversation. The sun is setting by the time they get home. Thomas flicks on the lights and feels a pang of guilt about the teller. He did exploit the teller at the power company. But he really didn't do anything wrong. He didn't get her in trouble; he almost helped her in a way. She's not losing her job and it's not like the power company is going to miss the money. No harm, no foul. It takes little effort to restart the fire he built in the morning and after it comes to life, Thomas pulls out the sub-sandwiches they stopped to pick up.

"I don't get it," Madi says through a mouthful of bread. "We had to rush to pay a bill and ended up getting sandwiches?"

"Yep. Don't overthink it Madi. Sometimes good things happen to good people." If you make them happen, he thinks.

Chapter 13

Life returns to normal over the next week and Thomas goes through the motions like a robot. Take care of Madi, go to school, listen-in to people, repeat. Everyone else seems to do the same thing they always do, and the simplicity and monotony of their lives make him crazy. He can barely stand it. His life is filled with experiences most could never dream of. It's too much to bear.

Sunday morning comes, and Thomas wakes to an empty house. The twins had a slumber party for their birthday and Madi slept over. Thomas thinks Mary never got over the loss of her husband, so she keeps the house too noisy to ever sound empty.

Outside it's raining. Thomas lies in bed listening to the downpour when he feels the hairs on his arm stand up. Energy fizzles around him. *Here I go.*

The powdery white sand puffs between my toes. It's so bright out that I have to squint to see anything. I hear waves sloshing on the sand and turn to see Amos standing by my side.

"Thomas," he says.

"Amos," I say.

"Nice day," Amos says.

"This is a beautiful beach. It's good to be back."

"I'm aware. Shall we begin?"

"Um. Okay. I was wondering—"

"Ask your question."

"Really?" I say.

Amos frowns, his eyes flick. I know he doesn't like banter, so I have to be quick.

"I'd like to be able to initiate my visits, to have some sort of control over them. Can I do that?"

His eyes flash black to grey and back. "I might teach you to use the Way Stations one day."

"Really? What are they, exactly? How do they work?"

Amos shakes his head. "There are four Way Stations that can be used for travel between sides. They match up to four quadrants: North, South, East, and West, relatively speaking. We are near East Station."

"So, East Station matches up to the East Coast? Where I live?"

"Good Lord, no. They are simply where our worlds connect. Tendo has no direction; there is no North or South. You know nothing of this?"

"No. The only thing we've ever discussed was that I was to bring you thoughts while you decided what to do with me. And that was a while ago. I still don't know what's happening or when this ends. I don't understand anything."

"That is because the answers you seek are not useful to you or me. There is no point in your questions. You think they are rational, yet they are created out of emotion, which is not rational. So why bother trying to make you understand?"

"That's not fair. You can't assume what I'll ask."

Amos shrugs, "but I can. And what you want to ask cannot be explained. Things do not work between our universes like you think they do."

"Then how…"

"Enough," Amos stops me. "I can see this is pointless. I give will you a glimpse, and then we will not discuss this again."

Amos looks at me and I feel pressure in my eyes. There's a flash, and I can see tunnels running from Novo to Tendo. They twist and curve both vertically and horizontally and I can't make any sense of them.

"As I said, you wouldn't understand," he seems pleased with himself. A mocking grin tilts the side of his mouth revealing a twinkle of black. "Now let's get started," he says, his eyes gleaming. I briefly feel pressure but then it's gone.

"That was fast," I say.

"Yes. Nice use of the teller. Well done."

I'm not sure what he means, then realize he's referring to the teller at the power company. I feel a rush of pride. Amos isn't always bad. Granted, I thought he was going to kill me the first time we met, but we didn't know each other then. Plus, he's keeping my mom hidden to keep her safe. Even though he creeps me out, I can keep learning things from him until I've figured out how to get her home.

Rain pounds the roof. Thomas opens his eyes and smiles. There isn't much to do on weekends in Westchester when the weather is bad. There are no indoor malls, and all the shops in town line the streets, which, while charming, aren't practical to visit in the rain or a blizzard. The options for days like these are minimal. You can go to the movies, the library, or bowling. Thomas likes the library but it's too hard for Madi to sit quietly that long. Today, Madi chooses bowling when Thomas arrives at the Gleeson's to pick her up. He groans. It's the most expensive option. He'd hoped she'd pick the bookstore. He asks the Gleeson's to come but they can't. They're spending the day with Mary's parents. Mary takes one look at Thomas's wet coat and insists on giving them a ride.

Yellow marquee lights reflect off puddles of rain until Madi splashes through making the letters melt together. A sagging banner haphazardly hung between two posts reads: Lightning Alley is proud to host the Westchester Amateur Seniors Tournament. Looking up at the building Thomas notes several of the lights are out. It reminds him of the dangling sign from East Way Station.

"Call me later if you want a ride. It's supposed to rain all day," Mary calls from her window. "We won't be more than a few hours. I don't want to be on the road in the dark with the weather like this."

Yelling thank you at the same time, Thomas and Madi step into the alley. The smell of cigarette smoke and French fries assaults his nose, but Madi doesn't seem to notice. Bowling balls crash through pins loud enough to make his head throb. He pinches his sinuses. Madi is excited, so he'll have to suck it up.

Looking for the smallest ball, Madi runs up and down the racks while Thomas leaves his student I.D. for shoes and a lane. They play two games over several hours and decide to get a bite. Thomas checks his pockets. He has twenty dollars on him. That's not good, but it should be enough. They order fries and a large coke to share.

The waitress brings out their order and Madi dives in. Thomas hears laughing over his shoulder and tenses up, recognizing the sound. He turns as Nicole approaches with a girlfriend.

"Hi guys," she says and turns to her friend. "Katie, these are my friends Thomas and Madi. Katie is visiting from my old stomping grounds. Can we join you?" Katie looks displeased as they slide into the booth.

"Hello, ladies," the waitress returns and says, "can I get you anything?"

They order fries and sodas. Katie gets up to use the restroom several minutes later when the waitress returns with the food and tab. Nicole eats a fry then reaches into her jacket and feels around. Making a face, she frantically checks her pockets.

"Oh, no. I can't find my wallet. It must have fallen out in my dad's car."

"What about your friend?" Madi shoves a fry into her mouth.

"She doesn't have any money left. We spent it last night at the movies. Crap!"

Crap is right, Thomas thinks but gets an idea. "Don't worry, I'll get it," he winks and walks to the front counter thinking please God, let me make this work like it did at the power company or I'm going to look like a total idiot.

A waitress sees him and walks over. He recognizes her from school but doesn't know her name. "Hi. Is everything okay?" she asks.

Thomas focuses on her thoughts, pleading with her to think something that might help him. We have no money. Think of one thing to help us get everything for free today. Like you forgot to give us a receipt, so the meal is free. Come on, think it. Make it free.

Nothing happens. The waitress doesn't say anything, and he doesn't hear a single thought. Crap!

"Is it possible to add a few players to an ongoing game?"

New plan. He's got to get a hold of Mary and stall everyone until she gets there.

"Yes," the waitress says, "but I can't do it from here. You need to tell the front desk."

"Okay, great. We'll take a second order of fries and sodas as well," Thomas says. They might as well go all in. Either Mary comes with money, or he's going to juvey.

"I think I lost my cell phone," Thomas says. "Do you have a landline I could use?"

"Use this," the waitress hands him her phone. He watches her add the fries and drink to the bill as he punches in Mary's number. There's no answer.

"The fries will be right out," she says, reaching for the phone he's holding out to her with a shaky hand.

"Are you okay?" she asks.

"I am. Thank you. And thanks for the phone," he nods as she slips it into her apron.

"No problem," she winks.

"Are you okay?" Madi says when he returns. "You're all sweaty."

"I'm fine." He looks around.

"She went to the bathroom," Madi says. "Her friend is still in there. If you're looking for Nicole."

The fries take forever, and as luck would have it, so do the girls. There is plenty of time to kill. The place is packed. It's always busy regardless of the weather or condition of the building.

A group of older women walks by wearing shirts emblazoned with Alley Cats. One winks at Thomas. He cringes, and Madi laughs. The waitress walks by and sees him glance over her shoulder at the grandma and laughs.

"Better watch out for those gals. They're trouble," she winks.

Thomas laughs, happy for the distraction. "Thanks. Good advice."

The waitress returns to the counter and joins a girl in a matching uniform, who recently arrived. They talk for a bit, then his waitress pulls out a timecard and punches out. She waves over her shoulder to her friend and heads for the exit without looking at Thomas. We're screwed, he thinks. What was he thinking? He tells Madi to stay put and returns to the counter.

"Hi, I need to pay my bill, but I've misplaced my wallet."

"What bill?" the waitress asks.

"For the fries and the bowling. I'm going to have to call a friend to bring me some cash. Can I see the total please?"

"Your bill's been taken care of," she says.

"It was?" His heart speeds up.

"Uh-huh. Sarah, your waitress, said she told you. Anyway, take this ticket to the front desk for the shoes and they'll turn on another lane for you."

A smile spreads across his face. He thanks her and walks back to the table. The girls have returned. Everyone looks up at him and he is thankful they can't hear what he is thinking because he is giddy. He did it. He made someone do what he wanted without uttering a word.

"We're all set," Thomas says. "I got you girls a couple of games. If you take this ticket to the front desk, they'll give you some shoes."

"Really?" Nicole says. "That's so nice. You didn't have to do that. I could have called my dad."

Madi looks at Thomas, her eyebrows pinched. "I thought you didn't…" she starts but stops when Thomas shoots her a look.

"It's not a problem," he says to Nicole. "Did you want to play anymore Madi or should we get going? There's a break in the rain. If we make a run for it, we can probably make it home dry."

Madi frowns. "Why don't we call Mary?"

"Can't you stay?" Nicole asks. "Play a game with us? You guys haven't even returned your shoes yet."

"Please, Thomas," Madi says. "I don't want to walk. It's awful out there. Let's wait until Mary can come to get us."

"Looks like we're staying," he says to Nicole.

They bowl four games. Every time he passes Nicole to roll the ball or she sits next to him, he feels something like an electric current pass between them. He's glad they stayed. He doesn't get that much time with her and doesn't want it to end. Madi complains she's hungry, which is fair. He is, too. Since breakfast, they've only had fries. He feels guilty already but knows what he's going to do. He's going to take everyone out to dinner next door.

The group spends the next few hours devouring pizza and breadsticks followed by lava cakes. Thomas tells himself that this will be the last time he manipulates anyone; he only did it because of the circumstances. It will not happen again.

Nicole calls her dad for a ride and offers one to Thomas, but he tells her no thanks. He's not up for meeting her dad yet. Instead, and knowing this will officially be the last time, he calls a cab.

Winter break couldn't come at a better time. Mary is taking Madi and the twins to a cabin in the mountains. Thomas was invited but declined, choosing to stay home and work. Feeling guilty, Madi tried to stay behind but he wouldn't let her. She hasn't been on vacation since she was too young to remember.

During the break from school, Thomas hopes to spend some time with Nicole, alone. The past two weeks they've been inseparable, going for ice cream and burgers with Madi after school. He hadn't planned to use his ability again. He'd had enough money for school supplies when they entered Walls Bookstore; then, Madi saw the build-your-own cocoa bar by the espresso counter and the girl who made fun of her clothes holding a large drink. After she spotted Madi, she took a sip and smiled.

Madi's face dropped. "I wish I could get one."

Watching the brat taunt his sister felt like a punch to the gut. "Get one. I'll take one, too," he said. It's just cocoa. Not a big deal. With how hard I'm working, we deserve it.

"Really? But how?"

"Order the drinks Madi. I'll take care of it." In fact, he thinks, he'll be tapping into his ability from time to time. He won't abuse it; he'll stay in control. He and Madi have had a rough go at life; if he can make it a little easier, why shouldn't he? What's the harm? None that he can see.

Treating Madi and Nicole has been a nice change, but he's careful not to overdo it. Like he knew he would, he stays in control. A special dinner might be in the cards over the break, but he's debating it; it would be very easy to get carried away, and so far, he's behaved. Pulling on jeans and a sweater for the last day of school before winter break, he can hear Madi banging dishes in the kitchen. She's as eager for vacation as he is.

"Morning kid. What are you doing up so early?"

"Couldn't sleep. I'm too excited."

"I bet. You're going to have a lot of fun. Are you all packed up? Mary's picking you up in a minute so she can put your bag in the car. You're leaving right after school."

"Are you sure it's okay? You can still come."

"Nope, I'm good here. I have a lot to get done, so this works out for everyone."

Madi puts her bowl in the sink at the same time a car horn honks.

"That's them. Grab your stuff." Thomas walks her to the car and waves goodbye as they drive away. The phone rings and Thomas runs back into the house. He grabs it on the third ring. Nicole is crying on the other end.

"Thomas?"

"What's wrong? Are you okay?"

"My grandmother, she's, she died."

"Oh God, Nicole, I'm so sorry. That's awful. Are you okay? I'll come over."

"Nnn…no. We're leaving in a few minutes. My dad got us on a flight to California."

"What? California? But you can't. What about winter break?"

"Winter break? Thomas, my grandma died."

"I'm sorry. That didn't come out right. I just don't want you to go. I feel like I should be doing something to help. Can I do anything for you? For your family?"

"Thank you. But no. I don't know. I can't even think. I'm sorry."

"Don't be sorry. I'm sorry, Nicole. I'm so sorry about your grandma. Do you know how long you'll be gone?"

"I have no idea. My dad is so upset. He won't tell us anything. He said to pack enough for a few weeks."

"A few weeks?" But that's the whole break."

"He's yelling that the cab is here, Thomas. I've got to go. I'll call you as soon as I can. I'm sorry. Bye."

"Dammit," he throws the phone across the room shattering it. "Great. That's just perfect." Grabbing his backpack, he storms out of the house.

It's dark by the time the cab pulls in front of his house. It takes the driver and Thomas three trips to carry in the boxes and bags that fill every available space of the car. Thomas thanks him for the lift and walks to his front door. The driver sits in the cab, his eyes glazed over.

"You should go now," Thomas says. The cabbie nods and drives away. Walking inside and looking around, Thomas takes stock of what he's done. An unwelcome feeling fills his gut.

"This is going to take a while," he says to an empty house.

It takes hours to unpack everything he's brought home. The groceries are first, but after that, there's a tornado of work. Brand new pots and pans, dishes, and cups cover the floor. A red waffle iron and juicer balance on a griddle, a deep fryer leans against an ice cream maker. Looking around the room, he realizes he doesn't know how to use most of the stuff. There are new bedspreads and sheets, fluffy blankets and pillows, books and toys, new wardrobes for both himself and Madi.

He hadn't intended to do this. The plan had been to go to town for a new phone and to pick up a few groceries, maybe do some window-shopping, anything to distract him from Nicole for a few hours. But the saleslady was rude, and before he knew what was happening, he had directed her to fill up the cart with a cell phone and two e-readers, a portable speaker, and some movies. Feeling justified at the time, he watched her run around the store until the glazed expression on her face scared him. Okay-I overdid it that time. It won't happen again.

Then he walked into the grocery store, and things went bad fast. The manager was kind, but Thomas needed food. He didn't plan to take advantage of her or the store; he was only going to get a few things. But along came the monster child, and Thomas lost control.

"I want ice cream, the pink kind," the boy yelled at his mother who looked exhausted.

"No Michael, we already have ice cream and inside voices, please."

"But I want, I want…" he cried and screeched until his mother gave in.

Shut up, shut up, she'd thought. Thomas completely agreed. He gave her a small nod along with his I feel for you, lady expression, but the mother responded by thinking mind your own business along with a dirty look. So, when the brat started throwing things into the cart without reprimand, Thomas snapped. He'd seen enough, and no one seemed to care. And if no one cared, then neither did he. With that, Thomas turned his attention to the manager. I'll take two of everything that the lady and little boy are buying, and they will pay for it. And that was that.

For the next few hours, Thomas went store to store, planting thoughts into whichever person could give him what he wanted. When his pile of bags grew too heavy to carry, he loaded them into a cab and made the driver wait in a daze while he continued shopping. Now, Thomas looks around the house and feels justified. He thinks of Madi and smiles. She is going to be excited, but he's glad she isn't home. This is going to take some explaining. He bounces a few ideas around in his head, but nothing sounds plausible. A thought bubbles. He tries to push it away, but it pulses at the corners of his brain and he knows it's too late to stop it. It blooms like a poisonous flower. *Make her forget about it.* He can make her think anything he wants. And not just her, he can do it to anyone.

Chapter 14

A week passes before Thomas sees either Broker. He's home sulking that Nicole isn't back from California, and school is starting tomorrow. Madi plays in her bedroom with a robot set, one of the few toys she seemed vaguely happy about. He was surprised at her reaction to all their new things. He'd expected her to go crazy, both with excitement and questions, but neither happened. Instead, she'd looked around and made a weird face before heading to her room.

He replays that day over and over. He hadn't meant to manipulate her. It was barely a suggestion. He could tell she didn't understand where anything came from, and he couldn't explain. She gave a him a look that reeked of disapproval, and he cracked. Something inside him took over, and he did what he had to. He vows that it will never happen again. Madi did not deserve to be manipulated.

But at the same, how many people wouldn't use a gift like Thomas's to take care of the people they love? Wasn't it worth the tiny bit of interference he'd had to be run? Madi had gone without so much her entire life, that Thomas feels slightly justified in his actions. He ruminates, focused on the square tiles on the floor that turn to a blur.

I sit on a bench in town. Everything is quiet and peaceful. Simon sits to my left. When we look at each other, he smiles, but it doesn't touch his eyes.

"Hello, Thomas."

"Hello, Simon," I say and feel pressure in my head. I lock down as many thoughts as I can. The pressure fades, then disappears. Simon's eyes flash.

"You've been working hard."

"I wish you'd warn me before doing that."

"I do. You feel it coming."

"I don't know. It seems like with where we are, you could verbalize it instead of jumping right in. This isn't much of a partnership."

"How so?" Simon asks, eyebrows climbing north.

"You say we're partners, but we're not even close. You have all the information, and I do all the work. It's very one-sided,

with you being on the side that gets something. I thought you
said if I brought you thoughts, I'd be rewarded."

"You have been."

"When? How have I been rewarded?"

"You're alive."

"Thomas?" Madi taps his forehead. "Are you in there?"

Thomas wobbles in his chair. "Yes, yes, I'm here. What's
wrong?"

"I've been calling you for twenty minutes. Are you okay?
You look like you saw a ghost."

"What? No, I'm fine. Twenty minutes? Really?" His heart
thumps. "Sorry, I must have nodded off."

"Oh. Well, Mary called."

"Don't even ask Madi, it's a school night."

"But our play is coming up. We need to practice our parts
and Mary said she'd help with a costume. You said you'd help but
you haven't. We're running out of time."

"All right, all right, but tell Mary not to make the
costume. I'm working on it. I should have done it over the
break, but I forgot about it. Go pack up. I'll walk you over."

Madi hugs his neck and runs to her room to pack her bag.
She's back in minutes and Thomas throws on a coat. He drops her
at the Gleeson's and instead of returning home, walks to the
thrift store for the costume he saw a few weeks back that should
work for the play. With that accomplished, he walks outside
while checking his cell phone for Nicole's messages and cries
out when he sees Amanda standing in front of his house.

"Jesus Amanda, you scared me. How long have you been
standing there?"

Amanda looks at Thomas through glazed eyes.

"Amanda? Are you okay?"

Amanda blinks. "What?" she says after a few seconds.

"I asked if you were okay."

"I'm fine. Why?"

"Because you don't seem fine. How long have you been standing there?"

"Where?"

"Right there. Jesus. What is going on?"

"What are you talking about? I was walking by. You're so weird, Thomas. I've got to go. See you around."

Thomas watches her walk away, listening in until she's out of sight. He's baffled at what he's heard. Nothing made sense. What the hell was that? He has no idea why, but a cold sweat breaks over his skin. Back at home after dropping Madi, he slinks into the worn couch and thinks about Amos. It takes only slight concentration before he feels the pull and knows that it's time.

Amos sits on the steps of the water palace. "I thought you'd like a tour," he says and stands up. "I realize that your last visit was rushed."

My heart thumps. My mom is right inside. He brought me so close to her. I try to organize my thoughts and put her somewhere far away. I can't blow this. I think about the people I dislike, and all the bad things that have ever happened to me, anything to keep me distracted.

"Uh-huh," I say. It's all I can manage. Amos smirks.

"I know," he says. "I'd be intimidated if I were you, too. It is impressive."

I follow him through the entrance, turning my eyes to the massive columns I saw last time, but they are much different now. Where fire pillars once stood, are now tornadoes; one facing upright, and the other inverted. My mouth drops. I hear Amos laugh.

"I like them as well. I might leave them for a while."

The tornados twist and turn to invisible music, beckoning me to watch. Something flashes from inside of one and I squint to see it, my stomach dropping when I understand what it is. Inside the tornados are thousands of tiny animals. They flip and twist through the massive funnels, bashing into and off of each other. Sometimes they merge, and when they do, their faces contort with pain. When I look in horror at Amos, he shrugs.

"Tornados are indiscriminate. Anything inside those two got there of their own volition. I had nothing to do with it."

He walks away without another look. I follow behind as he moves through rooms and hallways, each one more bizarre than the last. Both dread and excitement fill me. I'm getting closer to her, my heart pushing me to move faster while my brain screams to slow down. I force myself to shut down my thoughts, to keep the ugly loop running that I predetermined should this day ever come. We stop at the water wall, and my breath catches. It's more spectacular than last time.

"What do you think?" Amos studies my face. It doesn't feel like he's trying to get into my head; it seems like he's interested in my opinion. I relax and admire the walls. Color floods my senses.

"It's the most amazing thing I've ever seen," I say and mean it.

"Thank you. Look closely at the landscaping. I've added something new since the last time you were here. It's inside the reef."

He stares at the life beyond the walls and points. I follow his fingers to the glowing pink reef. Underground vents gurgle, and explosions of colors burst into the water. I lean in to get a better look and watch the colors solidify and take form into fish.

"My God," I mumble, my eyes bulging like the fish I'm watching. The pressure in my head begins. I bear down against it and it stops. I look at Amos.

"Nice work, Thomas, thank you. You don't disappoint. You've also been choosing to do things to better your life. I respect that. Keep it up. The next time you're here, I'll teach you how to use a Way Station."

"Then, we're done?" I ask but can feel that it's too late. He's already gone. Everything turns black.

Inside his pocket, Thomas's phone rattles. He pulls it out to see a text message from Nicole. They're taking a family vacation, trying to regroup. She doesn't know when they'll be back and explains that her dad has worked something out with the school. She'll call him when she can. He clenches his fists.

Two weeks pass in a flurry. Thomas mills around the school and town, wandering in and out of restaurants and shops. He listens in on everyone without prejudice, except for Madi and the Gleeson's when he can avoid it, but sometimes it happens. Amos has brought Thomas back to the beach several times but only to drain him of information. There's been no mention of using a Way Station, which is crucial. It might be the only way to get to his mother. The entire situation has become a blank jigsaw puzzle. How do you solve a puzzle without pictures? All he can do is what he's already doing, but he's beginning to loathe everyone and their sticky thoughts that seem to be shedding. Each one feels like it's left a tiny piece of itself behind in Thomas. The bad ones are the worst. They feel like poisonous glue. He can't wait to be done with them.

Winter is painful in the northeast. This year is no exception; only Thomas doesn't notice it much. These days, he spends most of his time on the other side to be closer to his mother. Adam's beach, or what began as Adam's beach, has been a blessing for Thomas. Not only is it beautiful, but it's where he can escape the cold and try to forget about Nicole, if only for a short time. Besides, Amos is here, and Amos has the information he seeks.

The sun beats on my skin, warming my entire body. I run my fingers through the familiar sand, enjoying the texture. I hate that I love it here.

"Why don't you add to this place? It's nothing more than sand." Amos says.

I jerk back. "I didn't hear you walk up."

"I noticed." He knows I hate it when he startles me.

"You come here all the time, yet you only rest. I'm surprised you don't do more with it."

"I didn't know I could. Besides, it's Adam's. He likes it like this."

"That's silly. This space is for changing. It doesn't belong to him."

"But he loves it. I couldn't."

"He abandoned this project. He's working on another. You can do whatever you want with it."

"Really? When? What's the project? Can I see him?"

"No. He's very busy, and the work isn't complete. It's not ready to be viewed."

I nod. There's no reason to press. He won't answer.

"You've wasted precious time here playing in the sand. You should be creative. That's the whole point."

"But I don't know how."

"That's nonsense. If you want to change it, do so."

"You say that like I was taught how to do something but decided against it. That's not the case. No one has taught me anything. I've had to do everything myself."

"You're being a child, Thomas. Regardless of what we've been taught, we do everything on our own, don't we?"

This annoys me. Learning here is very different from learning on Novo. And I don't need a lecture; I need instruction.

Amos laughs. I didn't realize he was listening. I must stop doing that.

"Nearly everything here works the same way," he says, his eyes twinkling with humor. "Even the Way Stations."

My ears perk up. "What about them?"

"If you want to build something here, you use energy to force its will. The same is true with the Way Stations. If you want to come here, you make it happen."

"But how? That doesn't make any sense. I wouldn't even know where to go or what to do."

"It is not about that; this lesson is about energy and how you use it. Energy is nowhere and everywhere, all the time. It moves, it does, it is. It is everything. With the Stations, if you focus your energy on a Station from your side, you'll find the opening on your side. It will take some practice, but eventually, it will draw you to it like a magnet."

"And then what?"

"And then I pull you in. Of course, I will still pull you in at my discretion, but using the Stations is a benefit for working productively with me. It is a way for you to travel and explore."

I can't think. My heart is thumping. I lock down my thoughts and look at Amos.

"Oh," is all I can manage.

"It's a manipulation of energy. It's different when you're here than when you're there, but it's still just a manipulation. The sand and sky work the same way as the Stations. If you want to change them, then do it."

"So, if I want to add more than sand, like sculptures or structures—"

"Yes. You already know the answer. I've explained enough." Amos rolls his eye at me. He takes two steps and vanishes.

I hate that he makes his exits look so cool. I grab a handful of sand and let it drizzle through my fingers. Is it possible that I can find a Station by merely wanting it? A single pebble sticks to my pinky. It sparkles in the sun. I focus on it. Bigger. Get bigger. Nothing happens. I close my eyes and picture rubbing my thumb along the grain of sand, lengthening it as it rolls along my skin. When I look again, it's bigger. I feel the smile spread across my face.

"I see you've figured it out," Amos says, and I jump.

"Are you going to startle every time I see you?

I grab my chest. "Dude, I didn't hear you.

"Dude?" Amos says.

"Sorry. I meant Amos. Did you forget something?"

"No. I came to tell you to be mindful of your time. I don't care how much you're here as long as you return to collect. Don't forget that you still have work to do. While you brought in quite a bit, you did lose some points for trying to re-read that girl. I meant to tell you that the last time you were here."

"What girl?"

"The one whose memory you altered. When you got into her car."

"Amanda?"

"I suppose. You needn't bother with her any longer. Her thoughts are no longer viable."

Dread washes over me. I don't want to ask what he means because I don't want to hear the answer. But I have to know. "What are you talking about?"

"Her memory, that block of information you stole from her some time ago. It was excellent, albeit unnecessary, and quite damaging."

"I don't understand."

"You stole her memory when you altered it, and she's beginning to suffer the consequences. Did you think you could make changes to someone's memory without it affecting them? You didn't only watch her; you joined in. And then as a bonus, you brought her male friend into your dream to show him what she was up to. You'd already fried her hippocampus. How much more did you want her to suffer?"

"I didn't want her to suffer at all. I didn't mean for any of that to happen! I had no idea that it had."

"Well, it did, and you destroyed a part of her brain she's definitely going to miss. Or not, come to think of it. Now she won't miss anything at all. She won't be able to. I guess there's some mercy in that."

"You can't be serious. If I've harmed her in any way, I need to know how to fix it."

"There's no fixing it. You ruined the part of her brain that people need. She can't make new memories and her old ones are jumbled. Her emotions are ruined, possibly her sense of smell, and the effects will become more pronounced with time. I don't know why your past Broker taught you to do such a thing. Don't you see why using memories might be a bad idea? You must have despised her."

"No, no, no," I shake my head back and forth as if the motion will erase the damage I've done.

Amos presses brows together. "Had you really no idea what would happen?"

"Of course not," I shout and flinch as it registers. I wait for Amos to explode, but he watches me with a curious expression.

"If you're that upset, there is one thing," he says.

"What is it? I'll do anything."

"If you want to fix Amanda, you can try to replace her memory with another, only it'll have to be a big one, and it might not work at all. A lot of time has passed."

"But if I do it again…even if I figure out how to do it again, the same thing will happen to the next person. Is that what you're saying? I'll have to break another person to fix her, and then fix that person by hurting someone else. It will go on and on forever. I can't do it to anyone else. I won't."

"You people can be so unimaginative. There must be someone out there you consider to be a worse person than Amanda. I think you know where I'm going with this. Continue doing your job, and when you come across some unsavory character, pull a memory, and I might try to help you fix Amanda."

"No. Take a memory from me. I did this. I should fix it."

"Don't be ridiculous. You're useful."

I steel myself. "I won't do it if there isn't a way to do it without hurting someone else. I'll stop working altogether. I'll be useless to you. I'll stay in my house and completely avoid people. I can do it, too; I have for years. You can pull me in here all you want, but I won't have anything for you. You obviously need the thoughts, so you must need me."

Amos jumps from the rock and faces me. "Don't threaten me, Thomas. You are being dramatic, and I don't like your tone. You will return and get busy, or she has no chance. That is your choice. What isn't your choice is whether you still work for me. You do. Now get home. You've been here much longer than usual."

I feel the breath leave my body in defeat. This conversation is over.

"Fine. But it hasn't been that long. You just left."

"You're mistaken."

"It's been like two hours."

"Your perception of time is incorrect, Thomas. You've been here, on Tendo, for roughly two months."

"Two months?" I feel the panic bubble in my stomach. "That's not possible. It can't be—you were just here! I would never have stayed that long if I'd known."

"Well, now you know. Calm down. Go back using the Station. Follow the path out of the palace and across the beach. Once you leave the cavern of palms, turn left and stay that way until you reach the square tower. Close the door behind you after you enter, and I'll feel when you're ready. And Thomas, I'll see you soon."

This time when I enter the Station, he doesn't push me through right away. Instead, he leaves me floating long enough to make it clear that I am at his mercy. I grind my teeth so hard I'm afraid they will shatter. He's got to get on with it. I need to get back. I can't begin to calculate what two months translates to back home. But then there's no point in trying to make that calculation anyway, like trying to turn metric into non-metric with a single formula. It doesn't work for a reason. They are independent of each other. What they have in common is that they are merely numbers that people need to understand versions of time and place. They are placeholders.

A puff of air spins me around, and I'm face to face with the grinning sun. It flashes brighter and brighter by the second, probably in preparation to burn to me but I'm pissed. I pull off my shoe and crack the sonofabitch across its stupid face. The stunned fireball is launched into darkness, a trail of fire left in its wake. Well, that felt good, I think, as the pulling sensation begins. I disappear into the darkness.

Chapter 15

Chills wrack his body. Thomas wakes in his living room. He pulls his phone from his pocket while scrambling to his feet and checks the date. His relief is overwhelming. It's late, but it's still today, and other than being cold the, house looks undisturbed. The phone rings in his hand. The display reads Nicole.

"Hello, Nicole?" Thomas says.

"Thomas?"

"Yes, I'm here. Can you hear me?"

"I can, thank God. I've been trying to reach you forever. Did I wake you? It's late there."

"No, I'm up. I'm glad you called. How are you? Is everything okay?"

"I'm okay. I think the vacation helped. My dad still has some estate stuff to deal with, but then we're coming back. How are you? What's going on there? I miss you."

"I miss you, too. Everything is fine here. Same old same old, you know?"

"I do," she says. Thomas can hear garbled voices in the background. "That was my mom," she says. "I swear to God, every time I try to take a minute for myself, we're on the move. I want to scream." She muffles the phone into her stomach, but Thomas can hear her yell furiously, okay, mom, give me a minute.

"We're going back to my aunt's now. We've been at my grandma's house all day going through her things. It was so depressing. Anyway, I've got to go, but I'm glad I got to talk to you for at least a minute. I'll call you tomorrow, okay?"

He tells her okay and goodbye and heads to bed, wondering how much more he can take. His life has turned into a circus, and he's the star of the show. Whatever tomorrow has in store for him has got to be better than what he went through today.

Western Memorial Hospital completed an expansion over the summer and, in the process, added a children's pond and park. Thomas has wanted to check it out since his art teacher talked about the architecture in class last quarter. So, when Madi asked what he wanted to do after picking her up from school, she was thrilled to learn they were going to the new park.

"When did they finish it?" Madi says.

"A while back; it took forever. You sure you want to go today?"

"Mm, hmm," she says. "Why'd they put it by the hospital?"

"The hospital paid for it so that kids would have somewhere nice to go if they came to visit or were patients."

"I wonder if they'll close it when it snows."

"I doubt it. It's on a big piece of land. That's a lot of potential snowman building. I bet they leave it open year-round. I'm surprised it hasn't snowed already."

Madi starts jumping back and forth when the park comes into view. "I see it; it's open. Can I go?"

"Go ahead. I'll catch up." She beelines for the monkey bars and stays less than a minute before running to the swings.

"Hey Thomas," she yells. "Can you come on the teeter-totter with me?"

"I was about going to ask you the same thing."

Madi howls each time Thomas pushes his weight down, sending her into the air. He glances to his right and sees Rob Greer walking out of the hospital with a kid trailing behind him. They stroll along, their steps a metronome, neither willing to break the pace. Rob talks with his head down, seemingly at the boy, not to him. He is so engrossed in his one-sided conversation that he doesn't notice Thomas and Madi sitting on the stalled teeter-totter until he's a few feet away.

"Hey," Madi calls as Thomas steps off the structure, lowering her to the ground.

"Give me a minute, Madi. That's a friend from school."

"Hi guys," Rob says, approaching. "Out for a teeter?"

Thomas laughs. "I heard it opened. Madi wanted to check it out."

"They opened it last weekend," Rob says, gesturing for his friend to join them.

"This is my step-brother, Adam."

Thomas sways on his feet. He's at a complete loss. Of all the people it could be, it's Adam. He found him. Adam stares blankly at the sky, his face expressionless.

"Hello, Adam," Thomas says. "This is…" he looks around, "uh, that was my little sister, Madi. She must have gone back to the swings."

Rob shrugs and squeezes Adam's arm. "Adam's not much of a talker these days. He's been at the hospital for a while, so I came to take him for a walk. Get him out of that stuffy place."

"What's wrong with him?" Thomas asks, his stomach in knots. "Can he hear us?"

"Hang on," Rob tells Thomas and guides Adam to a bench out of hearing range.

"Sorry. He's not always this out of it. We're still not sure what's going on. For the last few years, he's had these episodes, for lack of a better word. He's lucent one second and gone the next, almost like he has Alzheimer's, but they've ruled that out. We've tested for everything, but nothing sticks. Lately, he's seemed worse."

"Worse?" Thomas asks.

"His episodes, or whatever you want to call them, they used to last anywhere from a minute to an hour before he'd snap out of them. But this time he didn't. That's why he's in the hospital. This one has a better facility than the one in his town, so his dad brought him here to be monitored while he's like this."

"And you leave him here?"

Rob winces. "I'm always at school, and my mom has to work. My stepdad, uh—ex-stepdad, had to go back home to work to pay for all of this; the insurance doesn't cover everything. At least if he's here, he won't get hurt. It's not easy for any of us to leave him. It sucks."

"I'm sorry. I didn't mean it like that."

"It's all right. It's a rough situation, but we're doing our best."

"Is he healthy? Are there like, I don't know, brain waves?" Thomas searches Adam's face.

"Physically, he's fine. Outside of that, no one knows what's going on. The tests are inconclusive. But sometimes he seems more responsive, more present like he's right under the surface. I can see it in his eyes. Lately, though, he's been like this. Completely vacant. He's going to be fine though," Rob swallows the lump in his throat, "he's a tough kid."

Thomas can feel the fear buzzing off Rob's body. It's electric. He knows the feeling. He's felt it for Madi. "Oh shit," Thomas spins around.

"What's wrong?" Rob asks.

"My sister, I haven't heard her in a while," he moves toward the play area. "Madi? Where are you?"

Her head pokes out from under a slide. Thomas comes to a stop and gives Rob a thumbs-up. Rob nods and waves goodbye and heads back to Adam, but Adam doesn't seem to notice. He's looking at Thomas. They lock eyes. Thomas starts to shake. From inside Adam's mind, there is nothing to hear or see; the only thing present is a single overwhelming sensation. Terror.

"Thomas?" Madi tugs on his sleeve. "Are you okay?"

He shudders, shaking himself free from the spell. "I'm fine," he says, feeling anything but. In the distance, Rob and Adam walk toward the hospital. Thomas considers catching up to ask questions. There's got to be something he can do to help, but Rob wouldn't understand his interest.

"Do we have to go home?" Madi says, interrupting his thoughts. "It's still early."

Thomas sees the worry on her face and softens. "We've got time," he says. "How about the swings?"

Madi's face lights up. "I'll race you," she sprints away. By the time he reaches her, Madi's made friends with several girls at the swing set. They make up a game, leaving Thomas alone with his thoughts. He keeps an eye on the hospital entrance until Rob exits and not a minute too soon.

It's getting cold outside. "Madi," Thomas yells across the park. When she doesn't answer, he joins her and her new friends at the climbing wall.

"Hi guys," he says. The girls barely glance in his direction. "Okay, then. Madi, I need to run into the hospital. Where's your stuff?"

"Aww," Madi says, "do we have to go? We just got to the wall."

"We do, but I'll bring you back soon, okay? I've got to go inside, and you need to come with me. You can't stay out here alone."

Madi climbs down the wall with sloth-like speed. Thomas restrains himself from plucking her off and setting her down, midway through her descent.

"What do you have to do?" Madi drags her feet as they approach the hospital.

"It won't take too long. Do you remember the guys I talked to earlier?"

"Uh, huh."

"One of them is staying here. I wanted to leave a note for his brother."

"About what?"

"It doesn't matter."

"But—"

Thomas gives her a look, and she stops arguing.

Inside, the hospital is a flurry of activity. A nurse in pink scrubs ignores him, but the woman working the front desk looks up.

"Hello, I'm here to visit Adam Greer."

"Are you—"

"I'm family," Thomas cuts her off.

"No, you're—" Madi starts.

"Madi, go sit in that chair by the T.V. Put on some cartoons."

"Fine," Madi snaps and walks away.

"I haven't seen you before," the nurse says, inserting herself into the conversation. Over the intercom, a code blue is called. The nurse rushes toward it, along with several other hospital staff, leaving Thomas with the receptionist.

"Hi, Janet," he glances at her name tag. "I hope you can help me. I don't have much time, and I need to see Adam. Can I have his room number, please?"

Janet watches the commotion down the hallway, ignoring his question. For Pete's sake, he thinks and focuses on her head. Tell me his room number. She clicks on the keyboard and looks up.

"He's in 811, but that floor is secure. I'll take you."

The elevator closes after all three have stepped inside, cutting off the barrage of noise. It stops twice before they reach the eighth floor. Thomas and Madi follow Janet down a pale corridor before stopping at the last door.

This is it," she says and starts to walk away, but Thomas stops her with a thought.

Take my sister to the nurse's Station and wait for me.

Janet smiles at Madi, squatting down to Madi's height. "Would you like to come with me to the nurse's Station? I bet they have cookies; they always have something."

"Uh, sure?" Madi looks at Thomas.

"That sounds great, Madi. Go get a cookie while I leave a note for Rob."

Madi walks away with Janet, and Thomas steps inside Adam's room. Up until now, Thomas hadn't realized the significance of the eighth floor, which must be some sort of long-term mental health facility in this hospital. It makes sense. Adam is catatonic and can't be left alone, so his family had to put him somewhere. But here? Thomas chokes back tears. Adam should not be here. He is being punished for helping Thomas. By Amos. Thomas is sure of it. And if all Adam did was to help Thomas get home, then what else is Amos capable of?

The room is depressing despite the fresh flowers on the windowsill. Someone visits frequently he assumes by the stack of take-out boxes in the garbage. It's Rob. Thomas can feel his essence lightening the room but not enough to mask the gray lingering in the corners. This is no place for Adam.

Besides a small television mounted in the corner, there isn't much to look at. The space consists of a small couch and table set, along with a chair and tray table that you can roll over to the adjustable bed. The tile floor is dingy and hard, making it seem cold, even though it's so warm that Thomas takes his jacket off. It's as if the whole place was designed by someone who feared that the slightest bit of color or life might cause agitation; yet agitation is exactly what the room causes. Thomas finds himself pacing, then remembers why he's there. He pulls a chair next to Adam's bed and takes a seat.

Lying lifeless on his back, Adam stares at the ceiling with vacant eyes.

"Hey, Adam. It's Thomas. I don't know if you can hear me, but I came to tell you that I know you're here now and I think I'm responsible. Amos said you were working on something else and I believed him. I'm so sorry. I had no idea, and I'm going to do everything in my power to help get you out of there, and out of here."

Anger races through him. This kid is what, 14? 15? And he's locked up like a catatonic zombie because he helped me?

"I'm going to try to listen to you now, Adam. I need to see if there's any way to tell where you are, or how to communicate with you. I know it's an invasion and I'm sorry, but I've got to try." He peers into Adam's eyes and focuses, but there is only darkness.

"Come on, kid," he tries again, "don't make me dig. Show me where you are." Adam lies motionless, his mind a blank slate. Goddammit, Thomas screams inside. "Okay. Not today then. We'll try again tomorrow. Don't worry, Adam. I will fix this. If I can't reason with Amos, there's someone else I can talk to that might help. These guys, the Brokers, they need us, too.

Chapter 16

The world is blurry as Thomas walks from Adam's room. To stop himself from punching someone or something, he shoves his hands into his pockets and leans his head against the wall, slowly counting backward from ten. He feels a current tickle his ear, and blackness takes him.

The sound of breaking waves surrounds me, only they don't provide their usual comfort. In the distance, puffs of sand appear in the air, forming a trail heading toward me. Seconds later, Amos stands by my side. We stare at the water like vacationers admiring the ocean. I swallow.

"Where is Adam?" I ask. Amos raises an eyebrow at me.

"He is occupied."

"Doing what?"

"It doesn't concern you."

"I think he's here, and that you're keeping him here against his will."

"Be careful, Thomas. You speak to me sometimes as if you have the right to do so. You can very easily undo everything we've built together."

"I don't care. I'm not doing this anymore unless you let him go."

"I will do nothing of the sort. Adam is in no danger; he moves about as he pleases, only currently he's paying the price for his mistakes as will you if you're not careful. When he's done, he'll leave of his own accord. That being said, I've grown tired of the entitlement you exhibit. Do you think this is a game? That it's playtime? I assure you it is not."

"Playtime? Is that what you think? It was never that to me. You're unbelievable. I'm not doing this for you anymore. I'm done."

Amos snorts, and I realize he's laughing. He shakes his head at me.

"Silly, silly, boy."

I turn toward a strange sound behind me, but nothing is there. When I turn back, Amos is gone, and I'm no longer on the beach. I'm in the forest.

Fire screams from my leg as a razor snake slithers across me, tearing my skin as it moves. It is indifferent to the assault. I turn to run but trip over a root and land on my stomach. It's nearly impossible to stand, the ground below me is shaking violently. All around tree roots explode from the ground, knocking boulders free from the earth, splitting mountains into pieces. It's as if the forest is both expanding out and closing in on me at the same time. The faint river I heard when I arrived suddenly sounds like an avalanche, and I turn in time to see a wall of water racing toward me. There's no time to react; it's moving too fast. Then I am a part of it.

I flip and spin underwater like a rag doll while I crash through branches and hit rocks. Water pulls me in every direction at once. I fight for the surface and get my feet facing downriver, but I'm flipped back around or upside down every time I make progress. Somehow, I've managed to steal a breath or two, but the lack of oxygen has left me exhausted. I'm so weak, so close to giving up. I can't keep this up much longer. I need help.

A tree-root as thick as a car bursts through the water, nearly hitting me. I catch hold and am pulled clear of the river as it twists and twirls high into the sky. It snaps me back and forth, like a dog shaking a snake and I'm tossed onto an embankment where I have less than a second to roll out of the way before it changes directions and turns toward me, slicing through the side of my foot before it twists and plunges back into the river.

From deep in the trees comes a screech that sends my broken body back into motion, and I grab a branch from the ground while scrambling to my feet. Another sound comes closer now, but I can't place its direction and decide anywhere is better than here.

My legs are stiff and useless like they are in my nightmares, and for an instant I'm relieved; I must be dreaming. This whole thing has been one big night-terror, and this is the one where it's impossible to run. But even in dreams, you still try to run.

I force my muscles to work and shuffle away from the embankment. From the corner of my eye, I see an orb the size of a basketball flying straight at me. It's not until it gets closer that I realize it's not an orb; it's an insect; a giant, grotesque horsefly, the size of a basketball, and it seems determined to pulverize me.

It picks up speed just as I swing my heavy branch at it and connect with its jaw. It skids to the ground by my feet and gazes up at me with glassy eyes. All around its body are bloody teeth. Teeth—it had teeth.

There is applause, and I hear a voice bellow:

"Saaa-wing batter."

My heart sinks. Upriver, Amos is standing on a jagged boulder, his blond hair glistening in the sun. He flashes from solid to transparent several times, coming to rest as solid.

"You've killed a wolfbee, Thomas," he says, clapping. "I didn't think you had it in you."

I look down at the oozing thing I've knocked from the sky, trying to see any resemblance to a bee.

"I thought it was a horsefly," I say for no reason.

"Nope. That was a wolfbee," Amos says. "Canidae-Apis, my creation. It's similar to your honeybee; only if a wolfbee bites you, consider yourself lucky. You might only lose a limb. Get stung and well… I'd advise you not to get stung." He smiles at me with black fangs. I imagine being bitten by the bee, then by those black fangs. I stare at Amos, my emotions seething.

"I hate you, Amos."

Amos winks and is gone.

Thunderstorms billow in from the West, turning the blue sky to slate. A loud crack of lightning sounds, bringing Thomas back to his surroundings. He can hear Madi squeal from the nurse's Station; she's terrified of lightning no thanks to him. He retrieves her from the nurses, holding tight to her hand and reassures her that they can beat the storm home. She protests but lets Thomas lead her across the park, running toward their house. They scramble past the teeter-totter and the climbing wall while the wind blows swings with invisible riders and phantoms spin on the merry-go-round. Thomas shudders. When the bushes behind him rattle, he glances over his shoulder and sees an enormous, hairy tail, disappear into the park. There's no telling what it was, but the size was alarming. With urgency, he presses Madi forward until they've made it to the edge of town.

Madi slows to a stop to catch her breath. A group of people has formed into a small circle up ahead that seems to be attracting others by the second.

"What's that?" she points.

"I have no idea, but we're not —"

With a burst of energy, Madi sprints toward the commotion.

"Madi," Thomas chases after her, catching up as they both reach the group. Thomas recognizes nearly everyone, having spent the last few months digging through their minds. He feels exposed, shameful. Surely, they know what he's been up to. But no one looks away from what they are focused on. They point and talk over one another, their frantic questions bouncing around like ping pong balls. Madi fights her way through the crowd with elbows and determination until she reaches the center and stops.

"What is it?" she asks, but no one answers. It's as if seeing her next to what they've been looking at has put things into a collective perspective. One of fear. "Guys," she tries louder, "what is it? Is it dead? Thomas, what is that?"

Thomas pushes through the crowd to see what everyone is looking at. His world tilts. Laying on the ground in the middle of the group is the giant, dead, wolfbee from the forest. Its mouth is stretched open at a ghastly angle to show the bloody holes where its teeth used to be. Oh no. No, no, no. It's here. Did Amos do that? Can he send them here? The growing crowd presses them forward, but Thomas pulls Madi free. He tells her to keep up, and she does without arguing.

"What was that Thomas?" she asks when the front door closes behind her.

"How should I know?"

"You're lying. I can tell. You know what it was. I watched your face when you saw it. Your eyes did the same thing they do when you figure out a problem. So, what was it?"

"It was a bee, Madi. It must have had some kind of mutation and wasn't normal, but it was still just a bee."

"A bee? Are you crazy? It had teeth. And it was huge! That was not a bee, and you know it. It was already dead, but we still ran. The only reason we would do that is if you were scared of it. So, what was it and why won't you tell me?"

He shrugs. "Because there's no point in scaring you, too. All I know is that it wasn't good. I don't think there will be any more, but if you see another one stay away from it. Understand? Do not get stung. You run or knock it away, don't worry about hurting it. Just get away."

"But why? What will happen?"

"What do you mean why? Did you not see that thing? If you see another one, get away from it. Sometimes nature spits out bad things. And when that happens, you want to be as far away as possible. Okay?"

"But—"

"Oh my God, Madi. I'm not asking; I'm telling you. Please listen to me."

"Okay, okay. I get it," she rolls her eyes. He can tell she wants to push for answers.

"It's late. You should get some rest," he says. "I'll make you a sandwich and you can do your homework now or in the morning before school."

She yawns and walks to her room, shrugging off his questions.

Later that night, despite the cold, Thomas falls asleep in his parent's old room. In his dream, a train blows its air horn, and Thomas steps away from the tracks. It picks up speed, and he watches in horror as Madi and Amanda appear in the distance holding hands. They approach the tracks, and Thomas screams for them to stay back but they don't hear him or notice the train bearing down on them. As the iron monster passes Thomas, he sees that his mother and Adam are on board. She looks out at him, her fingers pressed against the window. Cool steel appears in his hand, and he looks down at the switch he's now holding. Leave it alone, and the train will follow the tracks that Madi and Amanda have stepped on. Push it forward, and it will derail, taking his mother and Adam with it. He hears Amos in his ear.

"Do you see?" he whispers.

Even as Thomas retches, the yellow shag carpet has never looked so good. Wiping the sleep from his eyes, he takes several breaths to slow his heart and scans his room for abnormalities. *The train is my life, and Amos is the conductor. I'm never going to be free of him. He took my mom, he has Adam, Amanda needs his help, and he's coming for Madi. I have no choice. I must do what he asks. What was I thinking?*

A sense of dread hangs over the kitchen the following morning as he goes through his life's motions. The morning radio host is ranting about the rain, and the havoc that it's creating for the local reptiles. His co-host chimes in that just that morning, she found a newt in her toilet. They laugh hysterically. Thomas changes the Station to a music channel and reminds himself to get on with it. Eat breakfast, brush teeth, wake up Madi, and make lunches. Little by little pieces of last night creep into his head, making his heart thump.

As he reaches into the cupboard to put away a dish, a sense of peace washes over him. He imagines a giant meadow covered with flowers and butterflies. Children run around laughing and singing; everything is fluffy and white. He sways on his feet. What is this? A warm wind breezes by his face carrying the scent of bubblegum. His heart stops. It's Madi. She's dreaming. Watching in fascination, he can see every detail. She is so happy here, that it makes his heart hurt. Somewhere between the skipping and twirling, he realizes what this means. He screams.

"Wake up, Madi, wake up, wake up," he yells, shaking her. She startles awake.

"What is it? What happened?" she cries, rubbing her eyes.

"I'm sorry, I'm sorry. I didn't mean to scare you. But I needed you to wake up."

"You could have just said so." She yawns and climbs out of bed, stopping at the bathroom where she yells through the door. "You're so dramatic."

Amos is going to see that if I can't block it. He'll know how much I love Madi, and that I'll do anything to protect her.

He'll use it against me. I will not let him have anything from her; not a single thought. How did that happen? She was in the other room and I went right into her dream, like it was mine to take. Of all the stupid...

"Are you going to eat that?" Madi points at his toast and takes a drink of milk that was sitting on the table.

"Huh?"

"Your toast. I ate mine, and your stack is sitting there. If you're not going to eat it, I will. You've been daydreaming all morning."

"Sorry. Go for it."

He sits in silence the remainder of breakfast, contemplating what to do. This mess he's made seems impossible to fix. Madi grins before she takes the last bite. The thought of Amos getting his claws in her is nauseating. He won't let it happen. She smiles at him through a mouthful of toast, and he knows what to do; even though he doesn't like it. He has to tell Simon everything. He needs someone on his side and between Simon and Amos, the choice is obvious. There will be ramifications, but he can't continue along this path without help, any longer.

After dropping Madi at school he returns home and lies in bed, hoping that it'll be Simon waiting for him when he open his eyes.

Thomas startles awake, realizing he fell asleep. Great, he thinks. Now he can't even get Simon's attention when he's trying. What a way to start the day. He stands and stretches, running his fingers through his hair, willing himself to snap out of it and wake up. Something seems off, but he can't put his finger on it. He surveys his small room and to figure out what's different then spots his shoes peeking out from the closet. This pair gives off such a pungent smell that he leaves them on the porch. But here they are, stinking up his room.

Soft laughter sounds around him, and the bedroom walls flicker light to dark, then disappear. The forest surrounds him.

"That's better," Simon says and takes a deep breath. "I have always loved the forest. Its potential is endless."

"I'll say. That was interesting. With my room."

Simon regards me, his eyes sparkling.

"How are you?" I ask, but I'm doubtful he'll respond. He doesn't interact with me like this.

"I'm well," Simon says through raised eyebrows.

"And you?"

"About as good as I can be."

"I doubt that," he says, his eyes never losing their twinkle. He knows, I think, and immediately regret it.

"I know what?" Simon says.

"That I need your help."

"With?"

"What if I told you that someone significant to me was trapped on this side and that I was her, uh, their, only chance of getting home?"

Something flashes in Simon's eyes, and his face is unrecognizable, the usual composure replaced with a look of fear or hope; it's impossible to tell. I feel that tickle, the one I've grown to hate, flutter around my head.

"Please don't," I say, and the sensation stops. An odd expression crosses his face, and this time, I recognize it. It's a look of understanding, close to the one my dad had in the cabin. I thank him.

"For what?" Simon says.

"For not rummaging around in my head. For hearing me out."

"What makes you think I didn't?"

"I don't know," I shrug. Simon only watches me. "Just, thanks, okay?"

Simon nods. "What is it you need from me, Thomas?"

"Well, let me start by telling you that if you help me get my friend home, I'll spend the rest of my life working with you."

"You'll do that anyway."

"I won't. And I think you understand that. I would rather die than leave things the way they are."

"I see that you believe that, but what you don't understand is that things can get much worse. And not just for you, but for anyone you find important. Surely you don't want that."

"I don't, Simon. That's why I'm asking for your help. It's to protect the people I love." Simon looks to the sky.

"Alright, Thomas. I will help you, but I want you to listen carefully. Everything that you do makes an impact. For every choice, there is a consequence."

"But that's living, Simon, and I've got to take my chances. I can't let anyone else get hurt because of my actions."

"Very well," Simon's eyes glass over. "What is it you need from me?"

Chapter 17

Sitting in the Westchester Public Library a week after he met with Simon, Thomas is amazed that the building can still have such an effect on him. He's seen things most people couldn't dream up if they tried, yet the library, once a sawmill, is breathtaking. After Charles Westchester used the Erie Canal to bring industry to this once nothing of a town, the lumber magnate's eponym was pasted on every building within a hundred miles. Even now, his name still graces the high school, library, and the town itself.

Thomas has spent half his life inside these wood and tin walls, yet he finds something new every time he steps through the heavy doors. His body tenses, his mind humming. *I feel this*

way about the palace, too. Something new, every time. He quickly
shakes it off. Today is no different, and as he looks across the
lacquered table at Madi, he can tell she finally gets it. Her
eyes move around the room as if she's seeing it for the first
time. He hopes she grows to love it as much as he does.

Madi turns to him and smiles. "Why are you staring at me?"
she asks.

Thomas blinks, then laughs. "Sorry. I wasn't. I was
daydreaming."

"What's new?"

Thomas laughs. "I do that a lot, don't I? I guess I always
have."

"I like this."

"The library?"

"No. I mean, yes, I like the library, but I was talking
about you. It's nice to see you look happy again."

"I'm getting there."

"Why? What changed?"

"It's a long story, but let's say I recently made a deal
with someone that's going to make our lives better."

"With who? How?"

Thomas smiles and drums his fingers on the table. "It'll
spoil the surprise."

Madi makes a face that wipes the smile from his and sends
goosebumps across his body. She looks like his mother does in
his worst nightmare, where he can't reach her in time. He
hardens his resolve. They are almost at the end of this thing;
he can feel it. He's sticking to the plan and following Simon's
instructions from end of their last meeting. Thomas is supposed
to cross between worlds as much as possible, but he should bring
Amos just enough thoughts to keep him from being suspicious of
Thomas's sudden work surge.

If only he could tell Adam to hold tight. If only he could explain to his mother that he's coming for her, it would ease some of the pressure. But soon enough, he'll get his chance to do both.

Madi yawns and stretches her arms over her head, signaling that she's ready for home. Thomas checks his watch and sees that it's almost 8:00 p.m. The library is closing soon, and he's tempted to call Mary. It's not only freezing outside but dark. Madi wraps up in a winter jacket and scarf, and Thomas decides to stop for hot cocoa if she complains. Otherwise, the walk isn't too far, and at least the sky is clear. He can distract her with a game about the stars.

Morning arrives with a bang. Then a boom.

"Thomas," Madi yells.

"I heard it, Madi. Stay inside," he pulls on his second boot and opens the front door. Across the porch lies a large tree-branch that must have sheared off from the old gum tree above their house. "Widow-maker," Thomas says, shaking his head.

"What's a widow-maker?" Madi startles Thomas. She's managed to get behind him without making a sound.

"Geeze Madi," he clutches his chest, "don't do that. I nearly had a heart attack."

"Sorry. Why'd you call it that?"

"It's what you call a tree when it has big, heavy branches hanging from it. At some point, one of them will fall and pulverize anything it hits. I told dad to cut that branch down at least ten times. I knew he wouldn't."

"It's not your—"

"It is my fault, Madi. I should have handled it. If you see something wrong, it's not enough to just complain about it. Thank God it didn't do the kind of damage I'd expected. Either way, we can't deal with it now, there's no time. I'll take care of it tonight."

Thomas drops Madi at school and heads for his own, stopping along the way to tie his shoe. As he squats down, rancid air fills his nose, and he fights the urge to gag. There is enough time for him to wonder what died when fire rips through his arm, knocking him backward. He screams in pain and confusion, pressing his hand against his throbbing arm when he sees it—his assailant. It approaches slowly on strong panther-like legs, a low guttural growl coming from its throat. Black eyes peer out of its monstrous face, something akin to a beaver-hyena crossbreed. Its eyes lock on Thomas, and it bares its fangs.

Before Thomas can move, it lunges, catching Thomas's jeans with a claw as he scrambles backward. He kicks the creature away with his free leg, but it continues its charge, catching Thomas's other leg. Screaming as skin is torn from his shin, Thomas rolls to his belly to get away and spots a boulder. He army crawls forward and grabs the weapon as the hyena-beaver clamps down on his leg again. With fury, he rolls over and smashes the rock against its nose, knocking it away. It staggers to its feet, lunging a final time before Thomas brings his weapon down again, smashing in its skull.

"Goddamn it," he screams, "I'm doing what I'm supposed to. Why did Amos send another monster here?"

Pain explodes through his body. His left arm and leg need to be bandaged; they're bleeding too severely to wait. The nurse's offices in both the high school and the middle school are close; he could visit either and say a dog had attacked him. But that would almost guarantee a call home to his parents. He has to go home. Or to Mary's; although he can only imagine how bad she'll freak out. The bushes behind him shake violently. He's terrified to look but finds himself turning around when a second hyena-beaver leaps from the bushes. Thomas holds his breath, expecting the worse, but the creature pays him no attention. Instead, it sets sights in a different direction altogether. Toward Merrimac Elementary. And it is moving so fast that there's no way for him to stop it. Thomas stands helpless, watching it disappear.

Oh God. Madi. Instinct sends him running. He doesn't stop until he can see her school. Nothing looks out of the ordinary. He stops to catch his breath and looks at his arm. His entire left sleeve is red. His leg is even worse.

"Holy cow, man. Are you okay?"

Thomas turns around. A kid from his school has pulled up next to him on a bike and looks at him with excited eyes.

"It's fake," Thomas forces the words. "I was filming a movie for school."

"Wow. That's killer. Who did your makeup? Is it a horror film?"

"Uh, yes. Zombie."

"Cool, man." He peddles away.

Covered in blood, Thomas knows he can't go into Madi's school; it would terrify everyone. He decides to wait and watch from a distance. If anyone saw that thing, there'd be a commotion by now. Plus, it was so much faster than him. If it were heading to the school, it would have made it by now. He'd already know. The steady trickle of blood running down his stomach is a problem. He's already light-headed, but that could be from adrenalin. Tugging gently, he lifts his shirt to examine the wound and winces as it pulls free from his skin. It looks bad but smells worse. It's warm out, and he's sweating, but pulls on a sweatshirt from his backpack to hide the blood.

Madi has a full day of school ahead of her but he can't chance leaving. If she comes out for recess, he has to be there in case the beasts return. Hopefully, the sweatshirt holds up, and his bleeding slows down.

A blur of fur moves by the bushes. *Oh no.*

A fang-beaver sprints across the field, seemingly headed for the school. He whistles at it, and runs in the opposite direction, hoping it will follow. It does. It turns and charges. Great plan, he thinks and searches the ground for a weapon as he runs. Blood soaks through his sweatshirt and pants, but he doesn't stop. Chancing a glance over his shoulder, he sees the beast closing the distance.

The sounds of snapping jaws and ragged breaths get closer with every lunge. Ten yards turn to five, then to three, then to one. Thomas waits for the pain, expecting it; imagining how it will feel. There is a squeal of tires followed by a loud thump, then silence.

Thomas spins to see a school bus stopped in the middle of the road. Several furry legs poke out from under a tire while the other two remain attached to a mangled carcass. Blood and gore are everywhere. It looks like the bus hit a buffalo.

Panting for air, Thomas drops to his knees. The blood dripping from his arm and leg don't seem all that important anymore. An enormous woman waving her hands over her head rushes from the bus. She takes one look at the pulverized creature and looks like she might faint. Her lips move, but nothing comes out. He isn't sure if she's gasping for air or words.

"Oh Lordy, oh Lordy, oh, oh, oh," she sing-songs when she finds her voice. "I am so sorry. I didn't see it. It came out of nowhere. I can't believe I hit it. It came out of nowhere. I'm so sorry, son. I think I killed your dog."

Thomas looks at her, eyes wide, his mouth hanging open. "Uh?" Thomas says. Can she see? He starts to laugh, a giggle at first, but soon he's in hysterics. Tears stream down his face as he laughs harder and harder. Seeing his tears, the woman starts crying, making him whoop with laughter. She thinks I'm sad. My God, she saved my life and thinks I'm crying over a dead dog. It's priceless. After a few minutes, he starts to feel bad. The poor woman doesn't deserve this. She deserves a medal he thinks, which sets him off again.

"Ma'am," Thomas says, wiping the tears from his face. "That wasn't my dog. I don't think it was anyone's dog."

"But you—"

"Ma'am, it had been chasing me for blocks. I was running from it. It was crazy—possibly rabid. I think it was foaming at the mouth."

"But, you're crying."

"With relief and fear, I guess. I don't think you understand. That thing might have killed me. You saved my life."

"But I didn't mean to. It was an accident," she says.

"Maybe, maybe not. You're still a hero."

Her eyes grow wide as she takes in his words. A dazzling smile spreads across her face and she hugs him, making him smile, too. And then he's there, in her imagination, watching her revel in her glory.

She rides through the city in a parade created for her. The mayor sits next to her in the backseat of a green convertible. Spectators line the streets and the high school band follows behind the convertible playing their best, but the cheering crowd swallows the music. This is her time. People see her. She is a hero.

Pulling free from her celebration, Thomas stumbles along in a daze, his feet pulling him toward the school but his mind traveling elsewhere. He glances back at the bus driver. She's where Thomas left her, lost in a world of her own. She stares at the sky, a broad smile stretched across her lips. He hopes she stays that happy.

Still dazed, Thomas trips over a curb that sends him flying. He flaps his arms for balance and rights himself but not before another jolt of pain shoots through him, reminding him how badly he's hurt. The blood loss he's suffered must be massive because he's so light-headed he might faint. It's torturous, but he makes his way to school's front as the recess bell rings. When no one comes out-front, he decides that they've gone to the back playground or stayed inside. If he's lucky, there should be enough time for him to get home and make it back by the time Madi is released. It's not an easy decision but hanging around in his bloody clothes seems like a bad idea. Before walking away, he turns to take one last look at the glowing bus driver. No longer in her daze, she's speaking with the kid on the bike from earlier. Thomas yells for the kid, waving him over.

The biker nod and peddles to Thomas. "Crazy scene," he says.

"It is," Thomas examines the bike and sees the pegs poking out. He decides not to steal it like he'd planned to do and thinks to the kid, run me home and back. I'll ride on the pegs.

"Hop on," the bike rider says through blurry eyes.

The elementary school release is chaos. Thomas is back with time to spare before several children and teachers spot him at the entryway and freeze. Madi steps between them, her expression tells him everything he needs to know. Even though he went home and cleaned up, he still looks terrible. When he feels fresh blood drip into his shoe, he angles his body away, hoping that no one notices.

A teacher restrains Madi, and another teacher yells for the principal. Thomas chances a peek at his leg and sees that his pants are dark crimson. There's no way anyone looking at him missed it, so standing here isn't doing him any good. Putting his hands up in a peaceful gesture, he ambles toward the teachers and Madi.

"Listen, everyone, this looks worse than it is. I'm okay. Everything is going to be okay. There was a crazy dog in the area that came after me, and when I tried to direct it away from the school, I fell and cut my leg. I must have sweated off my Band-Aid, and what you're seeing isn't all blood; there's iodine, too. Ask the school-bus driver. She saved me from the dog. Don't worry; the dog won't bother anyone now. Everyone is safe."

His old teacher, Mrs. Edmonton, holds firmly to Madi, eyeing Thomas as if she's never seen him before. His heart sinks. She was his favorite teacher—the one who seemed impressed with everything he did. Everyone needs that teacher. They are so important. Please don't look at me that way, he thinks. Be on my side. Madi resists against her, fighting to get free, eventually squirming loose to run to Thomas. She wraps her arms around his stomach, and her relief floods through his body. His pain subsides. Her relief is his relief.

"You look awful, Thomas, what happened? And are you sick, too?" she asks, her voice trembling. And just as he felt Madi's relief as his own, Mrs. Edmonton's fear surges through him. It's a terrifying sensation.

"I'll be fine Madi," he reassures her. "It looks worse than it is."

"You always say that."

"And I always mean it. But we do need to stop by the store for some supplies."

"We can go to Mary's. She'll have everything you need."

"Oh, terrific. She'll love this."

Chapter 18

Everyone they pass on the way turns to stare. Thomas waves indignantly, and most people look away. They have no idea what he's dealt with today.

"There's Mary," Madi points to a car, her voice perking up. "You're so lucky."

"Yep. The luckiest guy I know," Thomas says.

"Huh?"

"Nothing."

Mary toots her horn, waving them over. Thomas wishes they had gone straight home. Madi runs to the car, explaining to Mary what happened in frantic bursts. As expected, Mary climbs out of the car to inspect Thomas then insists he gets in. They arrive at her house, and she's just as demanding about determining his well-being. Thomas protests her poking and prodding but eventually gives in. She means well, and he knows if he doesn't let her make sure he's okay, this will take forever. He plops into a chair, defeated.

"It feels good to sit," he says down the hallway to Mary. "And before you say anything, it looks worse than it is."

"Everyone says that. Are you sure you're okay? There's so much blood."

"It's not all mine, don't worry. Plus, I don't think I'm bleeding anymore."

She brings him a wet washcloth and glass of milk. "Thank you," he mumbles and drinks the glass of milk. Color returns to his cheeks.

"Tell me what happened," she drops into the seat next to him, "from the beginning."

"Uh, dog chase?"

"What?"

"It's what Madi told you, a crazy dog came after me, and a bus hit it. There's not much to it."

Mary crosses her arms over her chest and peers at Thomas.

"I see that you're not satisfied with my answer," he says, forcing a smile.

"Not by a long shot," she says, then sighs.

"I need to make sure you're taking care of yourself. And you're sitting there covered in blood. What am I supposed to think?"

"I know, and I feel better. I promise. It was a freak thing, that's all."

"Well, you look awful," she turns on a teapot and sets a tray of muffins in front of him.

"Muffins?"

"Yes, smart mouth. You might need antibiotics, so get some food on your stomach. Then you can take a shower and we can clean up whatever it is that you're hiding under those bloody pants."

"Girls," she says to the three sets of eyes watching from the doorway. "I need you to stay out of the kitchen for a while. I'll let you know when we're done."

The twins shrug at each other and run to their room. Madi doesn't move. Mary looks between her and Thomas and sighs.

"Sweetheart," Mary says. "He's gotta eat. When he's cleaned up, I'll make sure he doesn't need stitches."

Madi stares at Thomas.

"I'll be fine, Madi. I promise," he says, looking her in the eye. Madi nods and walks out of the kitchen to join the twins.

"Thank you. You don't have to do all of this."

"Don't be ridiculous."

The teapot begins to whistle. Mary turns it off and returns with a thermometer.

"Put this under your tongue. You look feverish. It beeps a second later and she pulls it from his mouth. The color drains from her face.

"What is it?" His heart starts to race. He knows it's bad by her expression.

Mary takes the thermometer to the sink and runs it under cool water. She washes it with antiseptic and puts it under her tongue. When it beeps, she checks the results.

"Hmmm," she says and returns to the sink where she washes and re-sterilizes it. "Let's try that again." She puts the thermometer back into his mouth.

Thomas didn't think it possible, but she pales even further when she checks the results.

"Girls," she yells from the kitchen, "get your coats on and get into the car right now. We've got to go."

Perhaps sensing the urgency in Mary's voice, all the girls emerge from the bedroom with their jackets on.

"What's wrong, Mommy?" the twins ask in unison.

Madi looks back and forth between Thomas, the twins, and Mary but no one says anything. Her chin starts to quiver, and her eyes fill with tears.

"Madi, sweetheart; I know you're scared, but we need to go. I'll explain later."

The five travel in silence. Thomas chances a glance at Mary. She looks scared.

"Is 105.7° bad, Mary?" Thomas asks.

Mary's eyes widen as her mouth goes askew. At some point, she seems to become aware of her expression and snaps her lips together but keeps driving.

"It's um, wait, how did you know that, Thomas? You didn't see the thermometer."

"Mary, is that a high temperature?" Thomas asks. He watches her face strain as she struggles with a response and knows it will be something he doesn't want to hear.

"It's high. It's about as high as you'd ever want to get. I'm taking you into emergency and they'll have something that will help cool you much quicker than I could."

A thousand issues run through his head. He can't pay for this; they don't have insurance. It's not so much the bill. He knows he can deal with it when the time comes; it's the uncertainty of what they could find out about him and Madi. People will examine their finances, and there will be questions about his parents and why they aren't present. Surely, a teenager and his little sister wouldn't come to the hospital without their parents or legal guardians. This could be bad. It's impossible to know how much they'll learn. He's aware that he could do damage control after the fact, but it could grow out of control. How many people's heads would he have to mess with to keep everything quiet? No, this won't work for him. He has to get out of here as quickly as possible. He turns to Mary to voice his protest but feels the energy drain from his body. Unlike last time, when he knew it was coming, he doesn't have time to figure out what's happening before he faints.

The pile of leaves I awaken on is strangely comforting. I can tell what they are before opening my eyes. The smell alone is more than enough identification; it brings me back to a better time when family life was still good and leaves like these meant Halloween was coming. It's such a pleasant sensation that I could stay like this a long time, but instead, I open my eyes.

It takes a while for my vision to clear, and when it does, I marvel at the sky. The forest doesn't seem scary now, but that doesn't offer much comfort, I know it could change in an instant. I hear bushes crunching, and Amos steps in front of me.

"You're sick, Thomas," he says. "A fang-beaver's saliva caused an infection that is destroying your immune system. Your body is starting to shut down."

"I know," I say through a wooly mouth. I feel as ill here as I did on Novo. "The saliva stung. I knew I'd get an infection when it bit me, like it had the saliva of a Komodo Dragon. The worst of the worst. I knew it would make me sick."

"I don't think 'sick' is the appropriate term for what those lizards do to you," Amos says and flashes his teeth. I can almost see the glee he's feeling at my predicament. He smiles again, longer this time. "Dead is a better word choice. They poison your blood with their magnificent bacteria and venom. They're one of the more intriguing creatures from your world. But what bit you was a fang-beaver, easily a thousand times deadlier than your fancy dragon. And that was only a few hours ago. You're already septic. I sent a second to help you, but you went and bungled that by getting it pulverized. You see, the only way to survive a bite from a fang-beaver is to be bitten by another. The second bite's venom becomes an anti-venom to the first. You understand; you do something similar with snake venom on Novo. You make anti-venom out of it."

I smile at the beautiful sky. Tremors wrench through my body, pulling it into the fetal position without my consent. When they subside, I roll on my back, willing my muscles to unclench.

"I've won," I say. "You can't hurt me anymore. I don't have to do anything else for you. You've killed me with your own game and don't even realize it." I smile and enjoy how good it feels to know I beat him at this one thing. 'Now who's clever, Amos?' I think.

White-hot fire pierces my foot, and I scramble backward, the sickness in my body no match for the pain assaulting me now. I pull my leg to my chest, the two bloody puncture marks from my foot dripping blood down my shirt. My toes glisten and I still don't understand what happened until I see Amos proudly holding the leash of a fang-beaver with blood dripping down its face. He smiles at me, and this time it reaches his eyes. Right now, he is delighted. My pain brings him joy.

"Do you think I'd put this much effort into you only to kill you, Thomas? What would be the point of that? And you thought you owed me before," his eyes gleam. "You have no idea where we stand now. The amount of energy wasted on this event was so monumental I can't begin to explain. It's time for you to get up. There's much to be done."

"You're wrong. I'm out. Send those things as much as you want. I'm finished."

He laughs, thinking, and you think you're the clever one, Thomas. "I didn't send the first beaver, you imbecile. I sent the one to save you."

Chapter 19

Machines beep and spit out paper, people come in and out of his room to poke and prod, moving tubes from here to there. It's endless. Madi is somewhere close; he can hear her whimpers, which only serve to cause him pain. One nurse takes his temperature while another changes his bandages again. It's an odd sensation to be entirely under another's care. Blinking open exhausted eyes, he sees fluorescent ceiling lights passing overhead. He's being moved again, to another destination.

Dull pain pounds at the base of his spine and there isn't enough water in the world to quench his thirst. His throat is sandpaper, and this time when he opens his eyes it feels like someone blew dirt into them. Blurry figures come into focus, and he sees Mary reading in the chair across from him. He assumes that the three lumps under blankets in the adjacent bed are Madi and the girls. He refocuses his gaze on Mary, who must sense him because she looks up and smiles.

"How do you feel?" she asks.

"Okay," he lies. "Is there any water?"

Mary grabs the pink pitcher and straw left by the nurses and doesn't bother with a cup. She holds the straw to his mouth and encourages him to drink slowly.

"What happened?" he asks. Mary's eyes glaze over as if she's reliving the past few days. They must have been bad because when she returns her gaze, he can feel her pain wash over him. She tries to laugh it off, but the way she diverts her eyes from his tells a story.

"It was bad, Thomas," she says. "I can see your mind working a mile a minute. I was trying to wrap the series of events into one package so that you didn't have too much to digest."

"I appreciate that Mary, but you don't have to. Lay it on me. I can take it."

Mary shifts in her seat, adjusting her position. She takes a deep breath like she's preparing for a sprint. But it's Mary, after all. She's kind, and everything is significant to her.

"You had a fever so high I thought you might not…," she rubs her hands together, "I'll leave it at that. It was too high. Believe me, once you have kids you'll understand. Your kid goes north of 102°, and you're on your way to the emergency room. When I got you into the car, your temperature was 105°. My thermometer is old, but even so, I got a normal reading when I took my own." She takes a drink of water. "By the time we got to the emergency room, you were unconscious, and we couldn't wake you. The nurses had to pull you out of the car to get you onto a gurney. They each took your temperature and responded the same way I had; that there had been some kind of mistake. One reading came back at 107°."

Thomas listens to Mary recount the details of their ordeal as though he's in a tunnel. Her words sound strange and far away as though she's telling someone else's story. Were it not for her constant flow of tears; he might not believe that it had happened.

"Thank you for everything, Mary," he says, "I'm sorry that I scared you."

"Please don't apologize," she wipes her hands through the air, dismissing him. "Honestly, Thomas, I didn't know how you'd be on the other side of this—if there was another side."

Well, that's poetic, he thinks.

She cries for some time and he lets her. There's no reason to rush her. This was as traumatic for her as it was for him. She looks into his eyes, the gravity of what she is about to say written on her face.

"Thomas, a fever over 107°, can cause brain damage. Did you know that?"

"No, I didn't."

"You were above that. Minutes, maybe seconds more, could have killed you. I keep asking myself what if I hadn't checked your temperature? What if I'd given you some aspirin and told you to lay down and rest? I'm terrified of what could have happened. And there's so much more than that. This entire thing is crazy," she shakes her head. "You were so sick that you didn't feel it when they dropped you in the cold bath. You didn't even react."

Then they pumped you with meds and shouted back and forth. Everyone was frantic, like they knew that they were running out of options, and the last person to offer an idea would be the one left holding the bag. I'm no doctor, but I know what fear looks like, and that's what I saw on their faces. They were scared for you, and they were scared for themselves," she blows her nose. "Then," she says, "it happened. You screamed.

"It was pulverizing. The entire hospital went silent," her eyes well up. "Like we were frozen in time; stuck in a second that was too long on both ends."

"Mary?" Thomas puts his hand on hers. He understands her questioning herself, questioning the entire experience, because when she said that he'd screamed, he'd been pulled into her thoughts. The amount of pain she'd felt for him was enough for them both. And she was right to question herself. Who wouldn't? The hospital did seem to freeze. But he knew that it hadn't. He'd recognized the sensation instantly, from experiencing it so many times before. It was the same feeling he'd had after spending time on Tendo. The way time worked in both places was, in essence, the same, yet they didn't add up, and there was no logical accounting for the discrepancy. On Tendo, time was thick. It spread in every direction, submerging you within it. But on Novo, time felt linear, like a thin line that you were traveling along. Every experience trailed behind as you moved forward, toward a future you could never reach, because it was always ahead. Maybe it was just his perception of both places, but he understood what had happened the moment he saw it through Mary's eyes. She'd had a glimpse of Tendo, like everyone else in the hospital. And what's more, he realized that it probably happened all the time. It was just that no one trusted themselves enough to believe what they'd thought for that fleeting second. People who have crazy thoughts, are made to feel crazy, plain and simple. Poor Mary. Poor everyone.

"Then your temperature fell from over 107° to normal in minutes. No one could believe it. Twenty people in the room saw it. It was like watching a miracle," Mary says, her eyes flicking to life. Thomas thinks about what she's told him and compares her timeline to his experience on the other side. They match up to a degree. It wasn't the medicine on this side that healed him; it was the second fang-beaver's bite. He doesn't want to believe it, but he knows it's true.

A nurse shows up with medicine and check Thomas's vitals, so Mary takes the girls to the cafeteria to give him some privacy. The meds go to work instantly, and Thomas starts to doze off, but something nags at him about his time with Amos. He fights against his sleepiness to figure it out, but in the end, the drugs win. He closes his eyes and drifts away.

It hits him like a train. His eyes flash to the ceiling, and he struggles to sit up. *I heard Amos.* I must have made him mad or something. I'm not sure how it happened, but I heard him thinking. He'd been annoyed at me for thinking that I thought I was clever. And I don't think he noticed. Exhausted, Thomas lies back in bed, and falls to sleep.

Click-click, click-click. The noise repeats over and over, waking Thomas from a deep sleep. He's about to shout when it stops. He relaxes. It starts again, and Thomas realizes what it is. Someone is typing a message on their cell phone, and they have the keyboard set to register every time a letter is typed. There's a blip of silence, then it starts again. It's so annoying he can hardly stand it.

"Shut up!" he shouts. The noise stops. He opens his eyes and sees Rob Greer sitting across from him looking stricken, his cell phone frozen in his hand.

Thomas rubs his eyes then takes in his surroundings. Ahh. The hospital.

"Sorry man," Rob says. "I came to see how you were doing. I didn't mean to wake you."

"No, it's fine. I'm sorry, I didn't mean to yell. I've been out of it. How's Adam?"

"About the same. I came to see him and heard you'd woken up."

"Thanks. Jesus. Rough time for everyone."

"I'll say. Anyway, I stopped in to see how you were doing. Glad you're feeling better.

Thomas nods goodbye to Rob who does the same. The lump under the covers on the bed next to him moves.

"That you, Madi?" Thomas says.

"Mm, hmm," Madi pulls back the covers. "That was embarrassing," she says.

He pats the space next to him on the bed, gesturing for her to come and sit. She does.

"I know. I'm sorry. I haven't been feeling myself. But never mind that. How are you? You must have been scared."

Madi shakes her head. He can tell she's trying not to cry.

"I'm fine, Madi, I promise. I'm sorry I scared you; I'm sorry about all of this. The doctors gave me some medicine and I'm better now, okay?"

"You swear?" Madi says.

"I swear. And I'm starving. Should we buzz the nurse?"

"Na," Madi says, "Mary's bringing food."

"Of course, she is." He hands Madi the remote. "Why don't you put something on until she gets here."

The hospital wants Thomas to stay for several more days for observation and additional testing. No one can make sense of his 'remarkable recovery.' Mary comes by daily, and he knows it's wearing on her, even though she'd never admit to it. At Thomas's urging and much protest, she agrees that she doesn't need to be at his bedside 24/7, and that he'll call her when he's released.

"How is my boy-wonder today?" Thomas's favorite nurse steps into his room, scribbling on her clipboard.

"Better, thanks." He sits up in bed. "Think I can put my clothes on yet?"

"Sorry, sir, you may not." She clamps an oxygen monitor onto his finger and a blood pressure cuff on his arm, silencing him while she listens to his heart. He stays quiet, watching her work, appreciating everything that she's done for him. The doctor comes in while she is finishing up and reviews the chart, clicking his pen and mouth simultaneously. He does this often, click-click, click-clack, lips puckered like he's doing exercises with his mouth.

Trying not to laugh, Thomas waits for the news; be it good or bad, he needs an update. Sitting in this room day after day is making him go out of his mind. Please God, he thinks, let them tell me I can go, and not mention a word about my parents or how we're going to pay for this. Do hospitals do pro-bono work? The nurse fusses around the room, changing tubes and monitoring machines while the doctor reads the chart. Thomas holds his breath.

"Alright, Thomas," the doctor says, "everything looks good. You ready to get out of here?"

"What, today?" Thomas says. His heart races.

"You wanted to stay a little longer?" he says.

"No," Thomas says louder than he meant to. Both the nurse and doctor laugh.

"No, it is, then. I'll sign off but sit tight. I'll back in a few minutes."

Thomas waits for the doctor in a near panic. This is it; they're going to come after him and his sister. They found out about their parents. He's preparing to flee when the doctor returns, carrying a bag of Thomas's belongings and a new sweatshirt from the gift shop.

"Here's a clean sweater from the gift shop. We didn't have anything appropriate for you. We usually keep extra clothes around here, but it looks like we're running low."

"Huh?" Thomas says.

"We keep a donation bin of clothes that people can use if they need something to leave in. People don't plan on going to the emergency room, so they don't bring a change of clothes with them should they need one. We keep extras around. There wasn't anything warm enough that would fit you, so I grabbed this from the gift shop.

"Anyhow, I signed your release and am sending you home with a prescription for antibiotics. Take one pill three times a day with a meal. You can get it filled at the pharmacy downstairs. Make sure you eat before you take them, or they'll make you sick. Besides that, keep your arm and leg clean. I'll see you in three days at my office."

"What happens in three days?"

"Don't worry. It's a follow-up visit. But if you need anything, call my cell. And if your fever returns, go straight to the emergency room." He hands Thomas his business card.

"And the bill?"

"You're all set Thomas, free to go. Stop by the front desk and pick up the forms for your parents to sign. Once they've sent them back, accounting will get them squared away."

Thomas's mind is spinning. He manages to tell the doctor thanks and gets dressed to leave.

Chapter 20

"Are you still sick?" Madi whispers, waking Thomas up. He's been home for two days and has slept the whole time.

"Hi, Madi. I'm not. I think my body needed more rest. When did you get here?"

"Mary dropped me off. You were asleep forever. You must have had hundreds of dreams."

"I did," Thomas says, picturing his beach. He misses it. Amos has probably destroyed it. "I dreamt of a beautiful place."

"What was it like?"

"Well, it was a beach made of powder, and the ocean changed colors."

"I wish I could see it. Was I in your dream?" Thomas winces. No, thank God. "Not this time. You would have loved it, though. There were these crazy silver pyramids that balanced on glass spheres and floating waterfalls. Animals began as one thing but would turn into something else every few minutes. Nothing stayed the same."

"Why not?"

"Because I wanted it like that."

"That sounds sad. What if the animals didn't want to become something else?"

Thomas blinks. "Sorry. I'm not explaining it right. It was just a beautiful thing that happens in dreams, where the ordinary can be anything, even extraordinary."

"Well, it sounds sad. If something is happy how it is, it shouldn't be forced to change."

"That's not what I meant, Madi. It was a dream. You are way too serious sometimes," he shuffles her hair. "Let's go get something to eat. I'm starving. And look out there," he points through the window, "it's finally snowing. I know the perfect place."

Madi howls. "Mary said she'd take us sledding as soon as we got some snow. Maybe after school?"

"Not for me, but for you, we'll see. Get your boots, and you can go out after we eat. It's early, we've got some time."

By the time they've finished breakfast, the sky has opened and grown dark. Rough winds have transformed the fluffy snow into icy razor blades that stick to everything they touch. Thomas peeks out the window and frowns.

"I don't think it's a good idea to go out there now. It's pretty rough. But I tell you what, if it's like this after school, I'll take you to a movie if there's anything good playing. I'm going to run across the street and ask the neighbors if I can borrow their old work truck. Bill said I could use it the last time I cut wood for him." He builds a fire in the iron stove and he steps outside at the same time his neighbor, Bill, walks onto his porch.

"Hey Bill," Thomas yells across the street, "just the man I wanted to see."

Bill stands like a statue with his face to the sky. Snow sticks to his dark hair, making him look like a thin version of a dirty Santa Claus. He seems oblivious to the snow covering his face. His head clicks left then right, and he walks into the house without acknowledging the wind ripping his door open then closed.

What the hell? Thomas jogs across the street. The door swings open and closed with the wind, slamming every few seconds. He's letting out all the heat. Can't he hear it? Feel the cold? Thomas rings the bell but there's no reply, so he pushes the door back a few inches then holds it tight as a wind gust tries to tear it from his hand.

"Bill? Connie?" he tries again, "are you guys okay?"

There's no response, so he enters the house, calling their names. After several more shouts without a reply, he steps inside and closes the door. Walking through the house calling their names, Thomas gets the creeps but pushes on. Bill's playing a joke on him and planning to jump out and scare him.

"Hello? Anyone?" The house is silent.

In the kitchen, Thomas skids to a stop. "Holy crap, you guys scared me," he says to Bill and Connie sitting at the dinner table. Neither move. Instead, they stare into their dishes with glassy eyes. Thomas can see his breath with every exhalation. It is freezing inside. This is not normal.

"Bill, Connie, hello? Hey," he snaps his fingers in front of their faces, "wake up."

No one moves. Thomas feels his adrenaline surge, followed by panic. Maybe there is a gas leak. They could be comatose – carbon monoxide-ish. Or worse, drugged for some reason. Perhaps he's come in the middle of a robbery. In either case, he should probably leave immediately.

A metal spoon crashes into a porcelain bowl, and Thomas stifles a scream. Connie has reanimated and resumed eating. She scoops a spoon of soggy cereal into her mouth. She seems to chew on autopilot, and slowly, her eyes come back into focus.

"Darling, eh hem," she clears her throat. "Bill, wake up. Eat your breakfast."

Bill's head snaps up, and he looks around like he's never seen his kitchen before. His eyes land on Connie, and he visibly relaxes, his body sagging.

"Sorry, dear, you were saying?" he asks. Thomas doesn't know what to do. He's standing in the middle of their kitchen frozen in a Heisman pose, and neither Bill nor Connie have acknowledged him. Thinking it's about to get very weird, he decides to call attention to himself before they notice him on their own.

"Uh, guys?" he says.

Bill and Connie turn their heads to him in tandem, both sets of eyes growing wide.

"Hi, uh, sorry, I've been calling for you. I saw you leave the front door open. I was coming to see if I could borrow the truck. I knocked, but no one answered, so I came inside to make sure everything was okay. Sorry if I scared you."

They go back to eating their cereal without saying anything. What the hell? Thomas thinks but backs out of the kitchen. When he gets to the front door, Bill yells that the keys are on entry hook. Thomas snatches them up, and rushes from the home, slamming their door behind him.

"What's wrong?" Madi looks up. Thomas is panting. "What took you so long? Did you get the truck?"

"Yes. And nothing's up. I'm fine," he says through strained breaths. "It's cold out there. You need a hat and gloves. Better yet, put on the warmest stuff you have."

Madi makes no effort to move.

"It's getting late, Madi. Get your things together so I can take you to school." His tone gets her moving and he feels bad, but his neighbor's behavior was frightening. He needs to get Madi out of here.

He tries not to think about what might be happening with the neighbors. He's pulled a lot of thoughts from them. Maybe he had something to do with the way they were acting. It looked like their brains had temporarily shut down and he doesn't like it.

The drive is harrowing. The tires are bald and the truck slides everywhere. With few options, Thomas pulls the truck onto a snowbank next to the school and walks Madi in. Grumpy elementary kids mope around, complaining that school is open during a snowstorm.

"I'll walk you all the way in. Hand me your backpack."

"You don't have to."

"It's slippery, Madi. Come on."

"Okay."

"I'll see you after school," he says. "Don't be mad, they'll probably play movies since it's the first big snowstorm."

Besides the pile-up of cars who hadn't put on their snow tires yet, the high school drive isn't bad. The parking lot is full when he arrives, so he circles several times before finding a spot. It's dumping as he treks the short distance to building, his footprints disappearing behind him.

From the front steps, he takes in the scene. The school, ground, and air are all the same color. Everything is monochromatic. It is impossible to tell where one thing begins and the next ends. It's breathtaking. Turning his face to the sky, he lets snowflakes stick to his face and catches one with his tongue. He takes a final deep breath to savor what will likely be his last sane moment today, and walks through the doors.

Right away, it's clear that something is wrong. The halls are congested but no one makes a peep. Kids and teachers move around from one place to the next, some stopping at lockers while others enter classrooms, but there's no conversation, no laughter or arguments. No one is speaking. Everyone seems lost in thought, reminiscent of the scene with his neighbors this morning. Besides the creepy factor, there's something else bothering him that he can't put his finger on. He watches for a minute, trying to understand the problem and is horrified when he gets it. It's not just that everyone around him isn't talking; they aren't thinking. There's barely any brain activity.

Then pop-pop-pop. Gillian just thought about Spanish class. There's a quiz. Pop-pop. Andrea is thinking about Shayne, about the weekend and if he'll ever talk to her again. Two more pops, first from Jeff, who hopes there's a sub in math today, then from Sally. Did she forget to turn off the curling iron? Glassy eyes all around him seem to clear up at once. Thomas grabs his head as the explosion of thoughts hit him and runs from the building.

The parking lot has iced over, and he slips, landing on his tailbone. He might have broken his butt, but it's better than falling on his arm that's still healing. He lets the ice numb his tailbone and realizes his mistake when he stands up with wet pants.

"Sweet," he jokes, but doesn't really care. He can already leave. The minute he spent in the hallway gave him enough mindless information to appease both Amos and Simon for weeks. But it's Simon he wants to see. He has a lot of questions about his neighbors and his classmate's odd behavior.

Climbing into the truck, he marvels at how raw his legs have become at the hands of his frozen, wet pants. He's so preoccupied that he doesn't notice the girl standing at his window until she knocks so hard, he almost hits his head.

Wiping fog from the window, he's surprised to see Terri Greer waiting for him with a large, painful smile on her face. This'll be good, he thinks, rolling down the window. Terri opens her mouth to speak, but instead starts screaming. Thomas isn't sure what to do but images of lizards and snakes falling from her mouth flood his mind. When he realizes that he is seeing what Terri is imagining, he screams too and turns on the ignition. The truck lurches forward, nearly hitting Terri, and he fishtails out of the parking lot. Even down the road, he can still hear Terri screaming, imaginary monsters escaping from her body.

"No," he bangs his hand on the steering wheel, "what is happening?" But inside, he knows that all of this is because of him. He drives mindlessly until a road closure diverts him toward the hospital, and he knows that's it's time to face Adam.

Chapter 21

Red metallic hearts and plastic roses decorate the front desk and waiting room inside the hospital. Thomas feels a pang of jealousy that he might not see Nicole for Valentine's Day. He isn't sure how long it will be until he sees her at all. The nurse's Station is bustling, but Thomas quickly procures an escort to Adam's room when he lacks the patience to wait. Inside, the place looks empty, and he thinks that maybe Adam got better. That he woke from the darkness and simply went home on his own. Then a toilet flushes from the attached bathroom, and Adam emerges. He crosses the room and climbs into bed without a glance in Thomas's direction. Thomas stands awkwardly, uncertain of what to do. One of these times, he will make a plan before taking action. But Adam turns his head unexpectedly and looks at Thomas. Their connection is instant.

He's underwater. We're underwater, in the palace. It's changed dramatically; and that Thomas can't make sense of what Adam is seeing is highly unnerving. When the images become clear to him, Thomas starts to shake. Oh, my God, what have I done? Adam's in a nightmare worse than anything I've ever seen. Has he been here the whole time? While I was out making people give me things and pouting about a girl? Oh, God, Adam, I didn't know. I'm so sorry. If I'd known, I never would have wasted so much time while you were living in hell.

A dark shadow passes above Adam making him tremble. He knows what's up there. Thomas feels Adam's heartbeat change from a trot to a gallop. He's terrified. The shadow passes again; only, this time, it gets larger by the second until it's swallowed almost all of the light. Adam's fear spikes along with his pulse, then he's holding his breath and looking out into the water.

A yellowish glow lights up the darkness and begins moving closer. It's hard to understand what Adam is seeing. Now petrified himself, Thomas can do nothing but watch through Adam's eyes as the light comes into focus. What is that, Thomas thinks. It's like a stalactite, only it's too sharp. It's more like a spear. Wait, there's another, and another, and oh, my God. Those aren't limestone formations. They're teeth.

"Swim," Thomas pleads, but Adam doesn't move. He stands frozen, staring at the teeth heading toward him. "Goddammit, Adam!" Thomas squeezes his eyes shuts and screams, "Do something. You can build where you are, so do it! Make a wall, make a weapon, make something now. Put yourself in a Goddam force field."

Inside Adam's room, Thomas falls to the ground. He pulls open his eyes and sees Adam lying in bed, drool dripping down his face.

"No," he yells and pulls Adam's face back toward his own. In an instant, he's back inside Adam's mind, looking through Adam's eyes.

Adam spins in circles, examining the bubble that is surrounding him.

"What the hell?" he whimpers, something between a grimace and smile spreading across his face. The fish apparently can't see it. They come from every angle and bump into it, bouncing off in the other direction, their faces contorting when they hit the invisible barrier. Adam laughs, something that he probably hasn't done in months.

"Thomas?" Adam whispers. "I think that you are here with me and that you're helping. If I'm wrong, thank you to whoever is doing this, because I sure as hell didn't make this thing. Either way, I hope it's strong."

Adam doesn't seem to notice, but Thomas picks up the change in light in the bubble's reflection. Unable to move, or warn Adam, Thomas watches the beast appear, wondering what kind of animal has teeth like that?

The creature comes closer. Adam spins slowly and sees it. Thousands of razor-sharp teeth come into his focus before he's staring into its eyes. It stares at Adam, and both are still. Then it whips its tail from left to right. A violent jolt sends ocean debris flying along with millions of fish. Trees are ripped from their roots and sent hurling through the watery landscape. Adam is thrown across the bubble, but it flexes to cushion his fall. He gets to his feet, spinning around, looking for the beast.

The entire sea glows brightly as phytoplankton flash in every direction, temporarily blinding Adam, but when the intensity dulls, he sees it coming. The creature slides along the bubble with deliberation, its' shiny, black, back, a perfect contrast to its dark, purple, belly. Row after row of ossified scales run down its back and tail, each one sounding like thunder crackling as it connects with the bubble. There's no mistaking what it is, this giant Nile crocodile, only this one's as big as an airplane. And it's here for Adam.

It turns to face Adam and pulls its snout back, revealing more teeth. The effect is that of a smile. Goosebumps spread across Thomas's entire body. It's gone with one flick of its powerful tail, leaving only flickers of light and a tornado of particles floating around.

"Thomas?" Adam asks. "I need to get out of here. Do you understand? It's coming back. You know it, and I know it, and I need to go, now."

Thomas thinks, I don't know how Adam. I don't know what to do.

"Please Thomas, or whoever you are, focus. Do something. I can't die like this."

Thomas feels the explosion knock Adam to the ground. Even with its flexibility, the jolt to the bubble is so rough that Adam gets whiplash. Through Adam's bleary eyes, Thomas watches the crocodile circle around and press its snout against the bulge of the barrier, his jagged teeth blocking the view of anything outside. It thrashes its tail back and forth, pushing against the bubble, trying to penetrate it, to shatter it. The bubble holds its shape, and Thomas's doubt gives way to hope.

It's holding, he thinks. Then he hears it, the unmistakable sound of glass cracking.

Adam sinks to the floor with his head in his hands. This is it. He wishes he could have said goodbye to his brother, Rob. Rob, who worked so hard to help him, to save him. This is going to crush him. He weeps.

Thomas feels pain radiate out of his chest and through his body. This is his fault. He should be inside the bubble, not Adam. Adam sits on the floor, listening to glass crack all around him, resigned to his fate. The croc pushes forward, his victory only inches away. The pain in Thomas's chest turns to fury. The bubble shakes. Water begins to seep in.

Thomas feels tears fill his eyes, and his rage turns white-hot. He takes a deep breath, focusing his energy, wanting to save Adam more than anything he's ever wanted in his life. Please, please, let me fix this. I can do it. I put the stupid bubble there. If I can pop it, he'll have a chance. He can swim away under the debris. The croc will never see him. Come on, bubble, pop. Pop. Please pop, he yells. Focus, he tells himself, then he screams it.

There is an explosion of glass and trees, fish muck and sand, teeth, and scales. Thomas doesn't realize that he is still screaming until the nurse shaking him, yells for him to stop.

He blinks his eyes and spins toward the bed. Adam is gone. He looks back at the nurse, confident that he's lost his mind.

"There you are. Shh, okay, take it easy, take it easy. Let's get you to a seat, and I can call a doctor."

"Wait, no, please don't. Just, what happened to the kid?"

"Shh," she says in a quiet voice, "you should take a seat." His mind races to put the pieces together and his legs begin to shake. Oh God. Adam. He reaches out to the table to steady himself, but Adam steps forward, catching him first. While he looks like he's been to hell and back, he's managed to hang on to his dopy grin. Thomas is speechless.

"That was close," Adam says.

Thomas's legs threaten to give out, but Adam helps him to the couch before he collapses. He hears Adam talking with the nurse before she leaves. Adam wakes him sometime later by slipping a glass of water into his hands. Thomas drains it, then has two more.

"Listen," Adam takes a seat next to Thomas, "I want you to know that what happened to me was my fault. I can't exactly explain why, but I know that you feel responsible. You're not. And I also know that you helped me get out. So, thank you. I don't know how to say that in a way to make you understand how grateful I am."

Thomas faces him. "All of that was because of me. You should hate me. You should be furious."

"I don't hate you; you have no idea what you did for me. And I know you're going to try to put all of this on you, but you can't. You still don't understand."

"Don't understand? Are you crazy? That nut job put you in hell because of me, and I went about my merry life like everything was okay. I understand exactly what I did."

"Don't do this. You didn't do anything anyone else wouldn't have done. Look, we've got a lot to talk about, but I'm starving. Can we get out of here? The nurse won't be back for a while, and this room sucks."

They walk briskly to the elevators. The smell coming from the cafeteria isn't horrible, but it isn't great, either. It's not what Thomas would want to eat after being in a hospital for so long. Adam doesn't seem to care, so Thomas follows along; laughing as they enter the carnivorous room.

"Are you sure you want to eat here? Aren't you sick of this place?" Thomas says, following Adam through the galley line.

"I need food. I don't care what it is as long as there's a lot of it. Besides, I can't leave. My mom would freak."

Adam wolfs down three sandwiches and what looks like taco pie. Then he leans back in his chair and studies Thomas.

"Here's the thing," he says, "I know you're not going to let this go, this blaming yourself. I'd probably do the same thing. But you shouldn't. Most of this mess is my fault. You came along when I'd started to make mistakes. I put myself in a situation that I shouldn't have, and because of that, I put you in harm's way, too."

"What situation? What happened exactly?"

"I can't remember everything. I mean, I remember the crocodile and the bubble, but the rest is murky. I thought I was going to die in that bubble," he stares at the floor. "But you pulled me out. How did you do that?"

Thomas shrugs. "I don't know. It just happened, but let's get to that later. Have you been under water this whole time? Since the last time I saw you?"

"Like I said, it's blurry. I remember that everything was fine. I was going across a lot to work on the beach, and then I met you. After that, I only have flashes until the crocodile part. I know I've been gone for a long time and that I've been in the hospital. I could hear Rob when he came to visit, but I couldn't get back."

"You were trying to get back? Amos said that you were fine, that you were working on something else."

"That's bullshit. I'm not sure where I was, but I know it wasn't good," his eyes search Thomas's. "I made a horrible mistake. I didn't realize what he was. He's not good, Thomas. You need to stay away from him; from all of it. I know that now. The things I did were not beneficial for anyone; they created more problems than they solved."

"What mistake? What are you talking about? Start from the beginning. I need to understand."

Adam's face contorts into a type of pain. "My heads all mixed up, Thomas. He did something to me, so there's no way I can explain it right. It's like I can't string together a linear thought about our time together since I first met you up until the bubble. I can see all of the pieces, but I can't put them together."

"But in the room, it seemed like you knew what was going on."

"I do, in a way. I know Amos is bad. That's undeniable. When I brought him thoughts, it was bad for the people that I took them from. It took more from them than I understood." He squeezes his eyes shut, pinching the bridge of his nose. "I wish I could explain better. This is so frustrating."

"It's okay. Try to think. What do you mean that you took more?"

"Only that what I thought I was doing, taking a thought from time to time was no big deal. There are plenty to go around, right? Only, it's not like that at all. It damages them, Thomas. Every time I took a thought, I hurt someone."

Thomas feels his stomach drop. "How?" Please don't tell me. I don't want to know. I can't take it.

"Think of an essay you've written. The words and sentences you use are crucial, right? If you pull out a word or random sentence, the whole paragraph falls apart."

Oh, God, please don't let it be that substantial, Thomas thinks. "Right," he says.

"Well, pulling a thought or two from someone works the same way. Even though a thought might seem insignificant, it's still part of a bigger picture. So, every time I did it, I broke something in the person I took it from."

"Are you sure it was every time?"

"I have no idea. I still don't know how much damage I have done to a single individual or to anyone I have messed with at this point. There is no way to tell other than waiting for some horrific aftermath. Jesus. What if we start the apocalypse? This is a complete nightmare. And as far as I can tell, there's no way to give the thoughts back. I mean if we can take them, we should be able to give them back, right? But then what? We attempt to shove shit back into people's minds and see if they're cool? What if we make it worse?"

Thomas shudders, "We've got to try something."

"Maybe, maybe not. What I do know is that while I might not be able to fix what I did, I can try to stay away in hopes that no one else will get hurt."

Thomas closes his eyes and shakes his head. "Adam, you have no idea how bad this is."

"Why do you say that?"

"You think staying away will keep things from getting worse? They're already worse; this is a disaster."

"But what else has happened?"

"Everything is going nuts. People are going in and out of consciousness for minutes at a time, and I'm pretty sure it's my fault. I wasn't certain before, but what you said fits with what I've seen. I think that I took too much from certain people, and it might have messed with their thinking patterns. There were kids at my school who were completely catatonic for a few minutes, and I don't even want to talk about Bill and Connie."

"Who?" Adam says.

"My neighbors. God, they're so old I don't know what I was thinking of to mess with them. I figured that they'd have a lot of old thoughts floating around I could access. Christ," he drops his face into his hands, "what have I done?"

"You didn't know. I didn't either," Adam says.

"It doesn't matter now. What matters is that we try to fix this in a way that stops other Brokers from taking advantage of anyone else."

"You're talking crazy, Thomas. What would you have us do? Pick a fight with Amos? We'd be dead in seconds."

"I don't think so. I've talked to another Broker who agreed to help us. Once we get there, my mom will help. There might be a chance to turn some of this around."

"Uh, your mom? You're going to call your mommy. Are you joking?"

Thomas rubs his hands together, his eyes weary. "Yes, my mother. You know, L., from the water-wall?"

"Yeah," Adam's eyes narrow.

"Well, her name is actually Lilian, and she's my mom."

Adam drops his head and laughs. "You've got to be kidding me. I mean, seriously? What else have you left out? Are you my fairy Godmother, too?" He burns Thomas with a face, shakes his head and laughs or scoffs, Thomas can't tell the difference. Finally, Thomas decides that Adam has had enough for one day. He's been in the hospital for weeks, after all.

"Adam," he places both hands on Adam's shoulders, "you should go home and be with your family. I need to work all of this out, and when I do, I'll come to you and explain everything that I know, including what happened with my mom. In the meantime, get some rest and stay away from Tendo."

"You don't get it," Adam slaps Thomas's hands away. "I can't go home and relax. Amos can pull me in whenever he wants. What happens then? He'll read me and see all of this and then we are both as good as dead. I—"

"Adam!" Thomas stops him. "That's not going to happen. I won't let it."

"But there's nothing you can do. I know you think you can, but you can't help me." He drops his head, thinking I should have never brought you to his palace.

"How were you supposed to know what would happen? That's what anyone in your shoes would have done, and if you hadn't, I wouldn't know about my mother."

Adam gulps, staring at Thomas with wide eyes. "Did you just read me?"

"What? I don't know. It doesn't matter. What does, is that you go see your family and I'll worry about the rest. You need to figure out how to stay present, and you'll be fine. Don't daydream or nod off, stay focused so you can stay away from Tendo. I'll have something worked out by the end of the day."

"Thomas, couriers can't read other couriers."

"I didn't read you, Adam. I just told you to stay focused, and we're back to this?"

"What's your sister's name again?" Adam thinks.

Thomas steps toward Adam so that they're nose to nose.

"Adam, do not bring her into this. I'm trying to keep her as far removed from everything as possible. Don't say her name."

"You did it again," Adam says. "You read my thought, and it looked like you didn't even try."

"Adam," Thomas blows out his air, "it's not important. It's a parlor trick. You can probably do it too, but I don't have time to work on it today. I've made a horrible mess of things; we both have, now people's lives are in danger. And as a special bonus, we're in danger too, not that I care about myself anymore, but you're in danger along with our families and that's not okay. Please go back to your room so that the nurse can tell a doctor you've recovered. Then Rob and your mom can come to pick you up, and you can be a family again. Celebrate and enjoy your time together but stay out of Tendo and let me figure this out. Please."

"Christ, Thomas, you don't get it. At some point, very, very soon, we'll both be pulled back in, and if you haven't figured this out, you're never coming back. You can read couriers, and if that's the case, you can probably read Brokers, too."

Thomas's head snaps up, making Adam freeze.

"You can, can't you?"

"I did it once, but I haven't had time to figure out what to do about it."

"Well, now's the time, because you're everything they've been looking for, Thomas; you are them and us. A courier and a Broker. If you can figure this thing out, it could be our end game. And if not, it could be the end of everything."

Chapter 22

Branches claw against the window, like they want inside. Thomas sits in his kitchen, staring at a blank notepad. While he feels very alone, he's glad he dropped Adam at home with his family. They've been through a lot, and there's no telling how much worse things might get. What's important now is for him to focus.

The house shudders against the wind. Thomas gets up to throw some logs in the fireplace when Mary calls. She invites

him to dinner and he's about to say no, it's the worst possible
timing, but it occurs to him that he might not be coming back.
For Madi's sake, he tells Mary he'll see her soon. Things need
to be put in order in case the worst happens.

On the short drive over, Thomas wonders what to do about
Nicole. If he makes it out of this, he'd like to be more
involved if she's still interested. She's been different since
she lost her grandmother, and a lot of that is probably because
of how he reacted to the news that she had to leave over winter
break. How silly and immature he'd been. He's lucky she even
spoke to him again. But there is something between them that
could last. He could feel it the first time they met. She'd come
along at the most inopportune time, yet, the timing couldn't
have been better. He'd needed her. He'd needed to remember that
amidst the weight of the world riding on his shoulders, he still
had room for hope, and more importantly, love. He vows that if
he survives, he won't disappoint her again.

Wind funnels twist around his face as he approaches the
door. Mary opens it before he knocks.

"Hi," she says, "come in outta the cold. I thought I heard
the truck pull up."

"Hi, Mary," he says, pulling off a scarf. Mary's eyes knit
together.

"You've got something on your mind," she says. "I can
tell."

"Nothing's up. I'm just beat. It's been a busy day. Thanks
for having us for dinner. How's Madi?"

"She good; they're all in the back watching T.V."

"Sounds great. Thanks for having her so much lately."

"You're doing a good job with her, Thomas. I hope you know
that."

"Well, I'm not sure about that, but I'm trying. Anyway,
there's something I wanted to discuss. About Madi."

Mary stops fidgeting about the kitchen and points at a
seat.

"Sit," she says, taking the seat across from him. "Tell me. Is everything okay?"

"It's nothing bad. School is almost out, and I need to figure out what I'm going to do. It looks like I've got a couple of options, but I'm going to have to see what pans out with scholarships and which school I'll end up at. If I can't make it work with Madi initially, I wanted to see how you felt about having her for a while. I know it's a lot to drop on somebody."

"Thomas, it's not a lot, and I'm honored that you'd ask. I know I must seem like this pathetic woman, this Susie homemaker without the slightest bit of interest in anything outside of the house, but I'm not."

"I don't think that."

"Hear me out. I do want another life, one that is about me, but not until the girls have grown up and moved away. After John died, and I was left alone with the girls, I was so angry at the world that I didn't think I'd survive. I was angry that I had to live without him, and I was angry that I had to raise my girls without any help. But one day I saw them playing house, and it hit me that they lost someone, too. They were dealing with their grief as I was. It reminded me that not only were we still here, but that we still had each other. So, I started living again. Since then, I've wanted nothing more than to enjoy my life and love my children. I love you and Madi too, like I loved your mother; and I'd be honored to take Madi in. Your mother would have done the same thing for me. So, when you're hesitant to ask for even the smallest thing, like a ride, for instance, please don't. I am here for you always."

Looking at Mary with tears in his eyes, Thomas chokes back a sob. She smiles and messes his hair. His ears prickle as she thinks about his mother, and he listens in. This is for him; he won't share these thoughts.

He feels like he's turned to wax. Pieces of him melt away, and he disappears into Mary's loving memories of his mother, who was like her sister. Slowly her love is replaced with grief, as overwhelming as it was the day when Lilian O'Malley disappeared from the world. He feels Mary's pain along with his own, experiencing it in duplicate until it's too much to bear. Breaking free from her thoughts, he wipes away his tears. He doesn't know how long he's been sitting there, but when he looks up, Mary is quietly working in the kitchen, mixing something that smells of cinnamon. She sees him watching her and winks. Thomas knows Mary is no stranger to grief and appreciates that she gave him some time to muddle through this. His relief is palpable. Madi will be fine here should the worst happen. "That smells great," he says, gathering himself. "What can I do to help?"

Tonight's dinner is a happy event. The interaction between the twins is a riot. He's never really watched them communicate. They finish each other's sentences without noticing. Mary laughs every time they do it, and they look at each other with what must be bafflement about what's so funny. Madi gets the joke and laughs along with Mary, making the twins laugh. It's a circus. He watches in awe, amused at the silliness, and looks at Madi staring at him. He crooks his head.

"What is it Madi?" he asks.

"You're smiling. Your whole face looks happy."

Everyone's eyes shift to him. Heat rushes to his cheeks, and he feels his smile grow.

"I guess I am," he says and takes a bite of spaghetti.

After dinner, Mary sends him home with a massive container of leftovers. Madi stayed behind, and Thomas didn't argue. His only surprise was that Mary didn't question him about it.

In the small living room, Thomas lies awake watching the ceiling fan at work, blowing the warm air back down and around, its blades spinning like a clock. Time is running out. He closes his eyes and drifts off, thinking of Simon.

He wakes right where he went to sleep, his calls for Simon left unanswered. It can't end like this. His mother has been stuck in a watery nightmare for all this time while he wasted his own on simple, silly things. Everything was for nothing; what a waste of possibilities.

It snows so much overnight that school is cancelled Monday morning. Mary calls Thomas frantically. The entire house woke up with the flu outside of Madi. If she didn't already catch it, she will if she stays any longer. He has to pick her up right away.

He calls the Greer's house. Adam picks up.

"Thank God. You're still here. I need your help. Oh, it's Thomas."

"Yeah, I figured. What's going on? I'm freaking out."

"Me, too. I can't explain over the phone, but I've got my sister today. Can I pick you up? We can go to town, to the bookstore or somewhere so she can run around."

"Yeah, sure. Rob and I were going to catch a movie. I've been trying to stay busy but I'm tired, man. He's probably going to want to come; he hasn't let me out of his sight since I got home."

"Okay, I'll pick you up in twenty minutes?"

"That works. See you then," Adam hangs up.

Thomas races to get ready and runs out the door, hopping into Bob's truck. He owes Bob big time for letting Thomas borrow it for so long. He picks Madi up five minutes later then pulls in front of the Greer's house next. Madi watches him, her eyebrows arched in confusion.

"What," he says, pulling his fingers from his mouth.

"I was going to ask why you were biting your nails. You seem nervous."

"I'm not. Just cold."

She sighs. Rob and Adam appear a minute later and pile into the truck, Rob ruffing Madi's hair.

"Hi there," he says as if they're old friends. Adam stays quiet but gives Thomas the same look that Madi did a minute before.

"What?" Thomas says.

"So, bookstore?" Rob says.

"Yes. Why is everyone looking at me like that? Is going to the bookstore weird?" Thomas asks.

"It's um, slightly nerdy?" Rob tries.

"You won't think so when you've seen it," Madi laughs.

"All right then. Sounds small-town fascinating," Rob rolls his eyes. "Maybe after we can go to the DMV or the post office for some real fun."

Wall's Book Store is usually packed, but they're so early they find a quiet table in the back. With the way the weather is, it'll be standing room only soon.

"Did you figure anything out?" Adam asks after Rob and Madi wander off. "Should I be worried?"

Thomas looks around for prying ears. "Kind of. And I think I'll need your help."

"Name it."

"You might change your mind after you hear what it is."

"We're kinda past that point, don't you think? Tell me what you need."

"Alright. I can't reach the other Broker I was working with, and I need help getting into a Way Station. I used one coming home, but never going in," Thomas says.

"You can't just hop in one; you have to be pulled through by a Broker. They can tell when you're inside. But I thought the idea was not to get pulled through," Adam says.

"It's not to get pulled through outside of the Way Station. That's why I wanted you to stay focused. If Amos pulls you in that way, you go right to him. But when you go through a Station, you have some time after you get there. That's what I'm counting on."

"But he'll be expecting you," Adam says.

"Maybe not. I'm going to try for Simon once we find one. I'm hoping that he can tell I'm there, but if not, I have another idea."

"Do I want to know?"

"I'm thinking that if we both got in at the same time, it would throw Amos off, that he wouldn't be sure who was coming so he'd pull us through to see what was going on. But once he started pulling, you'd have to jump out."

"Are you nuts?"

"I don't think so. Why?"

"You can't jump out of one. You've felt it; it's way stronger than us."

"Not if you jump and I push at the same time."

Adam shakes his head, "But you don't know what he'll do. He might not even pull us, or if he does, then what? What's your plan when you get there?"

"I'm working that part out. I know it sounds lame, but I think if I can get to my mom, we can figure something out."

"It doesn't sound lame. It sounds like suicide, Thomas. If Amos is there, he'll either kill you or keep you. You think he's going to let you walk away?"

"I think I'm valuable enough to him that he'll trade me for my mother's release. That's the most important thing. She can finally come home. She can be with Madi again."

"You can't do this. I don't think you understand how bad Amos is."

"I think that my understanding of him is the only thing that I have going for me. I can use his pride against him. He's so egotistical that he'd never expect me to try something like this. It might give me the edge I need. Either way, I have to try. We're out of options."

"There has to be another way."

"You guys finished planning the end of the world?" Rob asks, approaching the table with Madi. Thomas and Adam glance up, both taken aback. Neither speaks.

"Weird, once again," Rob says. "I'm gonna go pay for this book, and then we should hit it. The movie is going to start soon. Thomas, are you and Madi coming with us?"

Madi shrugs. "They're only playing boy movies, but it's better than going home."

"You know what?" Thomas says, "a movie sounds great right now." It occurs to him that this might be the last time he gets to see one.

The movie's a flop, but no one seems to care. Despite the tension that pulses between Thomas and Adam, the day was a good one. They leave the theater and stop for burgers. Madi looks tired when the waitress asks about dessert.

"No, thank you. We'll take the check," he answers for everyone. She replies that someone already paid the check.

What a pleasant surprise, everyone thinks, but Madi raises an eyebrow at Thomas. She knows their money situation hasn't improved, and Thomas knows that Madi is aware. He doesn't take advantage of people as much anymore, but sometimes he gives in to temptation.

The ride home is awkward. Madi and Rob seem bored while Thomas and Adam seem agitated. The storm has passed, and Thomas can tell that the weather will be nice tomorrow. For everyone else, it will seem like a typical day. But Thomas knows better because of what he's planning to do. And if he isn't successful, tomorrow could be the start of the end. Adam must sense Thomas's nerves because he tries to give a reassuring smile that ends up looking like a grimace. He looks as scared as Thomas feels.

The alarm barks early, but Thomas has been awake for hours. He stares at the ceiling and out the window, praying for it to start snowing again; for one more day of respite. Any kind of day would do; nice, windy, rainy, he'd take any of them. It's funny how quickly you can become nostalgic about something when you know it might not happen again. Then you look back at yourself with jealousy: How did you let so much slip by? Where did all the chances go?

Madi's going back to school, and there's no way Amos will leave them alone much longer. Thomas is out of time and out of excuses. Climbing out of bed, he starts the morning routine without thinking, but stops himself. Not this time. Today, he will enjoy his time with Madi and remember all of the days before this one that he took for granted. Time should be cherished.

Madi sits across from him, stretching her arms over her head. "Morning," she says, "What were you thinking about?"

"Huh?" he asks.

"You were making your serious face."

"Was I? I guess I was thinking about school. What's happening with you today? Anything interesting?"

"Not really." She gets up for milk.

Thomas watches her go; a feeling of love mingled with sorrow washing over him.

Drop-off is typical until Madi stops midway across the parking lot and looks back at him, giving him a sad smile before walking away. She must know something is up. She pays more attention to what's going on than he gives her credit for. He waits until she disappears through the front doors and drives away.

From the warmth of his borrowed truck, Thomas sees Rob and his mother leave their house together and drive away. He waits another ten minutes to make sure they're not coming back before knocking on the door.

Adam answers with a nervous smile, picking at his fingers.

"So, you ready?" he asks.

"Ready as I can be," Thomas says. He's feeling nowhere near ready, but Adam doesn't need to know that. Sometimes in life, you need to be the guide; to act like you're in control even when you're terrified, in order to put others at ease. Thomas decides that today is that day. Adam's obviously freaking out, and they've still got work to do. If he needs Thomas to be calm and collected, then that's how Thomas will act.

"Any thoughts on how we'll find the Station today?" Thomas asks. "Where should we start?"

"When I lived here before, I usually found my Station entrance on the way home from school," Adam says. "If I couldn't feel it, I'd head toward the hills on the west side of town. It was almost always at one of those places. A few times, I had to go toward town, but that's the last place I'd start."

"Then let's head toward school," Thomas says, walking toward the truck. "What'd you tell your mom? I saw them leave."

"I didn't tell her anything. I'm supposed to be here. My old school let me go on a homeschool contract after the hospital. When the semester ends, I'll enroll here. My dad's always gone with work, so he was bummed, but he knew I'd be in better hands if I stayed here through the end of the year. Anyway, don't worry about my stepmom, she won't come home today. She's got something happening at work."

"I guess you got what you wanted, in a way," Thomas says.

"What do you mean?" Adam says.

"You told me once that everyone had forgotten you; something like one day they'd know that you were important. They obviously think that now, even before you've made it to medical school."

"I don't understand. Whose medical school? Mine?"

"Uh, yeah. That was the plan, I thought. That you were going to go to school, and then your family would finally see what you were capable of. Um, do you have any idea what I'm talking about? You look lost."

"I'm completely lost. What gives you the idea that I wanted to be a doctor?"

"Nothing. Never mind. I probably dreamt it," Thomas inwardly groans. Please let this be a temporary memory problem, he thinks. If Adam has zero recollection of his life's plan, then everything might already be lost.

"Park up there," Adam points, his attention span baffling Thomas again. Still, he's relieved to end the conversation and pulls the truck to a stop. They leave the truck behind a motorhome parked near Westchester Middle School. The snow is waist-deep everywhere but the road.

"This sucks," Adam says. "I'd like to say I hope we find the Way Station fast, but I can't say I'm eager for what happens when we do."

Minutes turn into an hour without luck. Adam's teeth start to chatter. "May-b-bb-eee you should focus t-tt-tooo," he tells Thomas.

"I know. I'm sorry. I've been thinking about my mom, and how miserable this must have been for her."

"Well, for what it's worth," Adam says, "I don't think it's been too bad. I mean, granted, she didn't get to be with you guys, but she's never seemed depressed or anything. But who knows? It's so bizarre."

"Bizarre doesn't begin to describe it," Thomas says.

"Whoa, did you feel that?" Adam says.

"Feel what?"

"The shock. It's here, the Way Station. We're close. I got zapped, and that's never happened before."

"Maybe it's because we're together?"

"I don't know, but it was strong."

"Good. Hopefully, that means it's open. I'll go first and try for Simon, but we'll have to try together if nothing happens."

"Okay, but what if it's Amos that pulls you in and not Simon?"

"At this point, it doesn't matter. Either way, I've got to get to Amos's palace. I don't think there's time for anything else."

"I still think this is crazy, but I also know I can't talk you out of it. Whatever happens, I'm right behind you."

"Thanks," Thomas says and takes a deep breath. "So, it's right in front of me?"

"About two steps," Adam says, looking toward a non-descript chunk of snow. Thomas nods moving forward, then disappears. Adam paces until he hears Thomas call for him, and like Thomas, he steps forward, disappearing into the Way Station.

"Have you felt anything?" Adam says after a minute.

"I don't think so," Thomas says, "nothing's happening. Maybe we should focus on the same thing, to increase the intensity?"

"How about the mini-sun on the other side? At the Station? We both know it well," he snickers. Thomas almost smacks him.

"Perfect. Okay, then on the count of three, think about it as hard as you can."

Adam nods.

"And remember, when you feel the pulling start, you have to get out."

"I know."

"Alright. Then three, two—"

"Good luck, Thomas."

"One."

Someone is yelling in pain. Thomas tries to place where it's coming from but can't hear over the loud hum blasting through his ears. The smell is awful, like burnt carpet, but worse. *That's hair.* The thought jolts Thomas awake. He scans the ground and finds Adam lying on his back, his arms and legs splayed like a cartoon character. Tuffs of smoke float up from his hair and shirt. Dropping to his knees, Thomas beats away at Adam's smoldering parts until Adam kicks him off.

"Stop, you're killing me," Adam yells. "Get off me, I'm fine."

"You're on fire," Thomas continues to smack at the smoke.

"It's steam," he scrambles away from Thomas. "It's out. I put it out with the snow. Geeze."

"Are you sure? What the hell happened?"

"I have no idea. Everything seemed fine. I felt the pull start and tried to back out, but then the whole thing flashed out. It zapped me so hard it singed my hair. I dove into the snow, thinking I was on fire."

"What happened to the Way Station?" Thomas says. "I was inside, and then it was gone. Did it move? Is it still close? We've got to try again."

"I just told you. It flashed out. It's broken or they've sealed it. That was the only way in around here. I'm sorry, Thomas. It's over."

Thomas feels the breath knocked from his chest. Tears sting his eyes. He runs down the street with Adam yelling after him. Jumping into the truck and flooring it, his wheels spin the on ice as the world around him becomes a blur. It's over. I failed. I'm sorry, mom.

Chapter 23

The telephone rings, interrupting his thoughts. He doesn't answer. He glances around the kitchen, wondering how long he's been sitting there, how long he's been home. I can't believe I left my mom in there. I lost her again. Why didn't I wait for Simon? Amos must have figured out what we were doing and shut down the Station. What have I done? I've ruined everything. If I'd never gone there in the first place, things wouldn't be so screwed up.

He sits up, his chest tightening: Thump-thump, thump-thump. The first time he went to Tendo, he'd gone there on his own.

Isn't that what Simon said? That Thomas had written Simon into his story.

Goosebumps spread across his arms. He grabs a pen and paper from his backpack and sets them on the table. Then he slows his breath to focus on the task at hand and stares at the paper. Be clever. Be careful, he thinks.

He writes.

The rusty trunk sits in the sun where I left it. No one has been here to disturb it, nor has anyone ever visited this place. It is mine alone.

Leather straps dangle from the trunk to the musty ground. I tear one free and slide it into my pocket before climbing inside. My hands reach for the latch I know is there, blind fingers finding it instantly. With hardly any effort, I give it a push, and the floor gives way to the tunnel waiting for me, eager to take me to my destination. This time, it won't be the forest.

Dull green light shines around me as I exit the tunnel into the abandoned Way Station. Everything is quiet, with no sign of the familiar characters—no happy clouds or angry planets are in sight. I wonder where they are. Were they released into the sky, or did someone crush them into dust?

I pull out the leather strap I brought with me to tie open the door I thought I might find. I'd had a feeling I'd wind up here. With the door safely tethered, I walk through the exit and onto the platform, my blood growing cold at what I see. The road is gone. In its place is something else. Something awful. This isn't what I'd expected. Where there once was land, now there's water.

Muddy swamp meets the platform and splashes over its top like an ocean tide. Gone is the dirt road leading to the canopy of palm trees. What lies ahead doesn't seem passable. One step off the platform, and I'll be swimming. There's no way to gauge the depth, but from the look of the massive black gum trees barely peeking out their wet heads, it's not only deep, but it's dense, and it appears to stretch for miles. If the canopy is still there, it's not visible. It's either too far away to see or it's been swallowed whole.

There's no other choice but to swim. I'm running out of time. An unannounced countdown has begun. I am as sure of it as the air I'm breathing. I bend to untie my shoes, and strange bubbles appear around the platform and pop, spraying in my face. They increase in number and size, and I watch in fascination, knowing this sudden proliferation of bubbles can't be good. I'm right. A massive eye bursts through the muck and stops a foot away from me, blinking in its socket, then tightening like a diamond when it sees me. I'm not positive, but I think it winked right before slinking back into the water and sending pools of mud over the platform and into the Station.

That was the crocodile that tried to eat Adam. And I think it recognized me. I can't go in there. It's suicide. There's got to be another way. There's always another way. Think. Think. Adam survived this monstrosity before; Thomas helped him do it.

The solution presents itself as quickly as the idea forms. Thomas takes off running on top of the swamp water in the bubble he's formed around himself, much like the one he put Adam in. He slips several times but gets the hang of the pressure needed to make the bubble roll forward. Using all his strength and endurance, he runs. Miles speed past him in minutes or seconds, he isn't sure; but then he sees what he was hoping for, the canopy entrance. It's still there, still framed by the line of palm trees. It looks like the swamp drops into a trench near the entrance, leaving a gap between the water and the land.

He runs harder now, closing the distance to less than a hundred yards. A rumble from below causes him to slip, sending the bubble bouncing along the water's surface. Scrambling to his feet, he sees a wave rise from the mud behind him and pulse forward, shaking him even harder. He's tossed like a doll, flipping along with the bubble but can see another wave building right behind it. He understands then. Those aren't waves. That's the crocodile, coming for me.

Its back crests, then it lifts its head and shrieks. Muck and spittle spray in every direction. It looks at Thomas for a fraction of a second, it's menacing eyes blinking once more before it thrusts under the water, speeding toward Thomas. The wave created by the massive force is still ahead of the beast and reaches Thomas first. The bubble is lifted and catapulted forward, long out of the crocodile's reach. It hits the swamp edge and bounces over the side, dissolving when it touches the ground. Thomas lands with a thud. He looks around, awed that he is alive.

"Yahoo," he screams, relief flooding his body, "take that, lizard." Filthy water splashes over the side of the swamp wall. The beast rises and looks over the edge at Thomas. It snorts once before sinking back into the swamp and disappearing.

Mud and debris fall from his body as he stands. Wiping the gunk from his eyes, he can't believe that something worked in his favor. He turns back toward the canopy and his glee dissolves. It isn't time to celebrate. Not even close.

Everything about the canopy has changed, and not for the better. Standing at least twenty times as large as before, the canopy scale is nearly impossible to process. Thomas isn't sure if it's the wind or not, but the trees seem to be moving in unison, dancing to an unheard song. The little voice in the back of his head tells him to flee, that if he goes inside the house of palms, he may not come out. But something from deep inside sets him into action, and he scrambles forward, making it inside the tunnel. At first, there's only darkness; the beautiful living lights don't respond like last time. Then a rush of air sweeps by his face, and the tunnel starts to wake, tiny lights jerking to life. Only this time, the light forms into moving blobs rather than illuminating the entire enclosure. And the color is off, dulled now, nowhere near as beautiful as before. "Come on," he whispers, "it's still too dark. What's taking so long?"

He hears the canopy tighten behind him, stealing even more of his visibility. More goosebumps arrive, and his entire body shudders. These lights are wrong. They don't belong here. Nothing belongs here. But there's no other way than through. He has a sense of dread that the canopy will completely close in on him if he tries to turn around. A bead of sweat drips into his eye, and he moves forward into the stale air that seems to grow hotter and thicker by the second. Red lights swarm around him, and he is thankful for the extra light until he's hit by one, drawing blood. Another light strikes, piercing his head. He screams in pain and tears it from his scalp, throwing it to the ground. It spins around on the floor, making wheezing, gulping sounds. Thomas kneels to see what he's done to the tiny hummingbird when it latches onto his hand. He slaps it away, crushing it when he realizes it's a bat, a tiny prickly bloodsucker with glowing red eyes. Three more bats attack, latching to his head and neck. Instead of batting them away, he runs and doesn't stop until he makes it through the other side.

Once there, he doubles over, resting his hands on his thighs for support. Every gulp of air burns his throat. When he's nearly caught his breath, he feels a tickle by his ear and screams, pulling a bat still attached to his neck. It snaps at him and wiggles free from his hand before flying back into the canopy. Thomas feels tears in his eyes. Everything he loved here is gone.

Pressing on, Thomas clears the corner and looks up. The sky is spectacular. It morphs from silver to green and purple to yellow before turning back to silver again. It's all he can do not to lay down and watch it, to embrace its peace. Under other circumstances, he wishes everyone could see such beauty, aurora borealis a thousand times over. A subtle shift in intensity startles him, and his dread returns. It's beginning again, and things are going to turn nasty. This whole thing is a joke. He understands that now. Amos knew he was coming and had no intention of making it easy or letting Thomas leave. He wanted Thomas to remember how magical this place was so that it would hurt him to see it the way it is now.

"So, what now? What's next?" he yells into the air. "Is the beach going to turn to lava before I cross it? Will the water turn to acid? What will it be, Amos? What's the best you can do?"

The endless beach stretches to the ocean. Thomas waits for the next series of obstacles to present themselves, but nothing happens. A breeze sweeps through his hair. He starts walking. The palace shimmers in the sky, and Thomas is frustrated that it still causes him such a visceral reaction. Every time he comes here, the same thing happens.

The palace is not there, and then it is. He knows it will happen, but it's still incredible. This time is no different, and walking through the entrance, he holds his breath, certain that a trap is waiting. Each corner he rounds feels like walking into a spider's web, but which one will catch him? The anxiety of the fear is worse than the fear itself. His knees start to wobble, and he forces himself to count to ten. The chamber is close. If there was ever a time to be steady, it's now.

Rounding the final corner, Thomas comes face to face with Amos, who sits on a swaying throne, writing on a metal tablet.

His eyes register surprise when Thomas enters but he quickly recovers.

"This is interesting, Thomas. What is it you think you're doing here?"

"Uhh…"

Thomas feels as if a lightning bolt strikes his face. He looks at the ground and spots one of his teeth. His shirt is spattered with blood. "My tooth?" Thomas slurs in confusion, holding his mouth. What the fff…"

"I asked you a question," Amos says, returning to his seat. "Why are you here?"

Swaying on his feet, Thomas can do little more than cast a glance at his orphaned tooth before meeting Amos's stare. There he catches a strange expression in Amos's eyes. It was minuscule, but it was there. *Doubt.*

Pressure assaults his head like a jackhammer, but Thomas presses it away. It returns as claws, shredding. He pushes back, this time not only at the invasion but at Amos as well.

In a flash, Thomas sees Rob walking around the park with Adam. Adam grows from a toddler to the boy he's become, leaning on his brother who shields him against fighting parents who love their boys, but seem to hate each other more. He feels grief turn to strength when Adam anchors to Rob. Adam's life explodes before his eyes. Then the strangest thing happens. He sees Adam in a hospital room lying unconscious with a cast on his arm.

New horrific pressure sets in, and he stifles a scream. What is happening? Images assault his mind, pouring in millions at a time. Countless lives and deaths, people worldwide being kind and terrible while others celebrate or suffer. There is an endless supply of scenes from the two sides that make up one world. It's remarkable. Thomas can't look away, can't break the connection until he sees himself through Amos's eyes. Holy shit. This is Amos. I'm in his head. I'm watching everything he's ever seen, and ever done. When Amos's last memory of himself passes by, Thomas severs the connection.

Amos stares at Thomas. He is pale and trembling. "How? You cannot—"

"I cannot what, Amos? Do to you, what you've done to so many?" Amos closes his eyes and points his fingers at Thomas. Thousands of eels drop to ground and speed toward him. Until then, Thomas hadn't realized they'd created Amos's throne. No wonder he'd swayed while he sat there. Thomas scoots backward, away from the slimy creatures, but not in time.

An eel wraps around Thomas's throat, squeezing so hard he feels pressure in his eyes. He claws at his neck for air, fingers tearing away at scales and blood, but it doesn't help. He is suffocating. Amos circles Thomas, glancing down in disgust, fury emanating from his body. Everything goes blurry, and Thomas goes limp.

I'm dying, Thomas thinks. He accepts it and feels his body detach from his brain. I wish I could tell Madi and my mom that I love them; that I could tell Adam I'm sorry. I'm sorry for failing all of you. I wish I had been better, that I'd done better. I fought until the end, against the worst things he could think of, but it wasn't enough. I'm sorry.

An eel shifts, giving his throat a sliver of air. Nerve endings fire throughout his body, and his brain comes to life.

Those weren't the worst things Amos could think of, Thomas realizes. He didn't think of them at all. The crocodile, the obstacles, they weren't in Amos's memories. He didn't see anything about me after the last time we met. He doesn't know Adam got out. He doesn't know about my mom. Why not? Think. Think.

It wasn't Amos putting the obstacles in front of me; I would have seen that in his memories.

The eel strengthens its squeeze and the sensation of fainting returns. Once again, his body goes limp. There are faint voices in the distance that remind him of listening to one of Maddie's plays from behind the curtain. They grow louder and louder, an argument turning into a battle. He floats in and out of consciousness. The eels loosen their grip. He struggles for breath. A woman screams. Oh, God. Please, not now. Don't hurt my mom.

Something inside him cracks, pulling him back from oblivion. Anger explodes from his body. There's another scream, then sobs. His anger continues to boil. The crying quiets to a whimper.

Blinking open his eyes to a cold, stone, ceiling, Thomas squeezes back the bile threatening to strangle him. Please, God, let her be okay. Forced to do the unimaginable, he turns to where the screams originated prepared to see the worst.

Although pale and disheveled, her eyes flicker fire when they lock on Thomas. His heart pounds. She's okay. She looks to the side, Thomas tracking her gaze. It lands on Amos, who is as disheveled as his mother. His eyes turn to slits when he sees Thomas looking at him.

Using what's left of his throne as support, Amos ambles to his feet. An eel drops to the ground and slowly heads toward Thomas.

"Don't," Thomas says.

Amos steps forward, freezing mid-step when Thomas locks eyes on him.

"Put your foot down and take a seat."

Amos drops into his chair like a heavy sack. His face contorts into a scowl. Lilian gasps.

"I forgot I could do that," Thomas says. "I haven't had to since my father wouldn't leave my house."

"Thomas?" Lilian says.

"We'll talk about it later, Mom."

Amos's mouth tightens, the resignation spreading across his face.

Thomas moves slowly, watching Amos work out that he's looking at mother and son, a bond that he'll never share or understand. It was his worst miscalculation. How could he not have seen it? Thomas grins.

"You know," Thomas says, "It didn't occur to me until I was suffocating that you didn't see past our last meeting. You didn't put those obstacles in front of me today, Amos; you didn't even know I was here. I was right. You were surprised when I walked in."

"I don't know what you're talking about, child. But whatever ability you discovered to orchestrate this, it won't last. If I were you, I'd get as far away from here as fast you can before I put an end to this."

Thomas smiles. "You're not listening. You didn't make the swamp or the crocodile. You didn't turn the hummingbirds into bats."

Amos tightens his eyebrows.

"See? You have no idea what I'm talking about. That's what I'm saying, Amos. It was me; all those things were a manifeStation of me. I finally understood something that my Broker said to me once; that he'd do or become whatever was necessary to make me understand what was at stake. Like you, he used fear. Other times, he gave me the ability to make things happen. But both of those things were mere tactics. The crocodile is what I was afraid of. I put it there because I expected it to be there. I was sure you'd have something waiting for me around every corner. The swamp, the bats—that was all me. You didn't have anything to do with them. Those things weren't in your head. They were in mine."

"Thomas, stop," Lilian says.

"We're leaving in a second, mom. I promise," Thomas says, not taking his eyes off Amos.

"I almost want to thank you, Amos. I wasn't aware of how miserable I could be until I met you. I have become my own worst enemy. I've expected the worst from everyone for a long time. I expected it from you, and you didn't disappoint. Your capacity for evil is remarkable, but I made it worse by fueling it. So now I'm going to do my best to fix everything that I've damaged."

"You can't change anything. It's too late."

"It's not. I'm going home. I'm returning the thoughts I stole back to the people I stole them from. I'm fixing Amanda, and I'm taking responsibility for my actions."

"You think you can walk away? The moment you relinquish your focus on me, I'll—"

"You'll do nothing," Thomas throws Amos across the cave with his mind.

Amos climbs to his knees, blood dripping from his nose. Thomas glances at his mother, whose face is frozen in horror. He's sorry he can't explain this to her now, but there will be time later. Right now, Amos is the only thing standing between everything he's come here for. Using all of his remaining strength, Thomas focuses on every experience he's ever shared with Amos, and every memory he saw of himself through Amos's eyes. Then he repeats it. Amos's eyes bulge. The trickle of blood coming from Amos's nose begins to gush.

"Like I said," Thomas relaxes his shoulders, "you'll do nothing. What you're experiencing now has got to be, what did you say? Frying your hippocampus? Something like that? If you're a good boy, I'll turn it off in the future. If not, I'll let the last few months of your life run on a loop until your brain is mush. It's your choice."

"I'll die anyway, Thomas. You know that."

"You won't. I know Brokers need thoughts to survive, and I'll stop in from time to time with my own thoughts to keep you alive. You'll survive. But it won't be pleasant. And you certainly won't be misusing the energy I bring on columns of fire or tornados. Did it ever occur to you how much pain you caused with your oddities around this place? I mean, that's what you were using the thoughts for, right? To build these bizarre things?"

"What are you talking about? That is not the case, Thomas. You'll never understand."

"Goodbye for now, Amos," Thomas says. "There's no point talking to you. You do nothing but lie."

Amos makes a sound that sends shivers down Thomas's spine. "I lie? I had no reason to lie, Thomas. You provided for me, and I rewarded you. You wanted the girl, so I gave her to you in bursts. You wanted things, you got them. You wanted your mother back, and here she is. I do not lie, Thomas. I fulfill."

"You fulfill? I wonder what Adam thinks about that. He was planning on going to medical school, and now he can't remember anything about it."

"That was his choice, Thomas. He knew the stakes when he left, as he knew the stakes when he came. Nothing was hidden to him."

"That's not true! He wouldn't have given up something like that. He would have never agreed to such a thing."

"But he did, Thomas, like everyone else who travels these lands. Why don't you ask your mother? She's conveniently close, wouldn't you say?"

"Thomas senses her behind him. "You will never be a part of her life again, Amos. It's done. No more."

Closing his eyes, he takes Lilian's hand. They walk away from the water palace across the beautiful beach, through the glowing canopy and into the Way Station. She hesitates at the entrance.

"These Stations only work if there's a Broker to…"

He smiles at his mother. "I've got it, mom. We're only here to get you back."

She grabs his hand so tightly he winces. "What do you mean? Aren't you coming? How will you—"

"I'm coming, mom, but we're using the Station to get you home. I don't need it anymore."

"I don't understand."

"You don't have to. It doesn't matter. You're going home now. I'll meet you there," he says. Lilian's eyes sparkle.

Chapter 24

Monday morning might be the best morning of his life. Thomas wakes to the smell of bacon and waffles. The kitchen sounds like a battlefield of fighting dishes and pans. But there's more; there are voices. He savors the sounds of his mom and Madi together in the kitchen. It doesn't seem real. It's better than real.

Breakfast is delicious. He hates to leave but has to get to school. There's something important to do. His mom asked to walk Madi today, and Madi couldn't have seemed happier.

School is as expected. It's horrifying to know that everyone is acting this way because of what he did. All the joy he felt earlier melts away as Thomas walks into the building. The only sound comes from shoes squeaking in the hallway. Kids move about, but no one seems awake. He shudders with guilt, taking a seat in his first-period classroom. Closing his eyes, he focuses on the bundle of energy gathered in the deep recess of his brain that's been pulsing since he left the other side. He begins to unravel it with his mind, layer after layer giving way like peeling bands from the ball they make up. Slowly, the ball starts dropping the bands on its own, moving faster with each release. They continue to drop until it has completely unraveled, leaving nothing behind.

Thomas stands up and walks into his next class, repeating the process. Once done, he goes to town and visits every store he's ever been in, ending up in the bookstore where he spends the most time. As an afterthought, he visits the market outside of town, the bowling alley, the hospital, and Madi's elementary school. No one notices him.

Tuesday mirrors Monday, only today he's eager to get to school to see if what he did worked. Did he make everyone whole, or is he responsible for destroying nearly every person in town? It's unbearable to consider. He tries to sneak out before Madi or Lilian wakes up, but when he passes his mother's room, he notices her notebook sitting on the nightstand. It's a bad idea to pry, but something makes him pick it up. Inside, he feels the breath slip from his chest when he reads her novel's first page. It is magnificent. He hadn't known she was a writer, but now that he thinks about it, the tales she told him as a child were beautiful. He'd assumed that she was retelling something she'd heard, but it occurs to him now that they were her stories. He sets down the journal and picks up another that contains hundreds of poems. Flipping through, each one looks better than the next. She is prolific in a way he cannot imagine. She's one of those people that makes it look easy. He may be prejudiced, that everything seems better because he missed her so much, but something tells him that's not the case; that these stories have more to do with Tendo than they do with Lilian, alone.

Closing the journal and feeling more than a little guilty for prying, he watches his mother sleep, thanking God that she's home. He can't wait to start his life over and see how much better everything is for Madi. He hopes the same goes for the town.

From the safety of his borrowed truck, the high school looks daunting. Thomas wonders what he'll do if it didn't work; if he didn't restore everyone's thoughts? How will he atone? There are so many unanswered questions, so many things that don't add up. Amos, the fang-beaver, freeing Adam. And what happened to Simon? He seems to have disappeared. All of this has something to do with Lilian, but he can't bug her about it. She needs time to reintegrate with her family. Getting this part right is the most important thing right now. He resigns himself to whatever fate has in store for him.

Bracing himself, he walks into the school. A paper airplane whizzes by his head. Two kids laugh, pointing at a girl with toilet paper stuck to her shoe. A substitute teacher races for her room. Noise roars down the hallway. Thomas stands in amazement, relief surging through him. The day passes like every other day, with no one aware that anything happened. He can't find Amanda, but he'll look for her after school.

At the intersection of Front and State street, Thomas waits for the light to change. He didn't bump into Amanda, and after checking with several friends, learned that she hadn't made it to school. He's a little uneasy, but Amanda's had a rough few weeks. It makes sense that she took some time off. He'll give her another day to get back into the groove, and if she doesn't, he'll seek her out. The light turns green, and he moves forward, just as a car barrels through the intersection from the wrong lane. Thomas inhales sharply; that was close. Too close.

He pulls into the one-way entrance for the pizza parlor to pick up dinner and comes face to face with a patron exiting through the entry-only line, honking his horn indignantly at Thomas, as if Thomas were to blame. Thomas takes a moment, tries to understand what is happening, but comes up short. It's just him. It's a weird day. That's all. The world hasn't started switching left to right, up to down, inside to outside, or right to wrong; because that would be a problem.

Everyone at the pizza parlor is happy to see him when he steps inside. He's picking up dinner for his family, after all. What could go wrong? Heading home with a pie in hand, he's flooded with relief. Everything seems to be okay. He thinks of Nicole and how much she'll like his mother.

Laughter floods the entryway when he opens his front door. Madi and the twins are on the floor, giggling. When he'd returned with his mother, he hadn't wanted to, but he'd placed a suggestion into Mary, Madi, and the girl's minds about where Lilian had been. If he hadn't, this reunion wouldn't have gone so smoothly. The way he'd explained it to his mother was that he could help them with a slight adjustment to their thinking. He wouldn't be taking anything away, but he'd be making some things hazy. Today, Lilian and Mary chat away on the couch like it's nothing more than a Tuesday, average in every way. It worked, and nothing could be better.

He smiles, making eye contact with his mother. She looks back, and there is a flash of dread that takes hold of him. She had looked at him the same way while they were still on Tendo, but he'd chalked it up to adrenaline and surviving Amos. He wonders what it is. It's like she wants—no, she needs something. She's eager for it. He resists the urge, but it happens anyway. He enters her thoughts before he can stop himself. She wants to go back, and she wants him to go with her. And there's something else. No one should have known that Lilian was his mom. She'd made that clear. But Simon did. Simon had said so the first time they met when Thomas climbed into the forest. He'd known who Lilian was all along. And now she wants to go back. For *Simon*.

Someone giggles. Thomas blinks, clearing his head. Stop it, he tells himself. This is not happening. Nothing is up. I'm just hungry.

Madi stares into space. Thomas steps forward to get her attention, and his mother says, "Earth to Madi, Earth to Madi, come in Madi." Her eyes find Thomas's, and she smiles, taking the pizza into the kitchen.

THE END/BOOK ONE

Acknowledgment

Ryan, Ethan, and Parker, thank you for your remarkable patience and love. About the Author Heidi Callan Heidi lives in San Diego with her husband, two sons, and hound dog.

Made in the USA
Monee, IL
13 September 2020